THEM

Carey Heywood

*Jennifer,
May your days
be filled with
love & books!
♡
Carey Heywood*

THEM

Copyright © 2015 by Carey Heywood

All rights reserved. Except as permitted under the U.S. Copyright Act of 1976, no part of this publication may be reproduced, distributed, or transmitted in any form or by any means, or stored in a database or retrieval system, without prior written permission of the author.

The scanning, uploading, and distribution of this book via the Internet or via other means without the permission of the publisher are illegal and the punishable by law. Please purchase only authorized electronic editions and do not participate in or encourage electronic piracy of copyrighted materials. Your support of the author's rights is appreciated.

Them is a work of fiction. Names, characters, places, and incidents either are the product of the author's imagination or are used fictitiously. Any resemblance to actual persons, living or dead, events, or locales is entirely coincidental.

DEDICATION

To Seth, my Him.
Thank you for always being there for me,
and for giving me my happily ever after.

1

Sarah

"Are you sure?"

I glance over at Will, who is napping on the couch, as I walk out of the living room.

He can sleep through anything, so my action is technically unneeded. In my opinion, it's rude to have a telephone conversation in the same room where someone is sleeping.

"I am. Will's asleep, though, so don't ring the bell. I'll leave the side door unlocked."

"It sounds like you're busy."

"I'm never too busy for my favorite nephew. Seriously, I can watch him all afternoon."

Christine relents, which is funny since she called me in the first place to ask if I could babysit. Then, after I said I could, started to worry over monopolizing my time.

I'm neck-deep in babysitting competition, considering both sets of grandparents and Christine's best friend also live nearby. Calvin is getting so big. Once Will wakes up, he's going to steal him, so I need to get my baby fix in now.

"Okay. Thank you, Sarah."

Christine and Brian don't live far from us, so I pull on my sneakers and a hoodie. Christine should have his stroller with her, so we can head down to the park and play until Will wakes up.

For as much energy as Will has, the first marking period of a new school year always drains him. He loves teaching, loves kids.

I scribble a quick note to him on a dry erase board that lives in our kitchen.

Our kitchen.

Crazy to think, we've lived here for almost three years together. Almost three years, watching the people closest to us have babies.

And, none for us.

The first year it was to be expected. We were newlyweds, crazy busy with making our house a home and I still had my birth control implant in. Sawyer and I both had them removed at about the same time. Stupidly, I thought we'd both get pregnant right away. At least one of us did.

Sawyer and Jared's daughter, Pascal is already three months old. When she was born, we rented a truck and brought Sawyer's family dining set back up to her as a surprise. Then we stayed the rest of Will's summer break to help her and Jared with the baby.

I couldn't help but feel like something was missing as I watched Will holding her. *All I want is to give that to him.* Even when we were still in school, I always knew Will would make a good father. He loves kids. It's part of the reason he's such a good teacher.

"Knock, knock."

I turn and smile as Christine peeks her head around the door.

Arms open, I walk over to quickly hug her before relieving her of my adorable nephew.

"How are you feeling?"

Both of her hands slide down to rest on her ever-expanding midsection. "I don't think I was showing this early with Cal."

My brother has been busy; baby Miller number two is already on the way.

"Is that normal?"

She shrugs. "I guess. I'm not happy about having to break out the elastic waistbands this early. Luckily, I saved all my maternity stuff, so I had Brian pull it out of storage."

I grimace. They had a storage unit because they were rapidly running out of space in their condo. They have two bedrooms, so unless they sell the place the new baby will have to share Calvin's room. This has been a point of contention between Brian and Christine. He wants to move, spread out, and maybe even find something in our neighborhood. Christine loves the location of their condo and the fact that they don't have to worry about yard work or the outside of the building.

And here Will and I are, four-bedroom house, just the two of us.

Doesn't seem fair.

Either way, Brian and Christine only have about five more months before baby two is here. Christine is trying to talk him into upgrading to a three-bedroom unit while he's trying to convince her to move into a house. My bets are on Christine; my brother would do anything for her.

"Thank you so much for agreeing to watch Cal."

I give her a look. "You know how much we love having him. Do you have his stroller in your car? I was thinking about taking him to the park since it's nice out."

After spending the summer in New England, fall finally making an appearance in Atlanta was great. September had been mainly dry and unseasonably hot, and the rain we did get managed to ruin every weekend. The temperature cooled off once October came, so I'm trying to spend as much time as I can outside before it gets too cold.

Sawyer would laugh at what I consider cold at this point. It's already snowed once where they live.

"It is."

I grab my house key and cell. "Cal and I will walk out with you."

She always brings a book bag of his stuff when he comes over. I slip it into the basket of Calvin's stroller. Christine packs for every possible scenario, so I know we'll be set.

"Be good for Aunt Sarah," Christine coos as she fastens his lap belt.

He pouts as we watch her leave, his plump toddler lip trembling as he murmurs, "Mama."

This is normal for him, though. He's over it once he recognizes the direction we're headed. We've babysat Cal enough for him to know the stroller usually means we're headed to the park. It isn't a large park, not like Piedmont Park, which is closer to Christine's mom's house. I'd have to drive if I wanted to take him there. The little park in our neighborhood is nice, though, with a separate section of smaller equipment for the littler ones like Calvin.

The park itself is on the newer side. Instead of the mulch-covered parks I grew up with, it has a solid gym mat-like covering beneath everything. It's kind of like walking on a giant sponge. After parking his stroller, he toddles straight for the swings. I lift him up, kissing his chubby cheeks before setting him into one then coax his legs through the holes.

I stand in front of him and, once he's holding on to the chains, start to push him. My nephew is a charmer, and a generally happy fellow. He favors Christine in coloring, with his blond hair and blue eyes, but his nose and mouth are all Brian.

"Your little boy is so cute."

Another mother, I guess, is placing a little boy in the swing next to us.

I fake a smile. "He's my nephew, but thank you. He's a sweetheart."

Her child squawks, trying to pull himself out of the swing. "It looks like you have a handful."

She nods, trying to settle him. "He refused to nap today, so now he's cranky. I was hoping the fresh air would cheer him up."

Cal's watching the other little boy fuss, rapt, and I do my best not to laugh. He's a funny little guy, on the quiet side. He's our little observer.

The other boy notices Cal's attention and settles into a staring contest. "This is Calvin, and I'm Sarah."

She reaches out her hand to shake mine. "I'm Jessica, and this is my son Marcus."

I internally roll my eyes at her name. For some reason, I've never been able to like the name Jessica after everything that went down. I'm an adult, though, so I'll try not to judge her by someone else's bad behavior.

"Nice to meet you both. Can you say hi, Calvin?"

We continue to make small talk until Calvin asks to get down. I follow him over to a small slide. He's good at going up the stairs but still needs my help getting situated at the top of the slide. He's just starting to climb up the stairs for another go when I feel two strong arms wrap around my waist and soft lips kiss my neck.

"Hey, honey," I whisper, leaning back against him.

It's amazing, the power he has to make everything better with only his presence. He's my true north, my home.

"Why didn't you wake me?"

I laugh. "You know once Cal sees you I'm going to be chopped liver."

My comment is proven seconds later when Cal's eyes find Will. His entire face lights up as he reaches for him. He's no longer interested in the slide now that his uncle is here. Will tucks me to his side and, with his free arm, scoops Cal up and sets him on his hip. As perfect as this moment is, it reminds me how much sweeter it would be once we have our own child.

"Hey, buddy." Will grins down at him as Cal reaches up to touch his face.

Cal seems fascinated by Will's scruffy face. Since it's the weekend, he didn't shave this morning and might have more stubble than he's ever seen him. I love his scruff. I've toyed with asking him to grow a beard but am scared I won't like anything covering his handsome face.

We head toward a seesaw. Will holds Cal in his lap on one side and I go to sit on the other.

THEM

"How long do we have Cal for?"

"Christine is going to call me when she's on her way, but I think she said it'd be around five."

"It was almost three when I started walking down here. Think we should head back?"

I'm on to him. "You want to play blocks before he has to leave, don't you?"

He tries to look innocent. "Maybe."

After the first couple of times we watched Cal at our house, Will went out and bought some toys for him to play with when he came over. One thing he got was this old-fashioned wooden block set. My man loves building things, and Cal loves knocking them down.

"Sure."

I say goodbye to Jessica and Marcus as we pass them. Will buckles Cal in and pushes the stroller as I fall into step with him. I can't help but wonder if the people we pass on the way home think Cal is ours.

Once we're back at the house, I change Cal and make him a snack while Will starts setting up the blocks. Calvin is working on knocking down a line of towers when Christine calls.

"They're on the way," I tell Will once I set my phone down.

I quickly pick it back up to snap a picture of them both pouting at the news. Cal cheers up once Will starts building another tower for him to knock down.

No more than ten minutes later, there's a knock at our front door.

Will gets up to answer it while I scoop Cal in my arms to get in some last-minute snuggles.

"Was he good?" Christine asks, already reaching for him.

I give him an extra squeeze before passing him to her. "He was an angel."

"I see you broke out the blocks," Brian remarks, bumping Will's ribs with his elbow.

"What?" Will asks innocently. "Cal loves them."

I cross the room, stepping over piles of blocks to slide my arms around Will's waist. "What movie did you end up seeing?"

"Um . . ." Christine looks away.

"No movie. We ended up touring a three-bedroom unit in our complex." Brian laughs.

"But I thought—" I start.

Brian kisses the side of Christine's head. "She's a sneaky little thing. I was dead-set against staying in a condo, but after seeing this place I might be changing my mind."

"Sorry I fibbed about the movie," Christine adds.

"No worries. So, tell us about the place. Are you going to get it?"

The new condo is in another building on the ground floor. Since it's a garden-level unit, it has a decent sized patio where the kids could play. The rooms are about the same size as what they already have, and one giant perk is it comes with two assigned parking spots.

"I think we're going to make an offer on it." Brian grins.

They hang out for a couple minutes before taking off to have dinner over at Christine's mom's house.

"What do you want to do for dinner?" I ask, sinking down onto our loveseat while Will picks up his blocks.

"Why don't we go out tonight?" he suggests.

I reach for my phone. "Want to invite your mom?"

If anyone said three years ago that I'd be saying that, I wouldn't have believed it. Now that she likes me, we've grown closer than I could have imagined.

Will reaches for my leg, sliding his hand under the cuff of my jeans and up my calf. "How about a romantic dinner, just the two of us?"

I've been in love with Will Price since middle school, and with a simple caress he can still make me warm all over.

"Okay," I breathe.

He stands, offering me his hand to help me up. Together, we walk up to our room. He showers as I decide what to wear in our shared, deep walk-in closet. I get distracted, trailing my fingers over his button-up shirts. Even though we wash our clothes together, there's always a faint hint of his cologne left on his.

Instead of picking out anything to wear, I'm standing in our closet sniffing Will's shirts. I still haven't made up my mind by the time he's done. His damp chest presses against my back, small drops of water falling from his hair to hit my shoulder as he wraps his arms around me.

"Maybe we should stay in." One of his hands drifts up to cup me through my bra.

I turn my face and kiss the underside of his jaw, licking stray drops clinging to his scruff.

"I'm taking that as a yes," he says.

Even though I'm not wearing much to begin with, he slowly undresses me. Like a gift, I'm unwrapped. I want to rush, drag him to our bed and make love to him, but Will is in the mood to take his time. Softly, gently, he kisses my skin until I'm standing in our closet shaking with need. Only then does he lift me up and carry me to our bed.

Afterward, as Will holds me tightly in his arms, I can't help but hope that maybe we've just made a baby.

We stay there, wrapped up in each other, until my stomach grumbles and he offers to go pick up sweet and sour chicken from my favorite Chinese place to make up for not taking me out to dinner. I watch as he pulls on a pair of faded jeans and a University of Georgia hoodie. It's not fair he looks so impossibly handsome without even trying. I'm certain I look like a mess right now, particularly my hair.

Will has a habit of pulling out whatever clip or band I've used to try and control my hair whenever we make love. If it didn't feel like heaven when his hands were in my hair, I'd make him stop. Too bad I don't look half as good with sex hair as he does.

"Want a couple eggrolls?" he asks before walking out the door.

I nod, making him grin in return. He loves knowing what I want.

Once he's gone, I grab my calendar. I've been charting my periods to try and figure out when I'm ovulating. Month after month, I hope that this will be the time it doesn't come. After Sawyer got pregnant, I talked to my doctor. He wanted me to relax and chart my ovulation schedule for nine months before we spoke again. Those nine months ended two months ago, and I've been avoiding calling him.

Part of me was certain I wouldn't need to, that since Will and I have a healthy sex life we'd get pregnant on our own. Based on my calendar, I'm due to start my next period in two weeks. If it comes, that will be my sign that I need to finally call him.

I put my calendar away. Will should be back soon, so I need to tackle my hair and get dressed. I'm downstairs getting a drink when he walks in. I can almost taste my dinner it smells so good.

"Where do you want to eat?"

"Let's eat in the living room and watch a movie," I suggest.

"My turn to pick." Will grins, setting the bag down on our island.

"Nothing too scary," I plead.

"But I like it when you try and hide behind me," Will teases.

I smirk at him until he rounds the island and kisses it off me. Once I relax in his arms he pulls back, smiling at me. I roll my eyes and turn to grab plates, handing one to him. This is a pretty standard night for us, Chinese food and a movie. I was excited when he mentioned going out, but there truly isn't anything I'd rather do than hang out at home with my Will.

Working from home has only perpetuated my homebody tendencies. When I still lived in Colorado, I had Sawyer to drag me out. She was, and still is, a social butterfly. I spent my time working on our new house and transitioning my business from having a physical office set-up to being one hundred percent remote.

I was too busy to establish new friendships. My house is a haven, with light creamy walls to balance out the rich craftsman-style woodwork that made us fall in love with this house in the first place. It's everything I've ever dreamed of. Only now that I'm not busy with work or redecorating, the stillness which greets me each day after Will leaves for work doesn't bring peace. It brings loneliness.

2

Will

"Mr. Price, is it okay if I eat lunch in here today?"

My head lifts as I notice one of my eighth-grade students standing in the doorway to my classroom.

Generally, the kids should be eating in the cafeteria, but Logan has been having a rough time so I'll make an exception. "Sure."

My classroom is shaped like a rectangle, with storage cabinets, shelves and a couple of sinks lining every wall except for the one behind my desk. I rearrange the tables depending on what we're working on every so often. Right now, all of the work tables are paired off to make squares.

He walks quietly toward the back of the class to the table where he normally sits and pulls out his lunch. Keeping my head down so it looks like I'm reading something on my computer, I watch him eat. It's hard to tell from this far away, but it looks as though all he has is popcorn. There's no way that will fill up a growing eighth grader.

THEM

I brought in leftover Chinese food from this weekend. I haven't started eating it, but Logan doesn't know that.

"Hey, Logan, do you like Hunan chicken?"

He shrugs. "Don't know, never had it."

I stand, lifting my container. "Are you allergic to anything? And do you like spicy food?"

He looks at the container in my hands. "No allergies, and sometimes."

"Mrs. Price was supposed to come meet me for lunch," I lie. "Something came up, and she can't come now. I hate throwing food away, but I'm stuffed. Want to try some?"

He gulps, slowly nodding.

"Grab an empty cup and get some water from the fountain first. I wasn't joking when I said it was spicy."

He does as I asked while I sneak a peek in his lunch bag, confirming there isn't anything else in it.

"It's on your table," I say, passing him as I walk back to my desk. "Let me know if you like it."

I try not to watch him eat, so I focus on loading grades into the system. The software allows students and their parents to log in and get the most up-to-date grading information. The system only works if I actually make the time to enter the assignments as we go instead of letting them pile up on my desk. Teaching art, I rarely have students struggle to pass my class. I'm an elective, so they all want to be here.

"Can I go get some more water, Mr. Price?" Logan asks, now standing beside my desk, my empty Tupperware container in his hand.

"Sure, did you like it?"

He nods, smiling. "It was good, just real spicy, like you said."

After downing his water, Logan heads out to his next class, pausing in the doorway. "Is it okay if I eat lunch in here again tomorrow, Mr. Price?"

"You're always welcome as long as I'm in here," I reply.

"Thanks, Mr. Price."

I nod and he's gone. I glance down at what was going to be my lunch, snapping the lid back on it and slipping the now-empty container into my bag. I have a stash of emergency granola bars in my desk, and I have enough time to inhale two of them before my next class starts.

I've had Logan in one of my classes for the last three years. His dad is a reservist currently overseas. His mom passed away when he was in elementary school, so while his dad is in South Korea he's living with his grandparents. From what I understand, both are in poor health.

Logan is a good kid. He loves coming to art class and he's one of those students I feel honored to teach. At the end of the day, I'm sure I learned more from him than the other way around.

THEM

After school, I stayed late to switch out the artwork hanging in the gym hall. With the exceptions of some bulletin boards dedicated to the PTA and certain subjects, the rest of the walls in the school were my canvas. It's my philosophy that kids are inspired by their environment, that somehow I can encourage their creativity by making art that speaks to them readily available.

Pieces with interesting shapes, colors and three-dimensional craziness were always popular. My favorite projects were the ones where my students had to share a piece of themselves through the art they were creating. The assignment could be something as simple as interpreting the lyrics of their favorite song into a drawing. That way, not only did I get to know their favorite songs, but I also learned how they envisioned the meaning of it.

One year, through a song, I discovered a student was harming herself and was able to get her help. My biggest fear is missing something with one of my kids. That's why, no matter what, I always make time for them.

I head home once I'm done with switching out the artwork. The middle school I teach at is a short drive from our house. I loosen my tie and waver between opening the windows and turning on the AC for my ride home. I'd be more comfortable with the AC going, but after eight hours of smelling tempura paint I need some fresh air. Besides, opening the sunroof always reminds me of Sarah.

The house smells like crockpot ribs the moment I walk in the door. Something about fall makes Sarah act more domesticated than normal.

"Smells good, babe," I call out, shrugging off my jacket and placing it on the fennel at the bottom of our wooden bannister. Sarah would rather I hang it up, but what's the point? I'm only going to put it back on tomorrow morning when I have to leave again.

There's a study Sarah uses as her office on the main floor. The room looks like something out of a magazine, from the buttery yellow walls to the matching curtains and rug under her desk. She has warm-toned, medium-height bookshelves running along the wall beneath the window and two cushiony armchairs with a matching yellow and light blue print facing her desk.

I sink into one of them and ask, "When're the ribs going to be ready?"

She swivels her chair to face me. "Hungry?"

I nod. "Starved. I gave my lunch to a student today."

Her brows pinch together. "Is everything okay?"

I chew the inside of my lip before I reply. "I'm not sure. He asked if he can eat in my class tomorrow, so I'm going to bring some extra food just in case. I don't know whether I should see if he opens up to me or talk to the school counselor."

Her eyes drift toward the ceiling. She knows both Christine and I aren't fans of the school's guidance counselor. I'll never understand why someone who seemingly dislikes kids so much went into her profession. On the surface, however, she's sugary sweet, her goal in life to give you a toothache.

I can't talk to her about Logan. At best, she would put a note in his file and forget about him. At worst, she'd publicly ask him if he needed free or reduced lunches. That's the last thing he would want his classmates thinking, even if it were true.

Sarah stands, walking over to sit in my lap and lean against my chest. "There'll be plenty of ribs left over to bring to school tomorrow."

That's my girl.

I dip my head and press my lips to hers as I wrap my arms around her and pull her even tighter against me. She's wearing a soft, woolen sweater which I look forward to taking off her tonight. When she still had an office for her business, before she decided to move back to Georgia to be with me, she wore nothing but business suits. Can't lie, those skinny skirts and heels she wore were sexy as hell.

I wouldn't trade her in yoga pants and big sweaters for the world, though. The changes she made by taking her company remote made a future where our kids could grow up near their grandparents possible. I'll never forget what she sacrificed for us. Living close to home meant she was also able to form a relationship with my mom. We've both now long since forgiven her for her role in our breakup.

I'm not sure she will ever forgive herself, though. She spoils Sarah now, her way of trying to make up for the years we lost. Too soon, I release my hold and follow her as she makes her way to the kitchen, listening as she tells me about her day. She's efficient, so much so that there isn't enough work to keep her busy eight hours a day, five days a week.

Before we got back together, she spent most of her time travelling. Now that she's taken over the more administrative functions of her business, I think she's bored. When we first bought the house, she filled her time with making it a home. Now that we've made this house ours, however, I worry that she regrets leaving Colorado for me. All I want is to make her happy.

"What sounds better with the ribs, baked or mashed potatoes?"

"I'm fine with either. Can I help?"

"Keep me company?" she asks.

I tug on her ponytail before sliding onto a stool. "There's no place I'd rather be."

Her eyes get soft as she smiles at me.

"Guess who I'm having lunch with tomorrow?" She pulls two potatoes from the pantry and starts washing them.

"Should we play hot or cold, or am I randomly guessing?" I tease.

She glances over her shoulder at me. "Oh, let's play hot or cold."

"My mom?"

She groans, shutting off the water with annoyance. "It's no fun when you guess it right on your first try."

I stand, moving over to kiss her neck. "She called me on my drive home and told me."

Her mouth drops and she halfheartedly smacks my chest. "Cheater."

I stay standing, hip pressing into the counter top, and watch her. She never stays annoyed at me for too long. Once she has the potatoes in the oven, I tug her into my arms.

"How'd I get so lucky?" I ask.

She looks up at me, her lips parting. It's an invitation I can't resist, so I dip my head to take her mouth. She is so sweet, my Sarah, the girl I've loved for most of my life.

When I lift my head, I take in the dazed expression on her face and ask again, "How did I get so lucky?"

It's not a question she ever answers. It's just my way of showing her how lucky I feel I get to call her mine.

"I'm the lucky one," she breathes.

3

Sarah

My period came today. I was a couple of days late and stupidly I started to hope. Nothing like crying as you sit on the toilet to make any hope you had evaporate. *What is wrong with me?*

I clean myself up and even though it's barely noon, I climb back into bed. Half of my day, I spend surfing the internet trying to stretch out my work so I can feel busy. I've run my company so well it no longer needs me.

So, what does that make me?

A stay-at-home, want-to-be mom of an empty home?

I call my doctor and make an appointment. Thankfully, he has an opening next week. I can pull myself together and wait six days. The hardest day will be Sunday and lunch at my parents, since Christine will be there with Brian and Calvin. My mom will want to know how this pregnancy is going, so she'll ask her all about it and then look at me.

The only person who knows we've been trying is Sawyer, and I'm sure she told Jared. If there's something wrong with me, I don't want anyone else to know. There's nothing worse than knowing someone is feeling sorry for you.

Will likes to ask me how he got to be so lucky. Will he still feel that way if I can't have his baby? He would make the best father. He's told me his children would never be emotionally abandoned the way he had been. That's why he's feeding that student of his every day at lunch.

My thoughts fall into a negative spiral of wondering if Will would be happy with adopting. I can pretend the thought of adopting wouldn't break my heart. It's hard to imagine another possibility when all you've dreamed of for years was creating a child together.

I'm mourning the miniature Will I've dreamt or of the little girl with the best of each of us. I want to be a mother. I want to carry my child inside of me. For as long as it took for Will and me to get our happily-ever-after, I never imagined there'd be a possibility we couldn't make a family.

Six days.

I reach for my phone and call Sawyer.

"What's crack-a-lacking, sweet cheeks?"

I sniffle, wiping fresh tears from my eyes, "I got my period."

"Aww, honey."

"What's wrong with me?"

"You stop that kind of talk right now. There is absolutely nothing wrong with you."

"Then why can't I get pregnant?"

"Have you talked to a doctor?"

"I made an appointment for next week."

"Good. Who knows? Maybe it's Will."

"Don't say that."

She starts laughing. "Maybe he has a late-night porn addiction and all of his spermies are ending up in some Kleenex."

I can't help it, I laugh. "There's nothing wrong with his sperm."

"How do you know?" she argues, teasingly.

"Trust me, I know."

"Oh, shit, Sarah. You know you can't get pregnant giving head."

"You are such an asshole."

Suddenly, I wish we were Face timing, since I'm certain she's smiling and I miss her face.

"I'm the best asshole ever," she replies.

"You are," I agree.

"Feeling better, my dearest?"

She always was the best at cheering me up. "I am."

"So, are you going to tell Mr. Price about your doctor's appointment?"

THEM

"I don't know," I admit.

"Want my opinion?"

I shift onto my side. "You know you're gonna give it to me whether I want to hear it or not."

"Don't keep this from him."

I sigh. She's right. I know it.

"I'm ashamed."

"Oh, honey."

I'm silent, as much as I can be as I begin to cry again.

"Do you want me to come down for a visit?"

Of course she would offer that. She's the most giving and generous person I know, aside from Will. I know she's breastfeeding, so if she came she'd bring Pascal. It's horrible to think, but I'm not sure I can handle having a baby in my house the same day I learn I may never be able to have one of my own.

"No, I'll talk to Will."

"You need someone to go with you to that appointment. Worst-case, you could always take Will's mom."

Sawyer has lost her mind with that suggestion. Why on Earth would I bring the woman who never thought I was good enough for her son to an appointment that proved it?

"No way."

"She loves you. I know you don't believe that, but she does."

"She had a jacked-up way of showing it back in the day."

I hear her inhale through her nose. "Sarah. I thought you had forgiven her."

I pull one of Will's pillows from his side of our bed into my lap. "It's hard to forget."

"I get that. All I ask is that you stop mentally punishing her for stuff that happened in the past. You don't want to be a bitter broad."

"A bitter broad?" I laugh.

"Yep. It'll make you get wrinkles and shit."

I sit up in bed, pushing his pillow aside and tugging the covers toward my lap. "Okay, I'll try not to be a bitter broad."

"So, what's your plan?"

I gulp. "I'll tell Will about the appointment tonight."

"Good girl."

"Thank you for being so awesome."

"I love you, babe."

"I love you, too."

After we hang up, I turn on the TV. I've already finished everything I had needed to do work-wise and don't want to get out of bed. If something else comes up, they can call me. I pick a movie from on-demand that I've seen before, a comedy, and try to relax. I'm asleep before the opening credits are done.

I wake to the bed dipping and two strong arms pulling my back against a solid chest.

"Are you feeling okay?" Will asks, kissing the side of my head.

I turn, tucking my nose under his chin, into his neck. There is something so comforting in the way he smells, and in the warmth that radiates from his skin.

"I got my period today."

His arms tighten around me.

I can't see his face, but I imagine his expression is disappointed. "I'm sorry, honey."

I pinch my eyes shut in an attempt to discourage the tears that are suddenly forming. "What if something's wrong with me?"

His arms tighten. "There is nothing wrong with you."

"Will you still love me if I can't ever get pregnant?"

He leans back, his finger coming under my chin and lifting my face until our eyes meet. "Don't think like that, ever. You are my entire world. There is no choice in whether I love you or not. I just do and always will, no matter what."

I dip my head and bury my face back into his neck. "I want to have your baby so much."

His hands move up and drift into my hair as he leans back to kiss my face. First my cheeks, then my forehead and lastly one hard kiss against my lips.

The intensity of his eyes pierces mine. "I only want you to be happy."

"I only want to make you happy."

"Don't you understand you already do?" he murmurs against my skin.

"I made a doctor's appointment for next week. Will you come to it with me?"

"Yes."

Silently, he holds me. I watch the light peeking through the slats of our blinds travel across our bedroom until the room darkens and they disappear altogether. Will pulls away to go downstairs and make us dinner. I stop in the bathroom first before following him. It doesn't happen often but there *are* times, even after almost three years of marriage that I wonder if I'm good enough for him.

He has this uncanny ability to make me feel worthy of his love nine times out of ten. It's just that last one time where my own insecurities doubt him. It's silly—stupid, even—and I try to convince myself I deserve him. Staring at my reflection in the mirror, it's clear that crying for most of the day did me no favors.

Will looks delicious all the time. How is that fair? From the moment he wakes up—even when he's still sleepy—to the moment he lays his head back down to go to sleep. He had the flu last year and still looked gorgeous. I wonder if people see us together and think he's too good for me.

I don't look gorgeous the moment I wake up. When I'm tired, you can tell by the dark circles under my eyes. I wear makeup most days to look average. Not a ton, just a touch of foundation and blush. If we're going out, I'll also wear eye makeup. Without it, I don't feel pretty. Will needs nothing to look so yummy. He's all mine, and still there are times when I'm struck speechless by how handsome he is.

Even now, he's downstairs making me soup in an attempt to make me feel better. I don't understand what he sees in me. I wash my face, brush my hair and change into a pair of flannel pajama bottoms and one of Will's old t-shirts before going to join him.

Our kitchen is bright and cheery. White shaker-style cabinets and subway tiles set off our granite countertops. Our island matches the cabinets but has a butcher block-style top instead of granite. The island helps with storage since we don't have much of a pantry. The picture window looking over our back deck and yard make up for it, though.

His back is to me as he stirs the soup, our toaster oven dinging as I walk in. Soup and warm bread, pure comfort food. As he turns to pull out the bread, he sees me hovering in the doorway. He sets the bread on the counter before coming to me.

His hands are on my hips, lifting his shirt until they can rest warmly on my bare skin. "Feeling any better?"

I nod before pressing my face into his chest and wrapping my arms around his waist. My Will. Maybe it doesn't matter that I don't feel so great about myself. Maybe as long as I have him, I can try to not be so hard on myself. I can't be that bad; he wouldn't love me if I was. I trust him. Maybe I can also trust that if he thinks I'm deserving, then I am.

"Hungry?"

I nod. "A little."

We sit side by side, each on a stool, pulled up to our island as we eat. Between bites, he rests his hand on my thigh and I cover it with mine. By the bottom of my bowl, I feel better. There's warm soup and bread in my belly and the love of my life beside me. Even if it would only be the two of us for the rest of our lives I know it would be enough. *Well, I hope it would.*

I clean up while Will hangs out, keeping me company. It's like he doesn't want to let me out of his sight. I'm glad, because his presence alone is keeping my negative thoughts away.

"Want some dessert?" I ask, once I'm finished.

"Come here," he teases.

I round the island as he turns so I can stand between his legs. He drops his lips to mine and feasts as I coil my arms around his neck and cling to him. His hands move down my back to my waist and wrap around me tightly. He bends me backward, deepening his kiss. I'm breathless by the time he straightens. He lifts his head slightly, breaking our kiss, but doesn't move beyond that.

My eyes flutter open and his handsome face is all I see. I grin, my smile widening when I see him do the same thing.

"So sweet," he whispers.

My heart is so full it feels weighted in my chest. I close the distance between our lips as I crawl into his lap.

"I love you so much," I tell him as I kiss him.

He returns my kisses and repeats my words, sealing me in his embrace. "The things I want to do to you."

We won't, though, not while I'm on my period. Knowing Will, he probably wouldn't care, but I do. That doesn't mean I can't take care of him. So I do, pulling back and dropping to my knees in front of him.

Crazy as it sounds, I love getting him off. When we make love, Will is absolutely in control. He's physical, moving me, powering into me, taking me. He's so different when I'm in control, though. He's almost frozen by what I'm doing to him, except for his face. There's no hiding he's enjoying every single thing I do. We lock eyes, and the lust in his sears my soul.

I recognize that expression. It's the one I wear when I'm looking at him. We were made for each other. If he is my perfect match, I need to stop second-guessing that I'm not his. I give him everything I can, all of my love, all of my desire, and I receive his, every last drop.

He pulls me up and back into his lap, cradling me, kissing me, loving me. It's early, but he carries me back to bed. He sets me down, quickly shedding his clothes until he's just in his boxers before climbing into bed and tucking me against him. We have a king-size bed, not that we need one so big since we always seem to end up together in the middle every night.

"Everything is going to be all right," he promises.

"Yes," I agree, because in this moment I can see there isn't another alternative.

As long as we are together, no matter what else happens, everything will be all right.

"Why are you so sure there is something wrong at all?"

"Sawyer and I both went off birth control around the same time."

His fingers coast up and down my arm. "Sometimes it takes longer for some people."

"It's been a year, Will," I argue.

He stills. "What if I'm the problem?"

I hate his choice of words. "Impossible."

He chuckles. "That's your expert medical opinion?"

I look up at him. "You're perfect."

He shakes his head. "No such thing."

THEM

I huff and he laughs at me, so I glare which only makes him laugh harder.

"It's not funny," I fume.

"Darling, it's outside of our control. But you are seriously adorable when you try to look mad."

I roll my eyes as his body shakes. "Happy to amuse you."

He shifts me to my back and kisses me hard. "You're doing a bang-up job."

I'm annoyed but I guess it *is* funny, and somehow his laughter is infectious. I fight it, I really do, pressing my lips together tightly as, in vain, I refuse to crack a smile. Will is on to me and sitting up, his legs straddling my stomach, he starts to tickle me.

Suddenly, I'm back in high school, on my back in the field by the parking lot as Will tickles me. I was so in love with him then. I had no idea that he even thought of me as anything other than a friend. In that moment, I could not have imagined that even after the time we were apart that I would be here someday. Here in bed with Will Price, married to him and in the home we share.

That does it. My face breaks and I'm not sure, but there's a chance that I've never been happier than I am in this moment. It took Will unintentionally reminding me of my high school hopes and dreams to make me realize how lucky I am. Is it human nature to always want more? When will it sink in that I already have everything I ever wanted?

Will's eyes shine as he looks down at me. "You are so beautiful."

I reach for him, pulling him down until he covers me completely.

4

Will

This weekend was hard on Sarah. It was painful to see the longing in her eyes as she looked at Brian, Christine and Calvin. She knows I love her, even if she needs to be reminded from time to time just how much. What she doesn't know is I feel like I'm failing her.

She wants a family, and I'm not able to give that to her. I'm going with her to the doctor today. I didn't tell her, but I did some research on infertility online over the weekend. The first thing they normally check is the guy. What if I'm the problem? I'm not looking forward to jerking off into a cup. I'm even less looking forward to the possibility that something's wrong with my sperm count.

I only want to make her happy. What if giving her a family is a physical impossibility for me? Would she be okay with adopting as an alternative? Maybe I should get her a puppy. Would she love it, or know it was a pathetic substitute to the baby she truly wants?

I'm losing my mind, actually considering replacing a child with a dog.

THEM

I hear the shower turn off.

I took a half-day from work. I wanted to take the whole day off, but Logan has been sharing lunch with me every day and I want to be there for him. He's starting to open up. His grandfather was put on hospice at the beginning of the year, which is bad news since he was the healthier one of his grandparents before his health took a turn.

His father is still in South Korea and he has no idea what will happen to his grandmother after his grandfather passes away. He's had a hard time getting his dad on the phone because of his schedule and the time difference. As far as he knows, his father has been informed and is working to get approval to come home.

Until then, Logan has become the main caregiver for his grandmother. The hospice people have been pitching in here and there as they care for his grandfather. That scares him. What if they tell someone? He's afraid someone will take him away from his grandmother because he's a minor and she's so sick.

That's a lot of crap for an eighth grader to be shouldering all by himself. Depending on how this doctor's appointment goes, I'm going to talk to Sarah about seeing what we can do to help. If the appointment goes badly, I'll do it by myself. I don't want to add any more stress to what Sarah is already dealing with.

She walks into the kitchen, and I'm surprised by how dressed up she is. She's curled her hair, is wearing more makeup than normal and is wearing a dress.

"Hot date?" I ask.

"Huh?"

"You look like you're going on a hot date, not to a doctor's appointment."

She blushes. "I felt like looking nice."

I tug her toward me. "You always look beautiful, but right now you look gorgeous."

"Stop." She lifts her hands to press against my chest.

I pull her closer. "How'd I get so lucky?"

Her mouth is right there so I kiss her. She melts against me so I kiss and hold her until we have to go. She acts annoyed that she has to fix her lip gloss before we walk out the door, but I know she really doesn't mind.

She drives, which doesn't happen that often if we're in the car together. We're going to her lady stuff doctor and since I've never been, I guess it makes sense. We have GPS, so I *could* have driven, but she wants to feel in control. I give it to her even though it makes me feel slightly out of control myself.

I'll drive on the way back. Hopefully, it won't annoy her. I'll even remember to put her seat back the way it should be this time.

THEM

This appointment is only a consultation. They won't make me leave a sample today, will they? Will I go into a room by myself while they all know what I'm doing? Great, now I'm having performance anxiety. Will they let Sarah go in with me? I don't know whether that would be hot or not. We've watched each other before, and that was sexy as hell, her hands all over herself. I'm not sure how that would translate in a sterile doctor's office.

Her hand is on my leg now and I glance over at her. We've parked; I hadn't noticed. Can she tell I'm nervous? Her hand squeezes my leg once before she gets out. I take a deep breath and get out, as well. We meet in front of the car, her hand slipping into mine, and walk into a grey brick building together.

"His name is Dr. Stacey," Sarah tells me in the elevator.

We stop on the fifth floor and walk past the offices of a dermatologist and a psychiatrist before reaching her doctor's office. I stand with Sarah as she signs in. The receptionist seems to recognize her, and they talk for a moment before she grabs my hand and we sit and wait. There's a couple, the woman clearly pregnant, and one woman all by herself, also waiting.

The walls of the room are peach, the upholstery of the chairs, as well. The effect makes the chairs seem to disappear into the walls; the only thing stopping them are the wooden arm rests. The carpet is sage with a peach triangle shape pattern repeating itself.

The solo woman is called back first. Not long after her, the other couple is also taken back.

"Is there more than one doctor?" I ask, curious as to how long we'll be waiting. The peach is getting to me.

"Yes, it's a practice. They have another office downtown, so I'm not sure how many doctors there are."

"This is a lot of peach."

She laughs, turning so she can press her face into my shoulder.

"It's tripping me out," I continue. "And giving me a weird craving for nectarines. Has that ever happened to you after an appointment here?"

"Stop," she pleads. "You're killing me."

"Only making an observation."

She lifts her head and beams at me. There's my girl. I press my lips to hers and her name is called. She blushes that we were caught kissing and stands as a nurse holds open a door for us. We pass empty rooms with examination tables. My curiosity gets the better of me as I pause to peer into one of them. *Huh. So that's what stirrups look like.*

The room we're led to is less examination room, more office. Her doctor, who I had incorrectly assumed was a woman but actually is not a bad-looking dude, stands to greet us. We are absolutely talking about this on the ride home.

THEM

"Mrs. Price, Mr. Price. Please, have a seat," he says after shaking our hands.

"Our normal course of action for couples concerned about fertility is to recommend the husband visit a urologist to have his sperm count captured. While you're here, I'd like to also get some blood work and do an internal sonogram today."

Internal sonogram?

Dr. Stacey stands and calls for the nurse who walked us back.

We follow her to a small room where she gets Sarah's weight, blood pressure, and draws two vials of blood before having Sarah go pee in a cup. After that, she leads us to another room with an examination table which also has a TV monitor.

The nurse asks Sarah to step into a bathroom attached to the room, undress from the waist down and come back into the room with a hospital gown on. After Sarah follows the instructions and gets situated on the table, the nurse shows her a wand-looking thing and explains that it's inserted inside her for the sonogram.

Inside her?

Sarah's eyes widen briefly and she reaches for my hand. The nurse turns on the TV thing and performs the internal sonogram. I think she can tell Sarah and I are nervous, so she tries to distract both of us as she explains that she's taking internal pictures which Dr.

Stacey will review with us. The whole thing is over in ten minutes.

The nurse prints off the pictures while Sarah gets dressed. Then she walks us back to Dr. Stacey's office. As we're sitting, she points one picture out in particular to the doctor.

After she leaves, shutting the door behind her, he speaks. "It'll be a week before we get the results of your blood work back. I'll give you a call at that time. My nurse did notice something during your sonogram that could be an issue."

He holds one picture up for both of us to see. It has a computer-generated circle drawn over a cloudy-looking spot with some numbers typed next to it.

"It appears there is a growth currently in your uterus. I don't want to alarm you. This is perfectly normal but may be a reason you're having issues conceiving. We'll still need to get a current sperm count to rule that out first before we investigate this further."

"Could it be cancerous?" Sarah stammers, clutching my knee.

"We will know more once we have your blood work back. However, in my experience and based on your history, this may be something as simple as a polyp, which are harmless. The reason it could be causing you to have difficulties conceiving is there is the potential the polyp in the uterus is taking up valuable real estate and tricking your body into thinking you're already pregnant."

Sarah exhales, her grip loosening. "So, you don't think it's cancer?"

"I do not."

My turn to exhale. "Do I need a referral for the urologist?"

He leans back in his chair. "Ask the receptionist when you check out. It depends on your healthcare provider."

I nod, lifting Sarah's hand from my leg and curling my fingers around it.

"Did you have any other questions for me?"

Sarah shakes her head.

"Okay. I'd like to schedule another appointment for you, two weeks out, where we can go over the results from your blood work and hopefully have the results from Mr. Price's urology appointment, as well."

We both nod and stand to shake hands again before we walk out. During check-out, Sarah makes her next appointment and finds out we do not need a referral. The receptionist gives her a printout with the contact information of three offices nearby.

When we get outside, she passes me the keys before walking right to the passenger side of the car. My hands shake as I unlock it. We both sit quietly for a minute before turning to face each other.

"What if he's wrong and it *is* cancer, Will?" Sarah whispers.

"He's not wrong." I have no clue but holy shit, she cannot have cancer.

"That was scary, Will."

My hand goes to the back of her neck as I lean forward, pulling her until we meet in the middle of the central console and I can hold her. This is going to be the longest week of our lives while we wait for the results of the blood work to come back. I hate that she's scared. I hate that I'm powerless to make it go away.

Now is not the time to tease her about getting dressed up for her good-looking doctor. I'm secure enough in my manhood and our marriage to not care what her doctor looks like. My priority right now is cheering her up. Sarah craves structure and absolutes; not knowing is not okay for her, and having to wait to find out isn't helping.

"Want a waffle cone?"

She lifts her head and, with unshed tears glistening in her eyes, smiles and nods. Waffle cones it is. I drive on autopilot to the ice cream shop we've gone to since we were kids. I order two scoops of chocolate chip for Sarah and, to live a little, I go for one scoop of chocolate raspberry truffle and one scoop of mint chocolate chip.

We sit inside where it's warmer and hold hands while we eat in silence. I don't know about Sarah, but

THEM

I'm wishing for simpler times that don't involve sperm counts or blood work.

When we finish and head back to the car, I walk her to her door and lean her against it to kiss her. I don't know what to say, but I hope my kiss does the speaking for me. I want her to know that no matter what happens, good or bad, she has me forever. That if there's a reason we can't have a baby of our own, I won't care. That I'll want her and only her for the rest of my life.

Sarah is it for me. Only once I've kissed all of that to her do I open her door. She reaches for my hand as soon as I'm in on my side. I lift her hand to my lips and grin at her. Whatever life throws at us, we'll figure out together.

When we get back to the house, I ask if she wants me to stay.

"No," she replies. "I know you're worried about missing lunch with Logan."

"Are you sure? You are more important to me."

She smiles. "Yes, I'm just going to go lie down. We can hang out more when you get home from work."

I lean over to kiss her. She's right; I do worry about Logan. I had a meeting with his guidance counselor and our assistant principal to clue them in on his lunch schedule. The family situation is not unknown with the school. Luckily, last I heard his dad should be on the way home soon. Thankfully, Mrs. Cobb, the guidance counselor for our school, wasn't adverse to him eating with me.

Logan is a good kid, and I have no idea if he's getting enough food at home or not. If he's on to me purposefully bringing too much food everyday so he has something to eat, he hasn't said anything. At this point, as far as he knows, he's doing me a favor. Since the temperature has been dropping, I also managed to get him to accept a couple of old hoodies of mine.

The kid is growing like a weed and outgrew his coat from last year. I know there are kids in worse-off situations, but I've made Logan my personal project. I was his age when I was a hungry kid, too. I was lucky to have the Millers to take care of me. Who knows what kind of trouble I'd get up to if I hadn't been assigned that project with Sarah.

Our ice cream pit stop has me running late. By the time I make it to my classroom, I see Logan walking away.

"Hey, Logan. I'm here. Sorry I'm late."

The relief that crosses his face kills me. I can't let this kid down.

"Hey, Mr. Price."

He stands next to me, waiting as I unlock my door and flip on the lights.

"So, how's your day going, Logan?"

He shrugs, and instead of heading to the back of the class like he did in the beginning, he now sits at the table closest to my desk. He's still on the quiet side but is opening up more and more every day.

"My grandpa had a rough night last night."

"I'm sorry to hear that, buddy."

He nods. It's terrible that someone his age has to shoulder this much.

"I can't wait for my dad to come home. I haven't seen him in eight months."

"What's the last thing you heard on that?"

I pass him a chicken salad sandwich. I've started bringing a cooler to work.

He takes a bite, practically inhaling it before he answers, talking around the bits of food left in his mouth. "He has to get out-processed from that base first. It's taking forever but should be done this week."

"That's great news, bud."

"So, why were you late today?"

"My wife had to go to the doctor and I went with her."

He keeps eating, but his eyes widen. "Is she okay?"

I nod, not knowing if I'm lying.

"That's good."

I grin at him and get to work.

5

Sarah

Why is the light on my phone blinking? I unlock my screen and see that I've missed a call from Dr. Stacey's office. A call I've literally been waiting for all week. I've had my phone next to me all day long except for getting up just now to go get the mail. Is there some sort of radar that ensures you will miss whatever call you're waiting for?

My leg shakes as I listen to the voicemail. Crap. They don't tell me anything, just ask me to call them back. Is that bad? I stand once the phone starts ringing and start to pace back and forth across my office. Five steps and I'm across the room. I groan and move out into the hall so I have more space to cover as I pace.

I have to stop myself from throwing my phone when the receptionist tells me Dr. Stacey is currently with a patient and will have to call me back. *But he just called me!* I want to argue. I'm too polite, though, so I save my frustrated venting for after I've hung up with them.

I head back to my office and make an unsuccessful attempt at sorting the mail I dropped on my desk when I'd noticed my phone was blinking. My head isn't in it; is this a bill, or junk mail? Who cares? Instead, I stare at my phone, willing it to ring. I also kinda-sorta have to pee but can't make up my mind whether to go for it or hold it. I double-check to make sure the ringer is on at least three times before he calls back.

I'm on my way, phone in hand, to the half-bath when Dr. Stacey calls.

"Hello," I answer.

"Mrs. Price?"

"Yes, this is she," I whisper.

"This is Dr. Stacey. I wanted to call and let you know your blood work came back and was normal."

"Oh, thank God," I breathe.

"Has Mr. Price made his appointment with a urologist?"

I sag against the wall, relief hitting me. "Yes, he's going tomorrow morning."

"Good. Well, we'll see you both back here in a week."

"Thank you."

As soon as I hang up, I call Will. I don't even know if he has a class right now, but I have to tell him. He answers right away.

"Sarah."

"My blood work is normal!" I shout.

"Oh, thank God."

I start to laugh. "That's what I said."

"I love you, babe."

I hold my phone with both hands, wishing I could hold him instead.

I'm suddenly choked up when I reply, "I love you, too."

"Babe," he says quietly.

I was so scared. I don't know why I'm about to cry. It must be a happy cry or my body relaxing after being so stressed this past week. Even though I feel silly for being emotional, I don't care.

"I'm taking you out tonight."

I laugh. "It's a date."

After we hang up, I can't hold it anymore and run to pee. Luckily, I have the house all to myself; otherwise, someone might wonder why I'm giggling on the toilet. I'm not even sure why I'm laughing. Maybe it's because I was so afraid, and now it seems silly to have worked myself up that way.

Even though my doctor had seemed certain whatever growth was hanging out inside me wasn't cancerous, I had been scared. So scared that neither Will nor I had told anyone about it, not even Sawyer.

It's impossible to keep anything from her, so I've been ignoring her calls and texts. I owe her a call big-time.

I only hope she isn't pissed at me for keeping this from her.

Phone still in my hand, I go right to her contact listing and call her.

"Oh, so you *are* alive," she answers.

"Hi, babe."

"You know, seeing as how my last text to you, um, two friggin' *days* ago was 'are you alive,' it's nice to finally know for sure. Let me guess: you and Will have gotten into bondage and you were handcuffed to your bed."

"There is a growth in my uterus, and we were waiting to find out if it was cancerous or not."

"Oh, shit. Is it . . . ?" She trails off.

"It's not. I just found out. That's why I haven't called. I'm so sor—"

"Don't even apologize," she cuts me off. "I completely understand. Is that what they found in your appointment? Do you need to have a surgery?"

"Will is going for his sperm count tomorrow. My doctor wants to confirm that before doing anything else. If Will's sperm count comes back normal then I guess we'll . . . honestly, I have no idea. All I know is I was so scared this past week. I wanted to tell you, but I didn't want to worry you if it wasn't anything serious."

"Oh, honey. That's what friends are for. I'm here for you to worry me about whatever you want, whenever you want. I can handle it. I don't want you to ever feel like you have to protect me."

The tears that formed as she spoke spill over as I try to talk. "I miss you."

"Do you want me to come down? Say the word, babe, and I'm there."

"I couldn't ask you to do that. Snow season is about to start."

Her husband, Jared, is a ski instructor and manages the rental shop at a resort near their house. He works year-round since the resort also has off-season activities, but winter is their true peak season.

"Who said Jared would come with?"

"Come on. Like he'd be cool with you bringing Pascal down here and leaving him." Jared loved his girls.

"You're probably right but for you, he'd deal with it."

"I love you. I'll be okay. Not going more than a week without talking to you will help."

"I get the radio silence, I do, but holy shit, I was getting so pissed at you."

"Still pissed?" I tease.

"Ugh, no, but if you ever shut me out again, we're going to have a problem, ma'am."

"Deal. Okay, I'm emotionally exhausted from all of this and Will is taking me out tonight. I'm going to take a nap so I won't pass out mid-meal."

THEM

"All right. Call me once you hear back on Will's appointment."

"It's not a real appointment. He went a couple days ago to pick up this cup. He has to jerk off at home and then run the sample over tomorrow. They'll call us and schedule another appointment if there are issues. If not, they'll tell him he can pick up the results and we'll bring those to my doctor."

Sawyer starts laughing. "So, you're going to help him prepare his sample."

"This isn't funny." I try to sound serious.

"Whatever, dude. Whacking off is hysterical."

I ignore the pile of mail downstairs and head up to our bedroom. "You're a mess."

"And you love me for it."

"I do."

"I'll talk to you later."

After we hang up, I feel lighter than I have in days. Sure I have a random polyp inside me, but at least it's not cancerous. It's strange, but because of the name, I've been imagining it looks like pulp from orange juice.

That's the last thing I think about as I stretch out on our bed for a nap.

I wake to lips on my neck and arms wrapped around me.

"Hmm." My eyes blink open and I see Will's smiling face.

"Hey, beautiful," he murmurs, pushing my hair from my face.

"Hi." I smile back and melt into him.

"How are you feeling? Do you still want to go out?"

I squint past him to look at the alarm clock. "Am I awful for not wanting to get out of bed?"

He laughs, dipping his head to kiss me. "I'm all for you never leaving this bed."

"That isn't what I meant," I huff.

"It should have been," he teases, his lips trailing across my jaw and down my neck.

My shirt is button-up, and his hands release me to start unbuttoning. "Can we, with your appointment tomorrow?"

He pauses, resting his forehead to mine. "Shit. I forgot."

I cringe. "I guess that means no."

He looks up, his blue eyes mischievous. "That doesn't mean we can't do other stuff."

Before I can reply, he ducks under the covers and starts pulling my yoga pants and underwear off.

"Will, you don't—" I stop speaking the moment his mouth hits me.

All coherent use of the English language is lost to me from that point on. I've always teased Will that he's good at everything he does, and this is no exception. I'm not stupid, though; I don't tease him for this. There is nothing sexier than how into pleasuring me he gets.

My body is fine-tuned to him. He knows exactly how I like it, but it's more than that. It's knowing that if *he's* doing it, I *will* like it. I trust him so much so that I've no reason to ever be embarrassed.

It's freeing and exhilarating and—"Oh, God, oh, God! Don't you dare stop, right, right there . . ."

He crawls up me, kissing me hungrily before pulling away. "I need a cold shower, stat."

I want to offer words of support but haven't mentally regained use of my tongue yet to form said words. I just lie there, blissfully limbless as I hear the shower turn on.

He's back in almost no time, now clad only in a towel. He shakes his head at me as soon as he sees I haven't moved, haven't even made an effort to put my clothes back on.

"You are welcome." He laughs, bending over to kiss my cheek.

I scrunch my nose at him and refuse to move otherwise.

"Want me to order pizza?"

"Mmmm."

"I'm taking that as a yes." He laughs again, pulling on a pair of track pants and an old t-shirt from our high school days.

Deciding it would be best not to eat pizza in bed, I pull my clothes back on and follow him downstairs.

He's turning off his phone by the time I make it to him. "Want to order a movie or watch something from the DVR?"

I'm two weeks behind on one of my favorite shows, but it's one Will thinks is silly. It would be horribly unfair to ask to watch it, considering he just went down on me and had to take a cold shower.

He knows me well enough to read my expression and rolls his eyes as he selects it from the DVR queue.

"Are you sure?" I grin at him.

He tugs me toward him and kisses me. "You owe me."

I like the sound of that. Owing Will Price always seems to be quite rewarding in the end.

"Deal." I kiss his neck, right under his chin.

His arms tighten before he releases me, stepping back. "The pizza should be here in thirty minutes. What do you want to drink?"

"Who'd you order from?"

We have different standing orders depending on which pizza place we order from. "Vinnie's."

Marguerita pizza, yum. "If we have any sangria left, I'll have that. Otherwise, iced tea sounds good."

I plop down onto our comfy sofa, put my feet up onto our ottoman-style coffee table and start my show. Will won't care if he misses the beginning. He's back in no time with a tumbler of sangria for me and a can of Coke for himself. I lean forward, making room for him to sit and then rest against him. I love staying in, just the two of us. When Sawyer and I still lived in Colorado, we went out way more than Will and I do now.

Sure, I miss living near my best friend but I wouldn't trade this, what I have right now, for anything. I've seen movies and read books where women are swept off their feet by some billionaire or celebrity, and into private planes or helicopters off to movie premiers or galas. I'm the one living the real fantasy, tucked up to my high school sweetheart, watching our DVR while we wait for a pizza to be delivered. This is it for me, my dream, all I've ever wanted. Well, *almost* all I've ever wanted. Hopefully soon we'll learn why we haven't been able to start a family.

Who knows? Maybe a year from now we'll be in exactly the same place, only with a baby of our own.

When the doorbell rings, I pause the TV and we both get up to go to the door. Will passes me the food while he pays the driver, and I take it to the kitchen to serve it up. He meets me in time to carry his plate back to the living room. We have it down to a science, the way we move in harmony.

Will even behaves as I catch up on my show. He only snickers a couple of times during the more melodramatic parts. It's a TV show about vampires, so the fact that he's watching it with me at all gives him a free pass to think it's silly. I don't care, though; Sawyer and I got hooked on this show when we lived together, and watching it reminds me of her.

She still watches it, too, and part of the text messages I missed from her were asking if I had caught up so we could discuss. Perfectly normal adult behavior. When I finish my pizza, I snuggle back into Will, since he eats faster than I do and finishes ages before me. Once I'm settled, he pulls a throw blanket off the back of the couch and covers both of us.

I don't notice until fast-forwarding through the next commercial break that he's fallen asleep. I pause the show to take a moment and watch his resting face. He's still so handsome, boyishly so while somehow also being all man. There are times, like this, when I have to remind myself that this is real. That he, we, together are real.

His chocolate brown hair is longer than usual. I can't help but wonder if all the worry about me or Logan has made him forget his regular haircut. I don't mind the extra length, though. It reminds me of the skater boy who tried to teach me how to ride by pushing me on his board around the neighborhood.

THEM

I still wear all of the rings he's given me: the plastic thumb ring, my engagement ring, and my wedding band. Doesn't seem fair, my three to his one. He is so giving, and he's all mine. I can't help it; softly, as not to wake him, I stroke his hair back from his face. He shifts, and I'm scared I've woken him but then he stills again, his lips parting. His lips, I could stare at them all day. Something as simple as tugging his lower lip between his teeth can absolutely mesmerize me.

They are perfection, how soft they are while also being firm. The moment his lips touch my skin, I am his to command. I've always been his, from the first day he kissed me and claimed me. Feather-light, I lower my lips to his and softly brush them against his.

Only then do I return to my show. These vampires may live and love forever, but I'm sure their love will never touch ours.

6

Will

Collecting my sample was a breeze this morning; I had one sexy-as-hell assistant. Handing it over to the nurse at the urologist, though, was something I never pictured myself doing. *Here, have a cup full of my sperm, stranger.*

There's a part of me that hopes I'm the problem. Sarah is stressed out enough already. If the reason we're not getting pregnant is me, she'll stop beating herself up about it. Sure, I want a family. I love kids, I always have and we're in a great place stability-wise to start a family.

Watching Sarah with Calvin leaves me with no doubt she'd be a great mother. She has this internal strength that my mom never had. When my sister died, my mom gave up on life and made no attempt to do anything other than go through the motions of living. It didn't matter that I was still around and needed her.

Sarah would never do that and even if she tried, I'm sure if I couldn't snap her out of it Sawyer would swoop in and kick her ass. If I wasn't so anti-snow I could see us having a blast living near Sawyer and

Jared. Brian would probably veto the whole idea, though, and Mrs. Miller would guilt-trip me considering she's been on cloud nine having Sarah back home. Seems like we're here to stay in Atlanta.

Even with the pit-stop to drop off my sample, I still manage to slide into school before the first bell. I love being a teacher. Having summers off is a huge perk. Downfall to that is it means I get almost zero personal time during the school year. This includes sick days, and not picking up something is sometimes impossible considering I teach walking Petri dishes.

Good thing I load up on hand sanitizer at the start of each school year. Another thing I've learned over the years is to look away if a kid looks like they're about to yawn, because nine times out of ten it means there's a sneeze on deck.

My first period class is an intro to art. There are some kids here who struggle drawing a stick figure. We're only three months into the year, though, so there's only so much magic I can do at this point.

What's fun about this class is since it's an intro, we jump around and focus on all different types of mediums. Those kids who struggle with stick figures tend to excel in something else. Being there to watch as they recognize their own untapped creativity bloom is pretty sweet. At the end of the day, it's the reason I teach.

Right now, we're doing a section on watercolors and impressionists. The kids love the concept of what looks like a mess up close coming into focus and becoming more beautiful as they step away.

It's fun but messy; by the end of class, my floors are looking rough. The moment the kids file out, I grab the Swiffer Wet I keep in the class to tackle the floors. There's three minutes before my next class starts, so I have to be quick. I'm just over halfway done when there's a knock on my door.

"Yes?" I lift my head.

"Mr. Price. Do you have a moment?" It's one of the PE teachers, Mr. Garrison.

"Sure. What's up?" I glance at the unfinished floor and figure it doesn't look that bad, so I put the Swiffer away.

"Would you be interested in assistant coaching the Decater High JV Lacrosse team?"

Didn't see that coming. "When would you need to know by?"

"Take the weekend and if you can let me know by Monday, that'd be great."

I nod and he leaves just as my students begin filing in.

Coach lacrosse?

Some of my happiest memories from high school, outside of the time I spent with Sarah, were playing lacrosse. Looking back, the aggression I was able to get out on the field had to have kept me from going off the rails. There was no reason to get into fights when I could wait until practice and whale on someone instead. As long as I didn't get too many fouls, I was good to go.

Coaching might be fun. It's something I'll have to talk over with Sarah because I know what a commitment time-wise it would be. There'd be practice every day after school and then games on Friday nights.

My next class is working on a project, so other than answering the off-question or doing a lap around the classroom to make sure the kids stay focused, I'm free to let my mind wander. The more I think about coaching, the more I want to do it.

Lunch is next period, so I can call Sarah and get her thoughts. Once the bell rings and my classroom empties, I grab my phone.

"Hey, honey. How'd the drop-off go?"

I laugh. "It was weird. I should have made you go with me."

"What, you didn't want to be alone as you spread your seed around?"

"That's just wrong, woman."

She laughs and I look up to see Logan hovering in the doorway. I motion him to come in.

"Hey, the PE teacher stopped by this morning and asked if I'd be interested in assistant coaching the JV lacrosse team over at the high school. I told him I'd think about it because I wanted to talk to you first."

"You would be the best coach ever. You should totally do it."

"Totally," I tease.

"Yes." Somehow, even on the phone, I can tell she's rolling her eyes at me.

"Cool. I wanted to run it by you first before I agreed to anything. I'm going to hop, though, since Logan is here for lunch."

"Okay, babe. See you tonight."

When I look up, Logan's eyes are on me.

"You know how to play lacrosse?" he asks.

I nod. "Heck yeah. I played lacrosse in high school and for University of Georgia."

His mouth drops. "You did?"

I grin and stand. "I might have some old black and white pictures. Want to see?"

"That'd be awesome." His excitement is palpable.

As I walk over to a storage cabinet, I ask, "Do you play?"

He shakes his head. "No, but I always wanted to learn."

Once I find the album I'm looking for, I head over to his table. "If I get the coaching job and it's cool with the main coach and your dad, do you want to come to the practices and learn to play?"

"That'd be amazing, Mr. Price."

THEM

It's been a few days since I've asked about his dad. "Things going better at home?"

The smile he gives me is halfhearted at best. His grandfather passed away two days after his dad came back.

"I miss my grandpa, but my dad got to say goodbye and spend time with him. My grandma isn't doing so well, so my dad and I are visiting her a lot. It's getting better. I'm just so happy my dad is finally home."

I pat his shoulder. "I'm glad you're doing better."

"I told him about you." He pauses to suck in air. "How you helped me while he was away. He wants to meet you, to thank you."

Talk about an emotional punch to the gut.

I gulp, reaching up to give his shoulder a squeeze. "I would love to meet your dad."

I leave the album for him to flip through as I walk back to my desk to unpack my lunch. At this point, I don't even ask if he wants to eat anymore. Pulling out one turkey sandwich and an apple, I walk back over and set them by his elbow. As cool as getting back into lacrosse sounds, Logan inviting me to meet his dad means so much more.

Speaking of news, my results should be back in forty-eight hours. I need to think of something to keep Sarah's mind off the waiting part.

"Mr. Price, is this the picture you won that award for?"

I stand and make my way over to him to see.

Nodding, I ask, "Do you recognize the street?"

All of my students get a kick out of knowing a place they see every day was the setting of my award-winning image. You can't see the school in the shot since my back was to it. I had been standing in the parking lot, about to leave when across the street, a little girl fell while riding her bike.

"Yeah. That's so cool."

"Are you looking forward to the photography section?" I ask.

He grins. "I am. I got a camera last Christmas."

We spent the rest of lunch talking about cameras and ideas on what the kids could take pictures of during our photography lesson. When I was in school, we had cell phones but none of them had built-in cameras. It's incredible to think that one technological advancement could make such a drastic change to the way we document our lives. Statistically, today we take more photos every two minutes then were taken in all of the 1800's.

I'm teaching the selfie generation. My students all have Instagram accounts and spend more time worrying over whether they should use Vallencia or Hudson to filter their images. It's easy to shrug off the things that appeal to them as idiotic, but I can't.

There is a lesson in the fact that they are currently more focused on how their lives are represented online than actually living them. The importance that is placed on how many followers they have or how many likes their pictures get is staggering. It's also a reminder how lucky I am that I grew up during a time where my teenage years weren't documented for public consumption frame by frame.

I took more pictures than the other kids I was in school with, but that camera was my shield. The difference between me and the kids today is there's only one person who saw all the pictures I took, not the whole internet.

Part of my lesson this year is the dangers and things they need to be aware of when posting pics. The fact that one person on Twitter can post a picture of a cute check-out boy at Target and set off an entire web storm is astounding. This kid, who lived in virtual obscurity one moment, went to having hundreds of thousands of followers and an interview on the Ellen show in the same week.

In his case, it was a flattering pic and the fandom that's blowing up in his honor has been mainly positive. What these kids don't understand is that virtual popularity is a double-edged sword. What is the draw of being adored by faceless, nameless strangers?

I hope to gain some insight into their motivation during our discussions. Nobody understands pop culture trends better than your average middle school student. When the bell rings and my next class starts to file in, I have to get my mind back to the subject at hand.

We're wrapping up our watercolor week. Each Friday, we have a quiz covering the mechanics of what we covered over the week. We have some topics that take more than one week in total. Then at the end of each marking period, we review and retest over everything we covered during that time.

While the kids work on their quiz, I try to come up with ideas to distract Sarah. It's been a while since we've gone anywhere, just the two of us. That's an option, packing the car up and heading toward the coast. It'd be a better plan if it wasn't so cold. November was definitely making its presence known.

I've never been a fan of scraping ice off my windows. Sarah surprised me last Christmas with a remote starter for my car, so now I have a cup of coffee and watch the ice melt away from our living room. She's better than I am at presents. I think it's because she's detail-oriented and observant.

She's in charge of birthdays and Christmas presents for both sides of our families. When the answer comes to me, I feel stupid for not thinking of this right away. Sawyer would know what to do or get her. I type out a quick text and get an even faster response.

~ *She needs a puppy.*

I reply ~ What? Is this a joke?

~ *Nope. Not joking. She needs something to take care of.*

Something to take care of?

~ Will she think it's a baby replacement?

THEM

~ Who cares. She needs company.

A puppy.

We'd talked about getting a dog after we got married but never got around to it. What Sawyer wrote about her needing company makes me pause. I had never thought about it that way. During the summer, when I'm home, we're together. Now that I'm back at school, she's alone all day long.

I have six periods of students to distract and fill my day. She has work that is, in her own words, 'not enough to fill her days.' A puppy might be perfect.

~ Thanks. You're the best.

~ Anytime, dude.

Since I promised her a date night, I know exactly where we'll go now. Sarah would never want a dog from a breeder. She starts tearing up every single time a story about a puppy mill comes on TV.

Once my final class is over, I don't linger. Depending on how busy my day was or how much I was able to accomplish over my lunch period, I usually end up staying at work for an hour every day to load grades or prep supplies for the next day. Not today, though; Mrs. Price and I have a date to go on.

She's still in her office when I get home, which is rare these days. "Everything okay?"

Her face lifts from her screen and a lazy smile spreads across it. No matter what else is going on in the world, knowing my wife is happy to see me every day when I get home from work is all I truly care about.

"Hey, honey. Everything is fine."

I cross the room and sit on the edge of her desk, leaning down as she tilts her face toward mine, offering me her lips.

After a gentle, loving kiss hello, I lift my head. "You're working later than normal."

She presses a few keys before pushing away from her desk and standing. "I watched a movie after lunch and was checking my email to make sure no one sent me anything."

My legs open for her to come stand between them as she drapes her arms around my neck. "Watch anything good?

Nodding, she grins. "I loved it, but it was a period romance so you would have hated it."

"Were there any boobs?"

She laughs and I lean forward to kiss her neck.

"No boobs," she replies, her breath catching as my hand slides down her back and into her yoga pants to grip her delectable ass.

"You're right. I probably wouldn't have liked it."

My other hand slides under her shirt to palm her breast. *Crap, sports bra.* Sarah owns four types of bras: lacy ones which are sexy as hell, cotton ones which are still sexy but not as much as the lacy ones, old sport bras which are a breeze to slip my hands into, and then these sport bras. These bras are like the Fort Knox of boob protection.

I hate them. Here I have my sexy wife rubbing against me while my hand is on her ass and I can't get to her breasts. The elastic is practically glued to her body. I enjoy undressing her, but she's going to have to handle that bra herself.

Giving up, I move that hand to join the other on her ass, kneading her cheeks as I kiss my way back up her neck. "Have we ever fucked on your desk?"

I had a dream once we had sex on my desk at school. The classroom was full of people watching us, but instead of my students it was Congress. I think it was around election time. Old dudes watching me bang my wife was weird, but I remember that image of her laid out across my desk and how hot it was.

She shakes her head. *Oh, it's on.*

7

Sarah

I'm never having sex with Will in a weird place again, no matter how sexy and good he makes it sound.

"I'm sorry, babe."

He would have sounded more convincing if he hadn't been laughing.

He's not the one with a blue ass.

Somehow, in our excitement, we broke a pen which leaked onto the top of my desk calendar. The one Will sat me on as he went to town on me. I was so turned on I didn't realize the excess wetness wasn't from us until we were done and I stood up.

Not only do I have a blue ass, but there are also blue ass prints all over the top of November. Good thing the month is almost over. Knowing my luck, it probably bled through to December. I forgot to check between Will laughing his ass off when he saw mine and spending the last twenty minutes in the shower trying to de-blue-ify my butt.

THEM

My cheeks have gone from a deep royal blue to a grayish, cold blue. At least it isn't summer. My bikini bottoms wouldn't cover this.

Will leans against the bathroom counter, all handsome and stuff. He's so annoying. I stick my tongue out at him as I pass him on my way back into our room.

"Still the sexiest ass I've ever seen." He tries and fails to keep a straight face as he says it.

"I should make you wait for sex until the blue is all gone," I grumble.

At that, he at least pales.

He sits on the edge of our bed as I get changed. "Where are you taking me tonight?"

Rubbing his hands together, he gets that look in his eyes when he's about to talk me into something. It was the same look he had before he suggested desk sex.

"I was thinking we could head over to the rescue center and pick up a puppy."

My shoulders sag and I still. "Are you suggesting we get a dog because you think I'll never get pregnant?"

He stands, crossing the room quickly to wrap his arms around my towel-clad body. "Not at all. We've talked about getting a dog in the past. I hate that you're here all alone while I'm at work. I thought you could use a partner in crime."

"A substitute baby," I argue.

His finger slips under my chin, lifting my eyes until they're locked with his. "We've only just started working toward having a baby."

"I've always wanted a puppy," I admit.

"And I've always only wanted to give you everything you've ever wanted," he replies, dropping his lips to mine.

I push him away with a grin. "No funny business. We need to get to the shelter before it closes."

Hurriedly, I get dressed in some jeans and a comfy sweater. I tug on my boots and pull on my coat once we're downstairs.

Will drives as I suggest dog names.

"What about Sam?"

"That's a people name," Will argues.

"Aren't most pet names also people names?" I ask.

He shakes his head. "Duke, Bruiser, Tank, Spot, Yeller."

"Yeller?" I laugh.

With a shrug, he turns into the parking lot. The animal shelter is a one-story brick building not far from the grocery store where we shop. I gave him a hard time for suggesting a puppy, but to be fair it's something we've talked about doing more than once over the last couple of years. At first, we held off as I struggled to find a new normal work-wise.

THEM

I don't miss the stress, but I do miss how full my days were back then. I know I started this company, and I'm proud of how well it's doing, but I'm not used to making money off the actions of other people. I've structured my company so efficiently I've made myself redundant.

There are plenty of people, I'm sure, who would have no problem sitting back and collecting a paycheck. That isn't how I'm wired, though. I love the feeling of accomplishment my work used to give me. I miss it. I have no idea if introducing a puppy will fill that hole, but it's clear that Will hopes it will. I hate worrying him.

Together, we get signed in and follow a volunteer back to where the kennels are. Given the amount of dogs, the room we enter doesn't smell that great. It's clean, but I guess there's no avoiding that dog smell when there are a bunch of them all in one place.

I want to ask Will if he thinks one dog all by itself will smell like this, but the volunteer is standing right there and that would be rude.

"What kind of dog would you like?" Will glances around the room.

"I'm not sure," I admit.

I was hoping that the perfect dog would somehow get my attention as I passed its kennel. Trouble was all of the dogs were trying to get my attention.

"Maybe we can narrow our options down by figuring out what you don't want," he suggests.

"Not too big," I say, picturing myself being dragged down the street by a giant dog. "And not too small," I add.

"So a medium-sized dog," Will teases.

I smirk; he's so clever. "Yes, a medium-sized dog."

There are still so many to choose from. It's daunting.

"Let's read their info tags." Will takes my hand and pulls me closer to the first set of kennels. "See." He points. "Some of them aren't good with kids."

We're able to eliminate a bunch based on that alone.

"What about this one?" I ask, approaching the kennel of a black puppy with a white triangle between her eyes.

"Rascal," he reads the name on her tag. "They think she's a rotty-lab mix. That sounds like she'll get pretty big."

I hold my hand up for her to sniff and her tongue darts out to lick it before her dark brown eyes hit mine. "I can live with that."

His arms wrap around my middle as he comes to stand behind me, resting his chin on my shoulder. "So, is this our new puppy?"

Turning my face toward him, I smile.

The volunteer comes over to tell us about a small play area we can sit with her in, to get an idea of her temperament so we can confirm we still want her before we start filling out any forms. She opens her kennel, and it's beyond cute watching her get so excited to come out and play for a while. After she clips a leash to her, we follow the volunteer to a small room with a floor-to-ceiling window that looks out into the area we were just in.

"Knock on the glass when you're ready to come out."

Will nods as she passes him the leash.

There are chairs in the room, but I ignore them and sink directly onto the floor. "Come here, girl."

She bounds over to me, topple-hopping onto my leg as she tries to lick my face. Will sits next to me and pets her back.

"She's so sweet," I gasp, gathering her up in my arms and giving her a squeeze.

"She's definitely full of energy. I think she might be a handful. Are you sure she's the one you want?"

I nod. "She's perfect."

He laughs. "Do you want to stay in here while I go fill out the paperwork?"

"Yes, please." I grin.

Once he leaves, Rascal starts licking and biting at my silver hoop earring. It tickles and she's set on doing it. I giggle as I struggle to push her down. She relents and is content to lick my hands instead. I pull out my phone and snap a picture of her to text to

Sawyer. It's blurry because she won't sit still, but it's still cute.

"Are you going to be my partner in crime?" I ask.

She doesn't respond, but she does look up at me so I take it as a yes. "And we'll go on lots of walks," I add.

The start of winter may not have been the best time of year to get a dog. At least Atlanta is much milder temperature-wise versus Denver, but that doesn't mean it doesn't get cold here. It'll give me an excuse to bundle up in my warmest clothes.

I continue to play with her until Will returns.

"Is she ours?" I ask.

He grins. "She is. Let's take her to PetRight so we can get her some food and a bed."

'Some food and a bed' morphed into half of the store by the time we were done. Will laughed as I loaded up our cart, but I wanted to make sure she had everything she needed.

When he had first suggested getting a puppy, I had balked at the idea. I wasn't sure what his intention behind getting her was and it had made me defensive, which was crazy. Sometimes, a puppy was just a puppy.

Before leaving the store, I put her new collar on and clipped her new leash to it. Will pushed the cart while I walked her. She wanted to sniff everything between the store and our car, and I do mean *everything*. For a little dog, not even ten pounds, she was stronger than I expected, and very determined.

"Hush." I laughed at Will as he cracked up watching me attempt to corral her.

She sat in my lap on our way back to the house. We stopped for fast food and had to put the bags in the back seat so she'd stop sniffing at them. Knowing where the source of good-smelling food was and not being able to get to it frustrated her. She struggled in vain to make her way into the back seat.

Our back yard is fully fenced, so I let her run around back there as Will and I carried everything in from the car. Even though she had all that space to roam, she stayed right by the gate and whined. It is irrational how devoted I already was to that little bundle of fur and how hearing her cry broke my heart.

"I take it I'm going to be the bad cop," Will noted, frowning at me.

"Huh?"

"I can tell. Our little girl does something bad, I'm going to have to be the one to train her."

I gape at him. "Rascal would never do anything bad."

Since everything is in the house, I walk over to the back door to call for her. It's dark out, Daylight Savings ensuring we lost an hour of light in the evenings. I could hear her approach but the sound stopped at the stairs to our deck. Flipping on the outdoor light, I walk out to investigate.

I find her sitting with her front paws on the first step and the most pitiful expression on her little puppy dog face.

"Oh, honey," I coo, hurrying down to scoop her up. "Somebody doesn't know how to climb stairs yet.

As I close the door behind me, I'm surprised by how much Will's already set up. Our dinner still sits in its bag, but Rascal's new food and water dish have already been washed, dried and set out in the corner of our kitchen on the cute mat we bought for them. Both are full, so I set her down and show them to her in case she's hungry or thirsty.

Will isn't in the kitchen, though. Glancing around, I spy his bent-over figure in the living room, putting together the crate we bought her.

"You don't need to do that right this second," I tease, walking over to comb my fingers through his soft, brown hair. "Let's eat."

When he looks up at me, his expression so impossibly boyish, I melt. I'm staring at the boy I fell in love with all those years ago. Sinking onto my knees next to him, I cradle his face in my hands and kiss him.

His hands drop the side of the crate he was working on as he moves them to band snuggly around my waist, deepening our kiss. We're interrupted by an excited puppy, who wants to play, and I leave them both to go collect our dinner. They're still roughhousing when I return.

THEM

Setting our plates on the coffee table, I ask Will what he wants to drink.

"I'll grab drinks," he replies, standing up.

Rascal trails after him, attempting to chew on the bottom of his jeans with each step he takes. We're sitting back, TV on, new puppy chewing on a toy, when Will's phone rings.

He frowns at the caller ID and mutes the TV before answering. I can only hear his end of the conversation.

"Hello."

. . .

"This is William Price."

. . .

"He's one of my students."

. . .

He drags his hand over his face. "Where were they taken?"

. . .

"How bad is it?

. . .

He stands, weary eyes finding mine. "Yes, I'm on my way."

As soon as he ends the calls, he turns to me. "Logan, you know, the kid who eats lunch in my class." I nod. "He and his dad were in a car accident."

"Are they okay? How did they know to call you?"

"They wouldn't say over the phone, so I'm not sure. Maybe Logan had my number in his phone. I gave it to him a while ago."

I nod, standing. "Do you want me to come with you?"

He reaches out, his hand gripping me by the back of my neck as he kisses me hard.

Too soon, he pulls away. "Stay here with the puppy. I'll call you as soon as I know more."

I pick up Rascal to keep her from trying to follow Will as he shrugs on his coat and then is out the door. Once he's gone, I flip the dead bolt as she licks my neck. The silence is comforting as I pray for Will's student and his father. I've never been overly religious. I don't pray regularly, or maybe I do without calling them prayers or addressing them to God.

I sink back down onto my sofa, where moments ago I cuddled with my husband in our new puppy glow. In moments like this, when life pauses to remind us how fragile it actually is, I think of my family and friends.

Rascal is distracting but not enough. I catch myself checking my phone over and over again as I wait to hear news from Will.

8

Will

When I get to the hospital, no one will speak to me. I'm not family. As far as I know, the only family around is Logan's grandmother and she's in poor health. Trying to explain to a hospital administrator that the only reason I'm here right now is because someone from there called me is equally frustrating.

"He's a reservist. If you won't talk to me, can you talk to someone from the military?" I ask, frustration evident in my tone.

That seems to trigger something and she picks up her phone. She didn't ask me to leave, so even if it's rude I listen to her call, my stomach dropping when she tells them arrangements need to be made to inform the next of kin.

When she hangs up, her expression softens as she turns back to me.

"Is Logan. .?" I can't finish my sentence.

She slowly shakes her head, and I cover my mouth with my hand. "Oh, God, his dad?"

She doesn't confirm but in doing so, I know it's true.

"What will happen to Logan? Can you tell me if he's hurt or not? Will Social Services be called?"

She doesn't answer any of my questions, just directs me back to the waiting room to sit until someone else can speak to me.

I call Sarah as I wait. Hearing her voice calms me, and I regret declining her offer to come with me. Sarah is the one person in the world I trust more than anything else. She gasps when I tell her I believe Logan's father may have passed away.

"What about Logan?"

"They won't tell me how he is or let me see him," I groan.

I don't hear what she says in reply as a nurse approaches me. "Honey, I have to go."

"Are you here for Logan Turner?"

"Yes." I stand.

"Someone from Social Services is here and wanted to speak with you."

In a daze, I follow her.

Logan regained consciousness the morning after the car accident. He had a broken arm and a concussion. I sat with him as his social worker told him his father had passed away. When the social worker explained he would be moved into a group home as his grandmother was not well enough to care for him and he had no other living relatives, I stepped in.

Sarah and I have been his foster parents since that night, three weeks ago. To say he's withdrawn is a gross understatement. We do our best to draw him out, but Rascal seems to have the most success. She now sleeps in his room and when we get home from school, he walks her.

One small blessing in all of this is Sarah is too busy to stress about getting or not getting pregnant. After my sperm count came back normal, she went and saw her doctor again. That same week, they performed an outpatient procedure to remove the polyp discovered during her ultrasound.

Logan rides to and from school with me, and still eats lunch in my classroom every day. He misses his dad. To go so long waiting for him to come home only to lose him is a tragedy I can't imagine. Every week, I bring him to see a grief counselor, and we visit his grandmother afterward. News of her son's passing, so soon after losing her husband, has taken its toll.

Logan seems hesitant to see her, but I don't want him to regret time lost with his last remaining blood relative before she passes. This kid has had to deal with more loss than anyone should in his thirteen years on this Earth.

Today, he asked me to take him to go see his dad. I glance over at his quiet profile as I drive to the cemetery. He was so strong, helping to plan his own father's funeral. There was some money, life insurance that came to him. He wanted to pay for everything himself, but Sarah and I wouldn't let him.

Brian drew up trust paperwork and once Logan agreed, those funds, all of them, are now waiting for him once he's eighteen. The cemetery his father rests in isn't a far drive.

After I park, I ask, "Do you want me to wait in the car?"

He shakes his head so I get out and walk next to him as we follow the now-familiar path to his father's grave. I never had an opportunity to meet his father before his passing, and I can only hope he died knowing how special his son was. There are days after Logan meets with the counselor where Logan will talk about his dad. Those days neither Sarah nor I can get a word in edgewise as Logan almost manically tells us one story after another.

It's as if he fears his father will be forgotten if there isn't anyone other than him who knew his life. Other days, more recently, he's silent, keeping everything tucked inside. That was why I gave him the option of me waiting in the car. I don't know if he wants to talk to his dad, and I don't want to intrude on that.

Being here at the cemetery brings his funeral fresh to the forefront of my mind. The day was blessedly dry, but the two days of straight rain prior had saturated the grounds. Logan looked so small and alone as he stood in a new suit and watched his father's coffin being lowered into the ground.

He had no family members to rely on. His grandmother wasn't well enough to leave the nursing home. There were some of his other teachers and a few of his neighbors who came, and a group of five soldiers from his father's reserve unit came to pay their respects and offer their condolences to Logan. None of them knew Logan or had known his father directly, though, so the meeting was awkward at best.

Logan didn't cry, but watching as his mouth tensed with emotion over and over that day is scarred on my soul. All I wanted to do was tell him to let it all out, that it was okay to cry. That wasn't my place, though. All I was at that point was a teacher turned unexpected foster parent. I was out of my depths and unsure of how to give him the support he needed.

Sarah wasn't, though. She saw his pain and curled her love around him. It wasn't until after everyone else had left that he turned into her embrace and sobbed. The force of his pain made her take a step back to hold them both upright. I moved behind her and held them both as he finally cried.

His tears spurred our own. It was gut-wrenching and a pain I had not experienced since the moment I first thought I had lost Sarah. Death has an uncanny way of reminding us how temporary our lives are. Almost three weeks ago, three of us stood and mourned as one in this cemetery.

"Am I cursed, Mr. Price?"

His heartbreaking question pulls me from my thoughts. "Why would you think that?"

THEM

There are tears in his eyes as he turns to look at me. "Everyone around me dies. I don't want you or Mrs. Price to die, too."

I tug him to my chest and hold him as he sobs. The pain, his emotion and fear so powerful, I get choked up.

"You are not cursed, Logan."

His voice is muffled as he responds, "How do you know?"

"I wouldn't lie to you. When I was younger than you, my older sister died, and a few years back my dad died, too. Life isn't always fair. It is hard and painful, but there are good things, too. You are having a lot thrown at you right now, but you are not the cause or reason for any of it. You are not cursed."

"Promise?" he cries.

I pull back so I can look him in the eyes. "I promise."

He nods, his hand jerking up to wipe his face. "Is it okay if I talk to my dad alone for a minute?"

I rest my hand on his shoulder, giving it a squeeze. "Of course. I'll wait for you in the car."

As I walk back toward the parking lot, I worry if I am capable of helping Logan get through this. I would never abandon him; I only worry I'm not good enough. Cursed? I shake my head, wondering where he could have picked that up from. He's been dealt a rougher hand than most kids but from what I can tell at school, he isn't being targeted by any bullies.

We have a zero-tolerance policy on that shit. I don't know why kids start acting all 'Lord of The Flies' from time to time, but we try to keep an eye out to make sure our kids feel safe at school. It seems like every single week, I'm seeing something on the news about a teenager taking their own life as a way to escape the torment of being bullied.

I'm not waiting in the car long when Logan walks back up and gets in. His cheeks are wet, so it's clear he cried again while he talked to his dad. Even though his dad was stationed overseas a couple of times while Logan was growing up, it's clear they were close.

Before I shift out of park, I turn to him. "Where'd this cursed idea come from?"

He shrugs.

"Any of the kids at school put that in your head?"

He shakes his head.

"You'd tell me if anyone was bothering you, right?"

He nods.

I don't know what's worse: him not talking at all or him asking me if he's cursed. I don't know him well enough to be able to tell if he's lying to me. I'll ask Christine to pay extra attention to him the next time he's in her class. I can discretely ask some of his other teachers to do the same.

"Coffee?"

THEM

This kid loves Starbucks coffee. Since it supposedly stunts your growth, we don't let him have it all the time, though.

He nods.

"Want to text Sarah and see if she wants us to get her something?"

He nods again, pulling out his phone. The bill for his phone and his dad's now come to our house. It'd be cheaper to turn off his dad's phone and add his phone to our plan, but we haven't done that because Logan likes to call and text his dad even though he's gone. In my eyes, whatever little amount of peace that brings him is worth the added expense.

His phone chirps with Sarah's reply.

"What does she want?"

"An eggnog latte."

I crinkle my nose. "That sounds disgusting."

He laughs and given our earlier conversation, that sounds like music to my ears.

Sarah is waiting inside the door with Rascal when we get home. Her eyes light up as Logan passes her coffee to her, and she gives him the puppy in exchange. Logan snuggles her to his chest and heads off toward the den. Once he's out of sight, I motion for Sarah to follow me upstairs to our room.

I close the door behind her and lean my back against it.

"How'd it go?" she asks, taking a sip of her drink.

"He asked me if he's cursed."

Her eyes round as her mouth falls open. "Why would he think that?"

I shake my head. "I asked him if any of the kids from school said anything but he said no."

She presses her hand to her chest. "That breaks my heart that he would even ask such a thing."

Taking her drink from her, I place both of our cups on the dresser next to the door before tugging her into my arms. "I know."

"Should we call his counselor?"

I kiss the side of her head, comforted by the fruity smell of her conditioner. "That's not a bad idea."

She presses closer to me. "You are a good man, Will Price."

"Hush, darling."

She pulls back, her eyes flashing. "I mean it. I was scared when you asked if Logan could come live with us. I know nothing about taking care of a kid, and even less about a teenage boy. I knew we could do it, though, because I'd have you and you'd know what to do."

I slip my hand behind her neck and pull her closer, tucking her face into my neck until I could feel her breath on my skin. "I have no clue what I'm doing."

She kisses my neck. "Well, you must be doing something right for him to confide in you like that."

"Thank you for saying that."

We grab our drinks and make our way into the den where Logan is playing a game called Minecraft. He's tried to show me how to play a couple of times. I have to be missing the point because as far as I can tell, it's nothing more than a glorified set of virtual building blocks. He's mentioned being able to interact with other players, but so far he hasn't.

As long as he doesn't have the volume up too loud, Sarah and I like to hang out in the room while he plays. Sarah reads on her e-reader and I play on the floor with Rascal, and Logan abandons that game not long after to play with the dog and me.

"Hey," Sarah says, making both of us look up. "Should we go get a Christmas tree tonight?"

Logan shrugs but doesn't say no, which is the same thing as saying yes, as far as Sarah is concerned.

Standing, she asks, "Do we want a fake tree or a real tree this year?"

I've been trying to talk her into getting a fake tree since we bought this house. Sure, a real tree smells nice and is more authentic, but I'm the one who ends up cleaning up all the needles and having to keep it watered. Plus, the fake ones can come pre-lit. All I want for Christmas is Sarah wearing a bow (and nothing else) and a pre-lit fake tree.

She looks at Logan, clearly not interested in what I want.

He looks back and forth between the both of us before speaking. "I've never had a real tree."

Real tree it is. Sarah beams at me.

"Someone put Rascal in her crate," I grumble, walking toward the front door.

The local YMCA is where we've bought our last couple trees from. They have a decent selection and the proceeds go to charity. We each get a cup of hot cocoa before walking into the lot, and Sarah deputizes Logan to be the official tree-picker-outer. He takes his position more seriously than either of us could have predicted and has to look at every single tree on the lot before he'll make up his mind.

Sarah and I patiently follow him. He decides on a Douglas fir, asking for my help to see if there are any bald spots. Once he's confident that this tree is the perfect one for us, we have a little bit taken off the bottom to level it off and the staff from the lot tie it down to the top of my car.

Logan helps me carry it inside while Sarah scurries up to the attic to find our tree stand. He goes to let Rascal out back before coming to help me with the tree, and we set it up in the front window of our living room. Sarah shows Logan where the water goes as I head up to the attic to grab the rest of the Christmas decorations. Once I'm back downstairs, I notice Sarah has holiday music playing.

"I know." Her eyes light up. "Let's have a fire."

I turn toward Logan. "Sound fun?"

THEM

His grandparents lived in an apartment, one that his dad took over once he got back from South Korea. I don't know if Logan has ever built a fire. He smiles shyly.

"All right, come help me bring in some firewood." I grin.

We have plenty right now since we had a tree come down during a storm this summer. It was a pain to cut up at the time, but since it didn't hit anything when it fell I can't complain.

This fire won't be to heat the house, only ambiance, so we won't need a ton of firewood. I make him hold out both arms and I stack five smaller logs on them. I manage to carry three bigger ones in myself. We drop the wood on some newspaper Sarah laid down near the fireplace and head back outside for another load.

"Have you've ever made a fire before?" I ask when we're back inside.

He shakes his head.

I wasn't a Boy Scout but Sarah's dad taught me to make fires at their house.

"First, we need some kindling."

"Kindling?"

"Yep." I grab a page from the newspaper and ball it up. "Something that will burn easily and give the bigger logs a chance to catch fire."

I make a pile of smaller branches and pieces of wood from the stuff we brought in, and then set a larger log half across the pile.

"Most fireplaces have something called a flue."

He laughs at the name, and I explain, "Not like a bad cold, but it's what blocks the cold outside air from entering the house when you aren't using the fireplace. If you don't make sure it's open before you start your fire, all the smoke will be trapped inside the house."

I motion for him to lean his head into the opening of the fireplace and show him the lever to open the flue. After that, Sarah brings me a long electric lighter she uses for her candles to get the kindling started.

"Keep an eye on the dog. I don't know how curious she'll get and we don't want her to burn herself."

Logan positions himself to sit on the edge of the brick ledge that comes off from the fireplace. There's no way that dog is getting past him. While we were making fire, Sarah unpacked all the decorations. I head to the kitchen to grab our stepladder and together, we string the tree with lights.

"Logan, want to put the star on the top of the tree?" Sarah asks.

He stands so quickly he almost trips over his feet. I take over guard duty so he can use the stepstool. Watching him on one side, Sarah on the other, her face turned up to look at him with the soft glow of the Christmas tree behind them is something I'll never

THEM

forget. They probably won't either since I scooped Rascal up and made them promise not to move as I ran upstairs to get my camera.

Sarah's rolling her eyes at me by the time I make it back downstairs. She only acts annoyed, though; I've been onto her game for a while.

I stand in front of the fireplace and snap a few pictures, content to know I'll be able to share how magical it looked with Logan later. Once the star is on top, Logan comes back down to watch the fire. The three of us take turns hanging ornaments. Once the tree is finished, we take some more pictures.

I use the timer and my tripod to get one of all of us, Logan holding Rascal.

9

Sarah

Logan's grandmother passed away today. It wasn't a shock to any of us, but we had hoped she'd make it through Christmas for Logan's sake.

That poor, sweet boy.

When he gets home from school now, I've been going with him as he walks Rascal around the neighborhood. The puppy is looking more and more like a dog every day. She's spoiled rotten. Well, that's not entirely true; she's spoiled, but overall has been an angel.

She still sleeps with Logan at night. She has a dog bed in his room but ignores it to sleep on his bed instead. The dog has been a saving grace when it comes to Logan. He adores her, and it's plain to see the feeling is mutual. She's never far from him when he's home. Unless he's doing something that requires use of both of his hands, one is normally reaching down to pet her.

I'll never forget the night of his accident. It's awful to think that everything happens for a reason. It's impossible to believe there could be a reason to Logan losing his whole family by such a young age. Even though I struggle to find the reason in that, it seems impossible to believe Rascal came into our lives that day for any purpose other than to be there for Logan.

Because their connection is so close, I made sure Logan was cool with me butting in on their walks before I started going. It's not like we talk on them, normally we don't. I enjoy his companionship, though. He's an amazing kid. I can't picture him in a group home. I'm happy Will stepped in and made it so we would become his foster parents.

It was a welcome distraction after Will's test came back to confirm I'm the reason we aren't getting pregnant. Under my doctor's theory that the polyp was tricking my body into thinking I was already pregnant, I had it removed. The procedure itself was no big deal; they didn't have to make any incisions. There was some cramping the next couple of days, but nothing worse than a lousy period.

There's no real way to tell if that was the problem or not. With all the running around we've been doing since Logan moved in, I haven't even thought about it, until today.

Walking the dog together, we headed toward the park I took Calvin to when it was still warm enough to play outside. We pass a mother pushing her child in a stroller. As we approach, I recognize her as the other mom from the park that day. We do the polite 'I don't really know who you are' half-wave to each other as we pass. I can't help but wonder if she thinks Logan is also my child. With his brown hair and eyes, he could easily be mistaken for a younger brother, or my son.

In a tragic way, he is.

"You met Mr. Price in middle school, right?"

It takes me a moment to realize he's talking to me since I'm so used to our quiet walks. "I did. We had English together and his desk was next to mine."

"When did you know you liked him?"

His question had me reeling from 'this is the cutest thing ever, he likes a girl' to wondering when kids are sexually active these days. "I think I thought he was cute from the first time I saw him."

He doesn't say anything in response, only nods. The rest of our walk is in silence. When we get back to the house, Logan heads upstairs to work on his homework. I find Will in the kitchen, starting dinner.

"I think Logan likes a girl at school." I grin.

He waggles his eyebrows. "Where'd you get the skinny?"

"Dork." I push his shoulder, laughing. "He asked me when I knew I liked you."

He grabs my arms and pins them behind me, arching my back as he hovers over me. All thoughts of middle school crushes fly out of my head as I gaze up into his blue eyes. I want him to kiss me, but instead, he teases my jawline with his lips and teeth.

"Will," I plead.

One of his eyebrows cocks up. The jerk knows what I want, but he's waiting for me to ask for it.

"Kiss me," I beg, frustrated that his lips are right there but I can't reach them.

A lazy grin spreads across his face as he gives me what I asked for. Before Logan, I'd be dragging Will upstairs right now to have my way with him. Now, I'm terrified Logan will hear us, or even worse walk in on us.

Will kisses me breathless before straightening and releasing my lips. I sag against him and he chuckles.

"There's more where that came from, Mrs. Price," he teases.

"I like the sound of that," I counter.

He arms flex around me, reminding me he wants me as badly as I want him.

"After Logan goes to bed?"

I nod, popping up on my toes to kiss the underside of his jaw. He has just enough scruff on his face to make me want to do very bad things to him. The hardest part will be the waiting.

We torture each other all evening. Stolen kisses and touches during dinner and dirty words whispered afterword work to amp both of us up. I try to watch a show Logan likes with him, but Will makes it impossible by repeatedly catching my eye and biting his lip. God, I love it when he does that. It's probably why he's always doing it.

I excuse myself, telling them both I plan to read in bed until I fall sleep. I use the time to change into some sexy lingerie. There's a decent chance it will only last a couple of seconds on me once Will sees it.

On the off-chance Logan would stop by and say goodnight or ask another question like he had on our walk, I pull a long pajama shirt on, as well. I'm asleep when soft lips start kissing my neck. My eyes flutter open and I smile up at Will's handsome face.

"Hey, honey."

His lips capture mine as he shifts over me. "You are so beautiful."

I push him off me. "Will, did you flip-flop the door?"

He smirks.

"William Ethan Price, you go flip-flop that door right now if you want any sex tonight."

Our house is older, and the doors have a habit of shrinking or swelling depending on what time of year it is. Not every door, but currently our bedroom door will shut but not lock.

"He's not going to open our door," Will tries to argue.

I glare at him until he gets up, grabs our sex flip-flop and wedges it under our bedroom door to act as a stopper. While he's doing that, I quickly tug my pajama top up and over my head. By the time he comes back to bed, I'm laid out ready for him.

THEM

"Hell, you had that on the whole time?" he asks, reaching out to drag his fingertip across the tops of my breasts.

I nod and he flashes me a wicked grin. The next hour is a blur. My sexy lingerie lasted all of ten seconds before Will had me fully bared to him. He knows me like no one else, knows how to make my entire body quake with just the simple touch of his fingertip.

He delighted in teasing me, in taking me so close to the edge where I could already feel the tremors of a scale-busting internal earthquake. By the time he finally did let me fly, I may have left my body. I did my best to return the favor, to wind him up so tightly he was dizzy when he found his release.

We lay, a sweating, tangled, grinning mess in each other's arms.

"What do you want to get Logan for Christmas?"

I cringe. "I have no idea. Has he mentioned anything specific that he wants?"

I've come to the conclusion that Logan either wants nothing or wants to make us happy by not asking for a ton of stuff, even if he wants something. No matter what we ask him, he is always good. No clothes; he's happy with what he already has. New video games? He's cool with the ones Will has and whatever he brought with him to our house.

He is the most content child on the planet, and it's driving me crazy. Do I want him to be some greedy kid who is constantly begging for stuff? No. What I want is for him to feel relaxed enough, considering that he's living here, to let us know when he needs something.

"I'm going to ask him," I huff.

Will laughs. "You know what he'll say."

I fold my arms across my chest and glare at him. "Maybe I'll find a way to ask it so he has to answer me."

Will leans down to kiss my temple. "Good luck with that."

Logan happens to pick that exact moment to walk into the kitchen. He pauses when we both look up at him.

"Logan." I grin.

He takes a step backwards.

"Get back here." I laugh. "I need your help with something.

Cautiously, his eyes flicking to Will's face more than once, he walks further into the room.

"Here." I motion toward the stools that line the island. "Sit. Are you hungry, thirsty?"

He looks at Will again, who shrugs.

"I'm a little thirsty."

"What would you like to drink?

THEM

"Ah, anything is fine."

See what I mean? Will moves to sit in the stool next to Logan's as I list off all the options beverage-wise I'd be happy to get for Logan.

"Apple juice would be good." He pauses. "Please."

"Of course." I busy myself pouring his glass then hand it to him.

"Um, what did you need my help with?" he asks.

"Well, Christmas is coming up and there are a lot of people in Will and my family who would like to get you gifts. The only problem is no one has any idea what to get you. I need your help making a list."

He stiffens. "I don't need anything."

I drop forward, setting my elbow on the top of the island and resting my chin in my hand. "Good thing I didn't ask what you needed; I asked what you wanted."

Will laughs. "Come on, man. Just tell her so she'll leave you alone."

I smirk at him before setting my sights back on Logan. "You should listen to him."

Straightening back up, I push a pad and pen across the island to him. "You need to come up with at least five things."

I've never seen a kid so scared to admit he wants stuff. He needs to get over that right now. Sure, I love the fact that he isn't greedy, but I'd like some balance on him getting or at least feeling confident enough to ask Will or me for the things he needs.

"And," I continue. "After you're done with that, we're going to the mall. You need new shoes and some new clothes."

"No, I don't," he tries to argue.

"Listen," I cut him off before he says anything else. "I don't know if you don't want to get rid of what you currently have because of any memories, or if you think you might somehow wear out your welcome if we buy you stuff. Let me be clear, you don't have to get rid of any of the things you came here with. That stuff belongs to you, and only you get to decide what happens to any of it. Secondly, you're outgrowing the stuff you have. We can go to the stores you like. I'm not going to pretend you're a doll and make you wear stuff I like."

"That's what she has me for," Will jokes.

Luckily, his joke seems to relax Logan.

"Okay, Mrs. Price."

While Logan works on his list, I start the dishwasher and work on my own list for the grocery store. "Will, do you want to go with us to the mall, or do you want to go to the grocery store?"

"I'll go with you guys and grocery shop after."

His response is one hundred percent for Logan's benefit. Will isn't a fan of clothes shopping. He was telling the truth earlier about being my doll. I end up buying most of his clothes for him. Otherwise, he'd live in ratty old t-shirts, and I need those to sleep in.

Once Logan is done with his list, I take a look at it.

- Lacrosse stick
- Other lacrosse stuff
- Xbox points
- Sketch pads
- New pencils

I can put Will in charge of figuring out the lacrosse stuff. The sketch pads and pencils are practically school supplies, not Christmas presents in my opinion.

"All right, let's go," I order.

Poor Logan looks terrified while Will tries not to laugh. You'd think shopping with me was a punishment or something. The mall I grew up with has long since been replaced by an open air, shopping center-type mall. During spring, summer and fall it's great, unless it's raining. I'm not a fan of the open-air concept in the wintertime, though.

"What are the stores that are popular with teenagers?" I whisper-ask Will when Logan isn't looking.

Will gives me a panicked look and shakes his head. "I don't know."

That means we'll have to walk around and try to figure it out on our own. "Hey. Do you like H&M?" I ask, seeing it on the right.

Logan doesn't reply so I pull him into the store to escape the cold, and also because I like their stuff and have shopped for myself here plenty of times.

"All the guys' stuff is upstairs. You two go look around up there while I take a quick peek at stuff down here."

Will gives me a look. He knows me well enough to know the phrase 'quick look' was a wild exaggeration.

"I swear, I'll be fast," I add.

They head upstairs while I look around at their new stuff for me. They have great long sweaters for layering over leggings. I like their dresses but wish the hemlines were longer. They look great on someone more petite, like Sawyer, but for me I'm scared about flashing my ass if I ever need to bend over. I find a few sweaters I like and head upstairs to check on Will and Logan.

So far, they've each picked out four t-shirts. "Come on, what about pants and sweaters?" I ask.

Will doesn't need anything, so he directs Logan over to the racks with stuff his size on them. I know sweaters aren't the most popular article of clothing for a teenage boy and because of this, they're not something that will make a kid excited to pick them out. I follow Will to see what size t-shirts Logan picked out and use that to grab some sweaters for him.

THEM

Once we have a decent pile, we send him off to the dressing room to try everything on. He pops out for a moment after each outfit change. He hasn't said much but I think, based on his body language, he's excited about his new clothes. On the way to the register, I make him stop to try on a nice, thick pea coat. It won't work for playing in the snow, but it's warmer than the hoodies he's been claiming are good enough.

There's a shoe store around the corner where we get him a new pair of sneakers and a pair of loafers in case he needs to dress up. He surprised me by pulling his new pea coat out of the bag and wearing it as we all walked back to the car. It could have been the cold air, but I had to blink away wetness from my eyes. Will didn't miss my reaction and drapes his arm around my shoulder, tucking me to his side.

Logan walks ahead of us, his back straight as he carries the bags holding his new clothes and shoes.

When we get home, I turn on the tree and read a book in the living room. Logan starts a load of laundry to wash all of his new things. I can tell he's excited to wear them to school tomorrow. After that, he tags along with Will to the grocery store.

Before long, they're back and bringing stuff in. I get up to help but they stop me, telling me they've got it. I'm settling back down on the couch when Logan comes over to me.

"Sarah?"

I look up, smiling.

"I'd like to thank you again for my new clothes."

I reach out to squeeze his hand. "I'm so happy you like them, honey."

He ducks his head, a blush creeping across his cheeks, and leaves the room.

It reminds me I haven't passed on his list to our family and friends. Christmas is right around the corner, so I know they want to finish their shopping. I head to my office so I can send an email.

My desk calendar catches my eye. Luckily, December isn't covered with blue ass prints like November was. Shaking my head at the memory I pause, my mouth opening as I look at the date. Of course I knew what day it was, I just didn't realize what day it *was:* ten days after the day I should have gotten my period.

What do I do?

Do I get a test?

Do I tell Will?

What if I'm only late?

What if I'm *not* late?

I push away from my desk. Heading out into the living room, I grab my purse and coat. I send Will a text letting him know I'll be right back and run to a convenience store near our house. I pick up a two-pack of pregnancy tests and hurry toward the register. What if the test is negative? What will I say I needed to buy at the store?

THEM

There's a display of greeting cards right by the register. I pick up the first one I see and set my stuff down in front of the clerk. She barely glances at them as she rings them up. I'm shaking as I walk back out to my car. When I get home, I find Will.

He's watching Logan play Minecraft. "Honey, can I borrow you for a couple minutes?"

"Everything okay?" he asks, getting up.

I nod and lead him to our bedroom, closing the door behind him. "I'm late."

It takes him a second to get what I'm saying.

When he does, he moves closer to me, setting his hands on my stomach. "Do you think . . . ?"

"I'm not sure. I got a test."

We read the directions together, Will standing pressed up behind me, his chin resting on my shoulder and his hands on my waist.

"Seems pretty straight-forward," he murmurs, his breath tickling my ear.

I splurged on the tests and got the ones that point-blank say 'pregnant' or 'not pregnant' in the indicator window.

"I'm so nervous."

His hands move from my hips to wrap around my stomach. "Stage fright?"

He's making a joke, lightening the mood. He knows I mean the results, but instead, he's distracting me to calm my nerves.

One of my hands moves to cover his, giving it a squeeze. "The show must go on."

My voice shakes a bit. He had to have heard it because his grip loosens and I'm spun around and facing him the next moment, his hands on either side of my face as he peers down at me.

"No matter what the test says, as long as we're together, I'm already the happiest man alive."

I blink away the wetness that threatens to escape my eyes as I stare up into his clear-blue ones. "I love you."

His face softens as he leans forward to kiss my forehead. "That's my girl." He spins me back around so I'm facing the door to our master bath. "Now, go pee on that stick."

I swipe one of the test packets from our bed and giggle as I walk to the bathroom. As close and together as we are, I still prefer to pee without an audience so he waits just outside the door. My anxiety makes a reappearance the moment I'm away from Will and his calming presence.

Be pregnant, just be pregnant, I tell myself, like thinking it will somehow will it into actuality.

"All done," I say, opening the door and motioning Will in.

THEM

He glances at his watch. "And now, we wait. Two minutes, right? Have you already looked at it?"

I grimace. "Yes, two minutes. You look at it; I'm too freaked out."

He grins and sits on the edge of the bathtub, reaching out to grasp my hand so he can tug me into his lap. There, in the warm cocoon of his arms, I let out the breath I didn't realize I was holding and tuck my face into his neck. I still love the way he smells. He's changed colognes over the years, but there's always been something uniquely Will there.

It has to be part pheromone, something that calls to the base of me, the root of who I am and tells me that he is my match. I nuzzle closer to him and smile as his arms tighten around me.

"Want to sneak a peek?" he whispers.

"It hasn't even been a minute," I whisper back.

"I'm impatient," he answers, still whispering.

"Why are we whispering?" I ask, my voice still hushed.

"So the baby won't hear we don't always follow directions."

My head snaps up, my eyes on his. "What?"

He's grinning, his eyes beaming, his expression possibly the most excited I've ever seen him.

"You're pregnant, Miller Lite."

My mouth drops. "You can't even see the test. Why are you saying that?"

He points to our medicine cabinet. It's mirrored and after tilting my head, I can see the reflection of the test sitting on the counter.

I squint at it. "You can read that?"

He laughs. "I can tell there's only one word."

I leap out of his lap and grab the test.

Pregnant. He's right; it only says 'pregnant.'

The directions said the word 'not' would appear first if the test was negative.

I gulp, turning back to him. "We're pregnant, honey."

I gasp as suddenly I'm lifted, crushed to his chest as his lips capture mine.

10

Will

We're both so excited by the news I end up ravishing her in the bathroom. There was a point in time, back when we first got back together, that I wondered if the intensity of my feelings toward Sarah would go away. I knew it never dulled when she was mine the first time around, but part of me assumed that was young love, that now that we're adults it would lessen.

The opposite is true, though. Getting to wake up each morning with her in my arms has only made my love for her grow. Now, knowing she's carrying my baby, a baby we've both been dreaming for, my love has impossibly grown even more. I'm excited to watch her body change as our son or daughter does. The actual birth part has me nervous, but I have nine months to get over that.

Worshipping Sarah's body has always been easy. Her skin, her curves, the way she reacts to my touch, it's addictive. Her belly is my new obsession, though. I want to call in sick to work for her entire pregnancy and watch her body change. It's early so of course there's no visible change, but that doesn't stop me from kissing every inch of her torso knowing my baby is inside her. I plan to make that a daily ritual. At night, after loving her, I will chart the changes to her body with my lips and fingertips.

I carry her over to our bed. "I'm pregnant, Will, not disabled."

"Hush." I kiss her forehead. "Let me take care of you."

She doesn't argue; instead, shockingly, she blushes. My beautiful wife, the mate to my soul, and I can still make her blush.

"Do we wait to tell people?" I ask, resting her in the sea of pillows on our bed.

"Maybe we should see the doctor first to make sure everything is okay."

"Do you think we'll get a picture of the baby?"

She lifts her shoulder, reaching out to lace her fingers through mine. "I don't know."

"Okay, so we'll go to your doctor before we tell anyone."

She nods, a small smile curving her lips. It's then that I see her eyes are wet.

I sink down next to her and hold her face in my hands, my eyes asking the question my lips don't.

"I'm okay," she answers, then pauses to take a shaky breath. "I'm just so happy."

My hands drop to band around her and her face tucks into my neck as I hold her to my chest.

"So happy," she repeats, and I know she's crying.

My nose stings and I blink away my own tears. I hate to see her cry, but knowing they are tears of joy settles somewhere deep inside my gut.

After my sister passed away, my family life was beyond dysfunctional. My parents both checked out. They lost themselves in their grief and not only forgot about each other, they forgot about me, as well. I'll never understand that. Making Sarah happy is my mission in life. Knowing that I'm succeeding is what, in turn, makes me happy.

"Go back down to Logan," she whispers. "I don't want him worrying."

"I know we're not telling anyone yet, but should we tell him?" I ask, pulling back so I can see her face.

She hesitates. "I think we should make sure everything is okay with the . . ." Her face softens. ". . . baby first."

I nod, leaning down to kiss her forehead. "I'll get your phone."

She looks confused and giggles. "Why?"

"You have a doctor's appointment to make."

Sarah is struggling with what to get Logan for Christmas. She's worrying herself sick with trying to make it perfect for him. That or she's using it as an excuse not to think about the doctor's appointment we have scheduled tomorrow.

"Let me handle his gift."

Her brows lift. "But . . ." she starts to argue.

"Nope." I lean down to murmur against her lips. "I've got this."

She relaxes in my arms, and I hate to leave her but Logan and I need to get to school.

"Have you shopped for Rascal?" I ask, knowing she hasn't.

Her eyes light up. "She needs a stocking."

That's my girl. I brush my lips softly against her again before I pull away. Logan is waiting for me by the side door.

On the way to school, I do some sleuthing to see what he'd like for Christmas. He's an active kid, and I've already planned to get him some Lacrosse gear so he can participate when I start coaching in the spring. That will be one part of his present but while I want him to learn what it feels like to be part of a team, I also want him to learn how to embrace solitude, as well.

There's a trick to being alone without feeling lonely. He's had a tough year, had to deal with more than any kid his age ever should in such a short period of time. We talk, and he meets with a counselor regularly, but he isn't dealing. There's something he needs to work out, and my guess is he needs to do it on his own.

When I was his age, I had my camera and my skateboard. While he thinks the pictures I have up around the house and in the classroom are cool, he hasn't had that spark of interest to show that photography is something he'd like to learn more about. He's active, though, and loves to be outside. When the weather is nice and he isn't playing Minecraft, he's in the backyard playing with Rascal.

I'd like to get him a bike or a skateboard, but I'm still trying to figure out which he'd be more excited about getting. Right now, it's a toss-up. Worst-case, I'll flip a coin if he doesn't give me more hints soon. Christmas is ten days away, so there's a decent chance things will be out of stock if I don't get a move on.

After I park, we walk in together. When we reach the main entrance, we split ways but he always waits for me to squeeze his shoulder before he takes off toward his locker. My classroom is in a hallway with the other electives like choir and band, the gym at the end of the hall. Logan has English as his homeroom, and it's on the other side of the school.

The week before winter break is always tough school-wise. The kids' minds are all elsewhere, so it's hard to keep them from getting distracted. In my advanced classes, we're going over self-portraits. It's amazing how the kids see themselves. For whatever reason that has to do more with psychology than art,

THEM

they always highlight perceived flaws. Year after year of different students and it still surprises me.

At the end of the session, we review self-portraits from other artists, some well-known, some not, and discuss them. It never happens right away, but at some point the kids always get it. They get that what they might feel is a flaw is also something that makes them unique and interesting. That if everyone looked the same life would be boring. That there is beauty in imperfections, that the imperfection in itself is perfect.

Sure, there are rules when it comes to art, and technique which is my job to teach these kids. The goal, though, after all of those lessons is to give them the confidence to allow their art and their expression of it to be free. That changes the way they look not only at themselves but, I hope, at the world around them. If I have a mission, it's to teach the kids to embrace curiosity.

Managing all of that while stressing over Sarah's doctor appointment and what to get Logan for Christmas is proving to be harder than I thought it would be. I'm relieved when the bell rings for lunch. Logan still eats with me most days, which is good because during my last class, I decided I was going to give up on my detective work and just ask him outright what he wants.

I'm waiting for him when I hear his voice from the hall. I don't try to eavesdrop, but since the hall has mainly emptied for lunch it's impossible not to hear him and the girl he's talking to.

"So, do you want to work on the project at my house or yours?" the girl asks.

"Um . . ."

I can hear the hesitation in his voice clear as day. Is he worried Sarah and I would care if he had a friend over? I don't want to interrupt his conversation, but . . . my thoughts scatter as he continues.

"Hang on. Let me check with Mr. Price."

I do my best to look engrossed with the portrait in front of me.

"Hey, Mr. Price." Logan pops his head in the door.

I glance up. "Hey, Logan."

"Is it cool if Amber comes over one day during winter break to work on something for history?"

I shrug, wondering who Amber is and mentally trying to place the name. "Sure, as long as it's cool with her folks."

He grins. "Cool. Thanks, Mr. Price."

Now I'm seriously wondering who Amber is. He turns, his footsteps echoing down the hall as he walks back to her.

"Let's work on it at my house."

My gut clenches. It's the first time I've heard him refer to our house as 'his.' For a moment, the air in my throat catches as the importance of that slams into me with an almost physical force.

I avoid his eyes after he's said bye to Amber and walks into my class. He drops his bag on the floor with a thud and slides into the chair closest to me which faces my desk. Once I'm certain my face won't give away what his words meant to me, I look up at him. He's still grinning.

I smirk. "So, tell me about Amber."

If possible, his grin widens. "She's this girl."

I bet.

"Do I know her?" I ask.

He shakes his head. "I don't think she takes art. She's in chorus."

"What kind of project do you have to do?"

"We need to make a movie about life during the Civil War."

"Just the two of you?"

He nods, still grinning. I pull the mini-cooler from under my desk and open it. Sarah made each of us sandwiches: turkey for me, ham for Logan. I lift his sandwich, wait for him to raise his hands and toss it to him. He catches it easily.

"So, do you know what you'll do for the movie?"

He tries to talk around the mouthful he's just taken but then holds up his hand and chews furiously before he starts again. "We're going to be married, and she's going to get all sad that I have to go off to war."

"Married?" My right eyebrow lifts up.

"Yep," Logan replies before inhaling more of his sandwich.

Sarah is going to love this.

Now, time to get down to gift business. "Logan, do you know how to skateboard?"

His head lifts and he shakes it. His expression is lost on me; I can't tell if he's interested or not.

"Want to learn how?"

"I tried before," he starts. "When I was in elementary school. I sucked at keeping my balance."

"Do you remember what kind of board you were on?"

He squints, and I can almost see the gears turning in his head as he tries to remember. "I think it had Spiderman on it."

"There are these boards called long boards. They're easier to keep your balance on, but they aren't really for tricks, mainly cruising. Would you like to try something like that out?"

His eyes light up. "I know some guys who ride long boards."

That's answer enough for me.

After lunch, I text Sarah to let her know I'll run out to get Logan's gift later tonight. She replies with pictures of the stuff she picked up for Rascal and one of Rascal sitting on Santa's lap.

That picture alone got me through the rest of my day. Once Logan and I got back to the house, I filled Sarah in on my plans and told her about Amber. She ate it up, excitement over meeting a girl Logan might like written all over her beautiful face. I made her promise not to grill Logan about Amber while I was gone. She pouted but gave in.

Not far from our place is a newer shopping mall and after kissing my girl senseless, I made my way over there to the board shop. Before I got my first car, I either rode my bike or skateboarded everywhere. I wasn't serious about either; they were solely a method of transportation at the time. Working in a middle school, I've been able to absorb what things my kids are interested in.

Long boards are huge with the boys right now. Half of the time I assign something where the class can pick the subject to draw, paint, mosaic or stipple, I get thirty long board pictures turned in. When I decided to get Logan either a bike or a board, I Googled both to get an idea of the different types out there. The second Logan mentioned balance being an issue board-wise, I knew a long board was the way to go.

It's both longer and wider than your standard board, so you can take a wider stance on it. Other than that, I was clueless so I let the kids at the board shop trick me out. I may have gone overboard, but it's Logan's first Christmas without his dad so I want to do whatever I can to make it easier on him. By the time I leave, I have a tricked-out board with a sick geometric design on the bottom, a helmet, plus a spare set of trucks, wheels and pads.

I load everything into the trunk of my Jetta and head home. Logan is in the kitchen with Sarah, telling her about his history project. I shoot her a look letting her know I'm on to her. She's sneaky, getting Logan to talk about Amber by asking about the project instead of asking about Amber. She tries to look innocent and fails, a blush reddening her cheeks.

Luckily, Logan is oblivious so I stalk over to her and kiss her instead of calling her out. They're making dinner together. Logan likes food, and not just eating it. Since he's moved in with us, he's helped both of us make dinner whenever he's finished his homework in time to.

While he sets the table, I tell Sarah his gift is in my trunk and I'll bring it in and sneak it up to our room once he's gone to bed. Sarah's in charge of wrapping presents. Whatever artistic talent I have fell short of that.

"So, how was Rascal with Santa?"

Sarah covers her mouth as she starts to laugh. "I had no idea Santa was going to be there, but once I saw him I had to get a picture of them." She points to the picture now proudly hanging on our fridge. "Rascal was hysterical. She tried to chew on the fur above his boots. His elf gave me some treats to distract her long enough to get her away from him."

THEM

"So, Rascal isn't a fan of fur?" I laugh.

She nods. "PETA would be so proud."

"Doesn't it defeat the purpose of Christmas gifts being a surprise if you take the dog you're shopping for with you?"

She waves me off. "Like she'll remember. Besides, she loves going to the pet store."

I bend down and clap my hands, calling Rascal over to me. She comes bounding over, her tongue lolling out of her mouth, and rolls over onto her back in front of me. I rub her belly and continue to listen in as Sarah tries to get more details about Amber out of Logan.

Since she's distracted and too close for me to ignore, I sneak a couple of squeezes to her ass when Logan isn't looking. Each time, she trips over her words and turns to glare down at me while I innocently go back to petting Rascal. I lift my hand to sneak in another squeeze, but she's on to me and gently kicks her foot back at me.

Foiled.

Giving up, I stand. "What's for dinner?"

"Spaghetti and meatballs," Logan answers.

"And garlic bread," Sarah adds, trying her best to look annoyed at me.

"Smells great." I ignore her glare and change the subject. "Has Rascal been out recently?"

"I'll let her out," Logan volunteers, setting the wooden spoon he was using to stir the noodles on the counter.

Once he's out of sight, I pull Sarah against me. "Now I have to you all to myself," I tease, kissing her cheek loudly.

She giggles, trying to get away, but I only tighten my arms around her.

"Will, I can't believe you were grabbing my butt in front of Logan," she hiss-whispers.

"Come on, he didn't see anything," I promise, grinning at her.

"You're rotten," she grumbles, but I know she's over it when she kisses me.

I love everything about this woman. She knows all my secrets, my fears, my insecurities and loves me no matter what. I have it all with her: laughter, friendship, and she still makes me feel like a horny teenager whenever I'm around her. All I need in life is to know that she'll be next to me each morning when I wake.

As my wife, whatever adventures life has in store for me, I'll have her by my side to face them. Our potentially biggest adventure starting tomorrow when we go see her doctor.

11

Sarah

We're pregnant.

I told myself I wasn't going to cry, but that went out the window the moment Will looked at me, eyes bright and wet as the doctor confirmed it. By his estimate, we are six weeks along. Any tears that came after that were all Will's fault. I hope he's paying attention to everything my doctor is saying, because I zoned out after he said we should be able to hear our baby's heartbeat at our next appointment.

Our baby.

After the appointment, we stop to have lunch together. Neither of us speaks; we just hold hands and grin at each other. It's not until we're back in the car so Will can take me home that we're able to speak again.

"Should we wait to tell Logan?" I ask.

Will nods. "Isn't it normal to wait until the first trimester is over to tell people? Isn't that what Brian and Christine do?"

"So, not until the middle of February? That seems so far away," I argue.

THEM

"I know." He reaches out to rest his hand on my thigh. "But with the year he's had, it's probably safest to wait."

I turn to glance out the window, hating the implication of his words. There's a reason expectant parents wait to tell people—the risk of miscarriage is greatest during the first trimester. A bubble of fear expands within my chest. After waiting so long only to have our hopes dashed time and time again to get pregnant, I would be devastated if something were to happen.

"You're right," I gulp, my emotions lodging in my throat.

He squeezes my thigh and gently runs his hand downward to my knee and back up again. "It will be okay."

He's always known how to calm me down. I do my best to relax my nerves as we turn onto our street. Walking me inside, only to make sure I'm all right, Will kisses me sweetly, pausing to let his fingers drift over my stomach. I could tell he'd rather stay with me than go into work, but for some reason I need a couple hours to myself to collect my thoughts.

"I'm fine. Go." I push him toward the door.

He leaves me after one final kiss on my forehead and I watch him walk back to his car. Once he pulls back onto our street, I close the door and hurry to let Rascal out of her crate. I left my coat on so we could go for a walk. We don't walk every day; on the colder ones, when I'm feeling lazy, I just let her out into our fenced backyard. Today, though, given how mild it is, I decide to collect my thoughts on a walk with her.

"Wanna go for a walk, girl?" I coo, clicking her leash onto her collar.

We head toward the playground I take Calvin to when I babysit him. Given the temperature, it's deserted. By next September, I could be walking this way with a stroller. The sky is clear of clouds, but the wind still has an edge that stings my cheeks as we walk. Its chill does nothing to dispel the warmth inside me, though.

Over the last few months, our world has changed so much; first with Rascal and then with Logan coming to live with us. Will and I want to adopt him; finding out we're pregnant does not change that in any way. It's so strange to think about the loneliness I suffered before when now it seems as though every day my world is filling with more to love.

I had been so certain a family was not in my future, ashamed that I couldn't provide one for Will. My joy at the difference of now versus then is only hampered by the fact that we decided to wait until I was past my first trimester to share with everyone. I can't wait to tell my parents, Sawyer and, crazy as it sounds, Will's mom. She fawns over Rascal and Logan so much already, I'm sure she'll lose her mind over her first grandbaby.

Heart full, I turn back in the direction of our house. Once we're back inside, Rascal curls up on her cushion in the living room. I start a fire and pull out Logan's gifts to wrap. From us, we're giving him lacrosse gear and his long board will be from Santa. Sure, he's probably long past the age of still believing in Saint Nick, but neither Will nor I wanted to confirm that. Worst-case, he'll roll his eyes at us Christmas morning.

I have Christmas carols playing in the background as I work. There's plenty of time for me to wrap everything before the boys get home, but I still start with the long board so I can hide it before I wrap anything else. It comes in a box with two of the wheels visible on one side, which somewhat defeats the purpose of the box. It's hard to disguise the outline of the wheels so I end up putting it inside another box, filled with balled-up tissue paper.

I'm excited about Christmas and hopeful that we can still give Logan a good one even after everything he has been through this last year. He could be in a group home right now, and the thought of that alone breaks my heart. That may be why I go a bit overboard on the ribbons and bows. I only want it to be special for him. Once I'm finished with it, I carry the box back upstairs and hide it in my closet. It's big, though, so I might have Will move it up into the attic tonight after Logan goes to bed.

Heading back downstairs, I get started on wrapping all of the lacrosse stuff Will got. There are gloves, pads, cleats, a helmet, balls, the shaft and a head. I wrap each one individually and place them all under the tree. Logan is going to flip when he gets home and sees all of it. Excitement from the day hits me and I stretch out across the sofa to rest. Even though I only intended to lie down briefly, I end up falling asleep.

Hours later, I groggily awaken to Will leaning over me and rubbing my back. "Hey, sleeping beauty."

I blink up at him. "What time is it?"

He smoothes my hair back behind my ear as his blue eyes shine warmly down at me. "Almost dinner time."

Stunned so much time has passed, I bolt upright, almost bumping heads with him. "Why didn't you wake me when you got home?"

He lifts his arm to wrap around my shoulders and hold me close to his side. "You looked so peaceful and besides," his voice lowers to a whisper. "You need your rest."

I gulp, *my rest*. Will this feeling ever go away? I'm barely into my pregnancy, so it's not surprising I'm in awe of the thought of it. I wonder if four or five months from now I'll still feel the same way.

"What's for dinner?"

He stands, pulling me up with him, and directs us toward the kitchen. "Smoked sausage, steamed broccoli, noodles and applesauce. Logan helped me make it all."

"Yum."

Logan is already seated when we reach the kitchen.

THEM

"Sorry I didn't help with dinner." I gesture toward the food on the table. "This looks great."

As we eat, I ask Logan how school was. It was the last day before winter break, so it will be fun to have both of my boys home for the next two weeks.

"What day is Amber coming over?" Will asks.

"The twenty-seventh. She's going to be out of town before that." Logan's cheeks redden as he answers.

"Oh. Do you know where she's going?" I can't help my curiosity.

"Her grandparents live in Florida," he replies.

"Does she have any brothers or sisters?" I ask, ignoring Will's attempt to hide his grin.

Logan glances between us, probably wondering why Will thinks this is so funny. "She, um, has an older brother. I think he's a sophomore."

If his name is Brian, I'll die laughing. I can tell Will is thinking the same thing I am.

"I look forward to meeting her."

Logan pales. "She's only coming over to work on our project."

Will snorts and I glare at him. Turning back to Logan, I reply, "Of course."

He doesn't look convinced but doesn't say anything.

"Do you guys want to watch a movie tonight?" Will changes the subject. "Logan and I can run out to

Redbox or we can order something through the DVR."

I clap; I'm always up for a movie night. "Let's go with DVR. I can make popcorn."

I clear the table while Logan and Will go to check out what movies are available. After giving me their top picks, we all agree on an action comedy. Logan helps Will bring in more wood for the fire as I make the popcorn.

Fifteen minutes into the movie, I pass out.

12

Will

Amber is in the house. Her dad dropped her off thirty minutes ago. Sarah is pretending to read a book in the living room since they are in the kitchen. How do I know she's faking? She hasn't turned a page in ten minutes. Sarah spent the first ten minutes Amber was here offering her something to eat or drink while Logan looked about as uncomfortable as I'd ever seen him.

I decided to come to his rescue and get her out of the kitchen so they could get started on their project. I had hoped to get her upstairs, but I only managed as far as the living room. She planted her ass on the sofa and gave me a look daring me to try and move her. I just shook my head at her and flipped on the TV to some college ball so I could keep an eye on her and make sure she doesn't go and bother them again.

Rascal ambles out of the kitchen to come curl up on her cushion by the fireplace. It's warmer today than it has been in the last week or so, which is the only reason we don't have a fire going. We haven't had one since Christmas day. It came in handy for a quick way to get rid of all of that wrapping paper, though. Sarah outdid herself on all of the gifts under the tree.

Logan loved all of his presents. I've spent the last couple of days either trying not to fall off my old skateboard or showing him how to pass a lacrosse ball in the backyard. Passing the ball is fun, unless either of us misses and Rascal is outside. She goes nuts after the balls, and they're a bitch to get back from her.

After we opened our presents here Christmas morning, we picked my mom up and headed over to Sarah's parents' house for brunch and to open even more presents. I know Sarah was bummed we couldn't tell anyone about the baby. It makes sense to wait, though. Besides, Sawyer and Jared are coming down to visit. We're having a New Year's get-together, and I have a feeling Sawyer and Christine will figure it out as soon as they notice Sarah not drinking.

I glance up at her, grinning when I notice her toying with the locket I got her for Christmas. It's empty now, but I know she can't wait to put our baby's picture in it. Considering the amount of money she spent on the new camera lens she got me, there's a decent chance I'll be taking the picture.

"What do you think of Amber?"

I was so distracted I didn't realize Sarah had set down her book and was now looking at me.

"She seems shy," I reply.

Sarah nods. "I like her."

I can't help but laugh. "After ten minutes?"

She smirks. "Yes, after only ten minutes."

That response right there is Sarah through and through. She's quick to trust, so open and loving with those around her, even people she's just met. It's one of the things I love most about her, and I can only hope our baby inherits that from her.

"All I know is I'm not ready to be a grandparent," I tease.

Her forehead wrinkles. "But they're so young. You don't think . . ."

I stop her before she gets too worked-up. "No. From what I know of Logan, anything above and beyond having a conversation with her is not on his radar."

Sarah exhales, relief evident in her expression. "After everything you see in the news with kids these days, though . . ." She trails off as her eyes lower to watch her hand drift over her stomach.

Looking back up at me, she continues, "I wonder what things will be like when our kids are Logan's age."

Time to nip this thought spiral in the bud before she makes herself sick with worry over what imagined struggles the future may bring. "All I know is that with you as their mom, everything will be all right."

She gulps, her eyes never leaving mine. "Do you think I'll make a good mom?"

She's too far away for me to answer her question properly. I lean forward, scooping her up in my arms and turning till I'm in her spot with her sitting in my lap. My fingers link behind her back, my arms loosely draped around her. Our foreheads touch as I stare into the eyes of the woman I've loved for more than half my life.

"I know you will be the best mom our kids could ever dream of."

Her eyes glisten with unshed tears as she replies, her voice thick. "I know you're going to be such a good daddy."

It's uncanny how the complete confidence in her words affects me. There are few things I want out of life: to be a good husband, a good teacher, and, more than ever, a better father than I had.

"All I need is you by my side, darling."

She melts against me, resting her head on my shoulder.

Both of our heads turn toward the kitchen when Logan calls out that he and Amber will be in the backyard.

"Should I make sure he put on a hat?" Sarah asks innocently.

My only response is a bark of laughter, loud enough for Rascal to shift in her sleep.

"Why do you think that's funny?" she grumbles.

I coax her head back onto my shoulder before looping my arms around her again. "It's not that cold out."

She humphs but lets it go. I go back to watching my game and before long, she's fallen asleep. Her daily naps have increased since we found out she was pregnant. At first, I was worried it meant something was wrong, but it turns out that it's completely normal.

All I know about pregnancies is from what I've seen in movies or from Christine and Sawyer. Brian and Jared both doted on them during their pregnancies, and now it's my turn. It's unnerving, knowing this miracle is growing inside of Sarah right now. In a way, I'm helpless, only able to watch as Sarah alone bears the brunt of that.

I'll do anything in my power to make her as comfortable and content while she carries our baby. There's no doubt about it, I'd give her the world if I could. After our doctor appointment, she bought a couple of books to give us an idea of what to expect. One of the books is a brick, each chapter broken down by month.

Sarah's probably read the first-trimester section ten times already. I'm behind the ball since I haven't even read it once. I'd go grab it now if I wasn't scared moving would wake her. If only it was the book she was fake-reading earlier. Nope, until Logan finds out about the baby, she's keeping anything baby-related in our bedroom.

THEM

I have a couple of options: I can move her and probably wake her, or I can lean back and watch my game while the love of my life is snuggled against me.

No-brainer.

An hour later, Sarah stirs, lifting her head to blink her pretty brown eyes at me.

"Did I fall asleep?" she asks, groggily.

I brush her cheek with my fingertips. "You did."

Her forehead wrinkles up as she frowns. "Did I miss saying bye to Amber?"

Her worried expression slays me.

I shake my head. "No, darling. They came back inside about thirty minutes ago and are working in the kitchen."

Her features immediately soften at the news.

"Why were you so worried?"

She shrugs, a blush creeping across her cheeks. "I think Logan likes her, and after everything he's been through that makes me happy."

The beauty of her love, even when it's not directed my way, astounds me.

When I don't speak, she hurriedly continues, "I'm silly, I know."

"Stop." I lean forward to hush her lips with a quick brush of mine. "You are the most amazing person I know."

Her eyes start to glisten as she quickly tries to blink her tears away and lifts her hands to dab her fingertips at the corners of her eyes.

"I didn't mean to make you cry," I confess, squeezing her gently.

"I'm just emotional, I guess," she rasps.

She stands, mumbling something about offering the kids a snack, with Rascal trailing after her as she makes her way to the kitchen to spy on them. I'd tease her about it, but I think it's cute.

"Will, honey, can the kids borrow one of your tripods?" she asks, walking back into the living room with a drink in her hand.

Logan and Amber are behind her.

"Are you two ready to start filming?" I ask, getting up from the couch.

Logan glances at Amber before answering. "We've written the script and thought it might be a good idea to do a run-through to see if the spot we picked in the backyard will work."

"All right, give me a minute and I'll grab one."

All of my camera gear is in a spare bedroom we've converted into a home office for me upstairs. I have more than one tripod, so I grab a sturdy but heavy one for the kids to use and lug it downstairs and outside for them. I picked this one since it'll be near impossible for them to break it.

THEM

Sarah stands off to the side as I explain to Logan and Amber where and how to mount their smart phones. I offered to let them use our video camera, but they weren't interested, something about having an app to make gifs for Instagram. Things sure have changed since Sarah and I were in school.

As a teacher, I've seen the progression first hand. Now, with Sarah carrying our baby, I'm curious to see how different our child's future will be. Logan tilts his head toward the house in a silent plea for Sarah and me to go back inside. She pouts as we walk back to the house, looking back over her shoulder a couple times, hoping Logan changed his mind. I can't disguise my chuckle as I drape my arm around her shoulders.

She claims to need to put away laundry once we're inside, but the real reason she wants to be in our bedroom is the clear view of the backyard. I'm not clairvoyant, but I don't need to be to see a lifetime of her driving our kids crazy in the future.

"Will."

Her shrieked cry has me taking the stairs two at a time to get to her. She's standing at the window, her hands clutched to her chest.

"What's wrong?" I pant, catching my breath.

Her dancing brown eyes find mine as she grins. "Logan just helped Amber up and then they stood there holding hands for a minute. They aren't doing it anymore." She shakes her head at me. "You missed it."

My mouth drops open before I can respond. I clamp it shut and frown. "I thought you were hurt."

Her lips form the letter "O" when she realizes I'm annoyed. She leaves the window and crosses the room to kiss my cheek.

"I'm sorry, honey. I was excited."

My tension ebbs as I stare into her warm eyes. "Let's lay off on the matchmaking for the rest of today, okay?"

13

Sarah

Now everyone knows.

We told Sawyer, Jared, Christine and Brian on New Year's. Sawyer surprised me by promptly bursting into tears. Even more shocking was when Brian had to turn away to discretely wipe his eyes.

Christine was thrilled that we'd both have babies in the same year. She's looking more ready to pop every day, though. She's not due until May, me not until September.

Logan's reaction broke my heart. He asked if he'd be going to live with someone else since he wasn't family. Will and I had a long talk with him, letting him know he would always have a home with us. That even though we aren't related by blood, we think of him as part of our family and always will. I'm not sure if he believed us, but he hasn't mentioned living anywhere else since.

Will's mom was over the moon that we're expecting her first grandbaby. My parents are no less thrilled, it just isn't their first time. Mrs. Price, or Mama Price as Sawyer calls her, has taken to stopping

THEM

by at least twice a week. She times her visits so we can have some one-on-one time before Will and Logan get home and then stays for dinner.

"How are you feeling?" She reaches over to pat my hand.

"Christine said the exhaustion is supposed to wear off after the first trimester, but unfortunately it hasn't yet. I feel useless," I confess.

"Has the morning sickness gotten any better?"

I shake my head, mentally correcting her assumption that I'm only sick in the morning. Sadly, it seems to be all-day sickness in my case. With the exception of my prenatal vitamin, I'm currently existing on ginger ale and saltines. As much as I love her, I'm sick with envy every time I see Christine these days.

She has energy in spades, jogging every day with Calvin in his stroller, and she's head-to-toe got that pregnancy glow thing going on. On my best day, my skin is tinged with a shade of green that would make the Wicked Witch of the West jealous. My multiple trips to the bathroom spent dry-heaving haven't done anything to erase the bags and dark circles that have taken permanent residence under my eyes.

If I had more energy, I'd probably worry about Will losing any desire for me, but these days I'm even too tired to stress myself out.

"I'll cook tonight," she offers, loving the opportunity to help out.

I give her my best grateful smile but considering she shooed me off to take a nap, I don't think it worked.

The noises coming from downstairs when I wake let me know Will and Logan are home. I stop by the bathroom before I go down to greet them. One glance in the mirror and I have to admit that nap helped. I don't look my normal awful, and considering I managed a shower earlier I look half-good. I'm halfway down the stairs when Will hears me and comes to meet me.

"There's my girl." He takes my hand and squeezes it. "How are you feeling today?"

He's been worrying himself sick over me. I'm certain he's called the doctor no less than a dozen times since our last appointment.

"Human," I joke.

"That's good news." He brushes his fingertips up my cheek and over my hair, then down to gently grip the back of my neck.

Leaning down, he touches his lips to mine. "It's good to see you're feeling better."

"You worry too much," I whisper.

"I gotta take care of my girl," he counters, unapologetically.

"How was school?" I ask, as he leads me toward the kitchen.

THEM

"The kids were not impressed that Vincent Van Gogh cut off his own ear in the name of love."

My eyes bug out and before I can ask, he explains, "It was my idea for something Valentine themed to learn about him."

"You are so morbid." I laugh. "That's so not cool, traumatizing those kids like that."

"Please." He smirks. "It's better than having them paint hearts."

"Remember the conversation heart still-life project you had them do last year?"

He nods.

"It was hearts and still clever."

He still has a habit of chewing on the corner of his lip when he's considering something.

"There was one kid who painted anti-love messages on all of his hearts. They were great."

"Do you remember what any of them said?"

We pause in the hallway before we reach the kitchen and he nods. "Instead of 'be mine' one of them said 'be gone' and another one said 'not you' instead of 'luv you.'"

"How unromantic," I reply.

"He didn't gain any dates from it."

"Speaking of dates," I change the subject. "Do you want to do anything for Valentine's Day?"

"Aren't I in charge of the wooing around here?"

"Wooing?" I laugh, leaning forward with my hand on his chest to hold myself up.

Will has this incredible super power of looking both incredibly adorable and sexy as sin simultaneously when he's annoyed. It works in his favor, so he always gets his way because I'm too busy trying to decide whether I should cuddle him or drop my panties. He uses that moment of weakness while I'm lost in indecision against me every time.

"I give good woo," he teases, recognizing I'm currently under his spell.

His arm snakes up my back until his fingers thread my hair at the base of my skull. Tugging me forward till my body is flush to the hard muscle of his own, he dips his lips to nibble at my jaw line as I suck in a breath.

His 5 o'clock shadow is deliciously rough against the sensitive skin of my neck.

"Here's what I'm thinking." His words caress against my ear. "Logan is spending the night at Mom's. I've made a reservation to your favorite tapas restaurant. From there, we'll stop and get waffle cones and once we're home, I'm going to have my way with you all night."

Neither of us speaks when he lifts his head to meet my eyes.

Finally, he adds, "That work for you?"

I nod. "If I wasn't already knocked-up, I think your words alone could have impregnated me."

THEM

His lips tip up, the skin around his eyes crinkling as he smiles warmly at me. I hope I'll never lose the way a sweet smile from my husband can light me up from the inside out.

Any chance I have to tell him this is interrupted by his mom clearing her throat and saying, "Dinner's ready."

"Can I do anything to help?" My offer is lame and most likely too late, but I was raised to pitch in. Besides, it will help ease my guilt over her cooking for all of us in the first place.

"It is all finished, dear," she replies, linking her arm through mine and moving us both toward the dining room table.

The table is set, drinks already poured and dishes brimming with pasta, chicken, vegetables and rolls. There's too much food for just the four of us, and I realize she's done it purposefully so we'll already have another meal ready to go from the leftovers. At the table, she sits to my right, with the both of us facing the boys.

I reach out to clasp her hand in mine and thank her. Knowing the woman she is today makes me mourn the mother Will did not have growing up. Back then, she was cold, living but only barely doing that. She pushed Will away, terrified to form attachments after the death of his older sister. His whole entire life could have changed.

If he had felt more at home in his own house, would he have ever come to spend the time he had at mine instead? It's sad but if Mama Price had been a better mother, there's a chance Will and I wouldn't be together today. Our paths in life shape us; they have both the opportunity to break us or strengthen us depending on our own unique circumstances.

I lost seven years I could have spent with the love of my life, all because I was an immature eighteen-year-old who lacked the confidence to believe someone like Will could love me the way he did. That is my burden to live with. I plan to spend the rest of my life making certain that man knows how much I love him and enjoying and trusting in the fact that he loves me the same.

I choose not to live in the regret of what might have been in those seven years we lost. It is possible that, as Will needed to be more at home in my house growing up, we also needed time apart to grow as individuals and understand how beautiful we are together.

After dinner, Will follows his mom home. She sold the house Will grew up in last year and moved into a condo not far from our house. She's made many changes in choosing to live life versus only existing in it, but Will still gets nervous when she drives at night.

Logan helps me with the dishes, but considering Mrs. Price cleaned the pots and pans she used, there wasn't much to clean. When we're finished, Logan goes to take Rascal for a walk around the block and I make myself comfortable in the living room. I've barely sat down by the time Will is back. He's shaking his head as he walks in the door.

"Everything all right?" I ask.

He shrugs off his coat and hangs it over the bannister post at the bottom of the stairs. "My mother had her turn signal on the entire drive."

"Good thing it was you behind her and not some other driver she could confuse." I laugh.

His only reply is to come and kiss my forehead before sitting down next to me.

"Did you stop and make sure she got in okay, and thank her again for dinner?"

He nods, untucking my legs from my side and pulling them across his lap.

"Head's up." He gently turns my chin until I'm facing him. "I saw some Babies R Us bags in there. The stuff could be for Christine, but I'm guessing Mom's already shopping for our baby and by the number of bags I saw, a lot."

"Don't mention any of this to my mother," I plead.

He laughs. "Why?"

I shrug. "You know my mom. If she finds out *your* mom is already baby shopping, *she'll* start baby shopping to try and out-grandma your mom."

"Out-grandma?" He's still laughing.

"Don't laugh at me. It's a thing, and if you don't believe me, call Brian and ask him what happened when Calvin was born."

He lifts his hand in surrender before dropping them back onto my legs. "I believe you."

Our heads turn toward the front door as Logan and Rascal barrel in, bringing a cool blast of air with them. Logan's nose and ears are red as he unhooks Rascal's leash and then pulls off his coat. Unlike Will, he actually hangs his coat up in the closet.

"You should have worn a hat," I remind him as he slumps into the loveseat.

He nods. "It's colder than I thought it would be."

"Want me to make a fire and we can watch a movie?" Will asks the both of us.

Logan grins while I reply, "Sure, but there's a good chance I'll pass out halfway through, so you guys pick the movie."

Logan chooses a movie while Will gets the fire going. As I predicted, I was asleep long before it ended.

14

Will

"Is there anything she can take?"

This isn't the first time I've asked this question. We had hoped that once Sarah was past her first trimester, the morning sickness and exhaustion would go away. It hasn't. In fact, her morning sickness is so severe it's called *hyperemesis gravidarum*.

Last month, she got so dehydrated at one point she had to spend the night in the hospital hooked up to an IV. If I didn't believe in that kind of thing, I'd wonder if we were being punished for some unknown crime by fate. This is supposed to be one of the happiest times of our lives, but Sarah is miserable and I'm worried sick about her.

Something is up with Logan, too, considering the way he watches Sarah when she makes it out of bed. It's like he feels responsible, but that's crazy. He's just a kid; how could he think that?

Sarah squeezes my hand. She worries about me.

Dr. Stacey goes over everything we already know: consuming a bland diet, eating frequent small meals, drinking plenty of fluids when not feeling nauseated, avoiding spicy and fatty foods, eating high-protein snacks, and avoiding sensory stimuli that can act as triggers.

This is all stuff we're already doing. It still didn't keep her from being hospitalized, though.

"There has to be an anti-nausea medication we can try," I urge, already knowing what he'll say.

"We've tried them all."

Sarah gives my hand another squeeze. "As long as the baby is healthy, I'll be fine."

She's the strong one at the moment. All I can do is sit by helplessly while she struggles. All I want to do is take care of her, to take away anything that causes her discomfort.

"With some women, the symptoms lessen when they're into their twentieth week." Dr. Stacey's expression is hopeful.

"Fingers crossed," Sarah continues to try and lighten my mood.

Dr. Stacey uses this opportunity to change the subject. "Have we decided on whether or not you'd like to find out the sex of the baby during your ultrasound today?"

Sarah answers for the both of us. "We want to be surprised."

Boy or girl, all either of us want is for him or her to be healthy. The whoosh-whoosh of hearing the heartbeat of our child is enough to improve my mood, slightly. That and the dreamy expression Sarah gets as she listens to it. I am humbled by the strength and grace she has shown as the daily battle with nausea rages on within her.

"You are so beautiful," I whisper against her temple before I press my lips to it.

She blushes. "I look like crap."

"Shut it," I mock growl. "That's my wife you're talking about."

She shakes her head at me but reaches for my hand, taking it in hers and lifting it to press a kiss to the back of it. I hate this, how powerless I am to do anything to take away her discomfort. Worse, by impregnating her in the first place, it's all my fault.

As we drive home, I ask, for most likely the hundredth time, if there is anything I can do. The answer is unsurprising, as it's the same one she's given me the ninety-nine other times.

"You're doing everything perfectly."

No matter how many times she tells me this, I still don't believe her. The last thing I want to do is leave her, but I have to get back to school. Since she's tired, I let Rascal out for her while she goes upstairs to lie down. Once I let the dog back in, I pop up to kiss her before I leave.

She's out, absolutely exhausted from only going to the doctor. It's been so bad she's taken leave from work. I brush her bangs from her eyes and kiss her forehead. She shivers in her sleep, and I lift the comforter to her chin then give one last, longing look before I leave.

I make it back to school in time for lunch. Logan is waiting for me outside of my classroom, and he's not alone.

"Would it be all right if Amber ate with us today?"

I'm speechless and manage a jerky nod before I unlock my door. They shuffle in behind me, and Amber follows Logan toward a table in the middle of the classroom. It's further from my desk than where he normally sits, but I haven't gotten the complete brush off that would have been if they sat in the back of the class.

"The appointment go okay?" Logan asks as he drops his backpack onto the floor.

He's been as concerned about Sarah as I have.

"More of the same. The doctor hopes the further she gets along that she'll have less morning sickness."

"My mom had really bad morning sickness with my younger brother," Amber adds, sliding into her chair.

"Did it ever go away?" Logan turns to face her.

She nods. "She hardly got sick toward the end of it."

Logan turns back to me, his face hopeful. "Maybe that will happen for Sarah, too."

I nod, my expression most likely mirroring his.

It's that hope I hold on to for the rest of lunch. I pretend-load grades into the system, but truly I'm reliving my friendship with Sarah through Logan and Amber.

Instead of talking about MTV, they're talking about YouTube. The subject matter might be different, but the sharing and learning of their mutual likes and dislikes is the same.

The nostalgia carries me through the rest of my day. No matter what happens, no matter what obstacles await us, as long as I'm going home to my girl nothing else matters.

Practice has started for the spring lacrosse season at the high school, and Logan acts as my assistant. I'm distracted though, so I spend the majority of practice having them run passing drills and then let them scrimmage for the last thirty minutes. As much as I'd rather be home taking care of Sarah right now, coaching is probably keeping me from smothering her.

Once all the kids have left or have been picked up by their parents, I call her to see if she wants takeout for dinner. Since certain smells can set her off, it's easier to grab food these days. As long as it's something bland; dinner has been the meal she has had the most success in keeping down.

I use the car ride as an opportunity to pump Logan for details about Amber.

Glancing his way at a red light, I ask, "So, lunch?"

He shrugs, turning his head so he's looking out the side window. "A couple of girls were being mean to her in the lunch room, so . . ." He trails off.

My back straightens. "She's being bullied?"

Years can go by, but for some reason there's always a few kids who need to torment their classmates to feel better about themselves.

Logan sighs. "There's this girl who likes me and she doesn't like it that Amber and I are friends."

"Do I know this girl?"

There's nothing worse than finding out a kid you thought was sweet and kind is actually a master actor or actress. I'd like to think I can pick out the troublemakers. The stealth ones who fly under the radar, making their classmates miserable right under my nose, piss me off the most.

"I don't think she takes art. She does drama."

I nod; knowing she isn't one of my kids helps somehow. "Do you want me to step in?"

He shakes his head. "She doesn't want to say anything and be a snitch."

That's another thing I'll never understand. It's like middle school aged kids have it hardwired into their systems to try and solve their own problems. Heaven forbid any teenager or preteen reach out to an adult for help; we're clearly all idiots in their eyes.

"What kind of stuff is this girl doing?"

I don't care if he wants me to step in or not, if this girl is putting her hands on his friend I'm reporting it.

"She talks about her clothes and the way she talks."

"The way she talks?" I ask as we pull into the parking lot of a local Chinese place.

"Yeah, Amber's family moved here from Minnesota a couple years ago, so she says Amber talks funny."

We park and I wait until we're both out of the car to reply. "I don't remember hearing an accent."

He rolls his eyes, "That's the thing. It's pretty much nonexistent, and she still gives her crap about it."

"Are you sure you don't want me to report this?"

He hesitates. "I'll talk to her about it tomorrow. Can she eat lunch with me in your class again?"

I nod, holding open the door of the restaurant for him. Since we didn't call the order in ahead of time, we have to sit and wait for it. The restaurant is in a small strip mall, with a hardware store on one side and an antique store on the other. When Sarah and I come, if we have to wait, she likes to go and walk around the antique store. It's a small space, with all sorts of treasures stacked up to the ceiling. She's gotten a painting or two from there and a tea set she doesn't use, just displays on a bookshelf in our living room.

Since it's only Logan and me, we wait inside the restaurant. It, like the antique shop, is small on the inside. One entire wall is mirrored, giving an illusion

THEM

of another room. The opposite wall boasts a metallic black and gold stripe print with large blossoms.

I use the extra time to try and pump Logan for more info about this girl who's giving Amber a hard time. Experience has shown that many bullies are bullied themselves. I know neither Logan nor Amber want to be a snitch, but if I had her name it would make looking into her a whole heck of a lot easier.

"So, this girl, is she in any of Amber's classes?"

He chews on one side of his lip, a nervous habit I can't help but wonder if he picked up from me. "They have gym together."

I cringe; that's a tough break for Amber. Out of all of the classes a kid could be stuck with a bully in, gym has to be the worst. There are so many opportunities where the teacher isn't able to be watching. The gym itself is huge, plus the track and fields if the kids are outside, and I don't even want to think about the locker rooms.

"You swear it hasn't gotten physical?" I press.

He nods. "You know girls. They're all mental warfare."

For being thirteen, he makes a decent point. A buzzing sound comes from the front pouch of his hoodie and he pulls out his phone.

He looks up at me, lifting it at the same time. "It's Amber. Is it cool if I go outside and call her?"

"Sur—" I reply.

He's out of the booth and to the door before I can finish the word. I'm torn between laughing and Googling chastity belts for boys. Either way, it's clear he's got it bad for this girl, whether he can admit it or not.

Watching the way he is with Amber takes me back to the very start of my friendship with Sarah. We reminisce about it from time to time, Sarah and me, talking about how unsure we both were back then about moving from friends to more. Part of me just curses the time we lost together, those years when we were both too afraid to make the first move and then when we didn't trust our love enough to fight for it.

Growing up seriously sucks sometimes. There we were with all of these emotions and desires that neither of us were mature enough to handle. I'll always curse the time we lost, but being apart to grow up on our own could be the reason we're as solid as we are today.

"Order for Price."

I'm snapped out of my mind and back to reality. *Time to go feed my woman.* Since she has okay luck with bland food, I got her some sweet and sour chicken. She skips using the sauce and sticks to only the rice and chicken.

Logan turns as I walk out the door with the food. He starts to say goodbye, but I motion for him to keep talking and he does. I have an ulterior motive of seeing if I can pick up any info through their conversation. Sure, eavesdropping isn't cool, but he knows I'm listening so if he says anything he doesn't want me to hear that's on him, not me.

Unfortunately, his side of the conversation consists of saying 'yeah' over and over. I can hear her through the phone but can't make out any words. By the time we make it to the house, I've given myself a headache straining to make out what she was saying.

Logan hangs up as I park.

"Everything okay?" I ask.

He shrugs. "She got all happy when I told her you were cool with her eating in your class."

"Hopefully after a couple of days she'll feel comfortable enough to talk to me."

"I told her you were cool, but since she doesn't know you . . ." He hesitates.

"She doesn't want to tell me," I finish for him.

Sarah is sitting on the sofa with Rascal curled up into a ball next to her when we walk in. Rascal immediately springs from the couch to come greet and sniff us, giving the bag of Chinese food most of her attention.

"Smells good." Sarah grins, standing and walking over to take the bag from me.

After Logan and I have shed our coats, we meet her in the kitchen.

"How're you feeling?" I ask, pressing a kiss to the side of her head and giving her shoulders a squeeze.

"I don't want to jinx anything," she starts. "But today has been a good day."

"That's great news," I breathe.

Good days have been few and far between.

"I know." She grins. "I might even risk sweet and sour sauce."

My eyes widen, wondering if that's tempting fate and I'll be holding her hair back as dinner makes a reappearance later on tonight.

15

Sarah

"I'm on my way to the hospital right now," I reply.

"Okay." Will sounds breathless. "I'll meet you there."

Snapping my phone shut, I focus on the road. I got the call fifteen minutes ago that Christine's water broke. All I can think is how excited I am to meet my new niece and how terrified I am to get a preview of how my labor might go.

Will and I were at the hospital when she had Calvin but not being pregnant at the time, I hadn't even considered what labor would be like from my perspective. This time around, it was almost all I was thinking about. Over the last month, my morning sickness had for the most part gone away. There were still some smells I, for whatever reason, could not handle at all. One of them being coffee, another being seafood.

Both have been easy fixes. Will picks up coffee on the way to school and since I'm not supposed to be drinking a ton of caffeine, I stopped drinking it altogether. Seafood has been an issue a couple of times going out to eat, and once when Mama Price surprised us with lobster ravioli. That was a bad night. I swear I could still smell it the next day, which made that day a not so great one, either.

Now, being pregnant myself and rapidly approaching my own due date, I've become slightly terrified of the actual labor part. I've only been in a room with a woman in labor once and that was when Christine had Calvin. Christine is easily the most evenly tempered person I know. Seriously, it's why she hasn't killed Brian yet.

During her labor with Calvin, I wondered a couple of times if she was possessed. Her head didn't spin or anything, but it was the first time I had ever witnessed her raise her voice and if I remember correctly, she even threatened bodily harm against Brian. That was so out of character for her, it was clearly due to the pain.

How would I handle it? I was only four months away from finding out. I've never been a fan of pain, and I'm pretty sure my tolerance to it is on the low side. I've pumped Christine for details about what labor was like for her, and she claims to not remember the pain. How can she not remember the pain? That doesn't seem possible.

My theory is there is some mom clause where you don't freak out moms-to-be while they're carrying their first kids. The only flaw in that theory is a woman having more than one kid. Either way, I'm freaked.

I park near the front entrance and wonder if I should wait for Will or head inside. I'm being a baby about going in all by myself. Squaring my shoulders, I decide to grow up and not wait. This is the same hospital we will be having our baby and where Christine had Calvin two years ago.

Other than new wallpaper, Labor and Delivery is in the same place it was then. By the time I make it to the nurses' station, I can hear Brian from the hallway so I don't need to ask what room they're in.

I knock lightly before peeking my head in. "Hi."

"Come on in," Brian says, walking over to open the door more.

Christine is in a hospital gown, a sheet and blanket pulled up to her chest. She lifts her hand in greeting, her pretty face strained.

I hurry over to her after hugging Brian to kiss her cheek. "How are you doing?"

She grimaces and Brain answers for her. "Her water broke. So far, she's already dilated to four centimeters. We're waiting on the anesthesiologist to give her an epidural. The contractions are coming pretty fast."

He points out a machine next to her bed. "They're monitoring the intensity of them on this. When these red dots go up this thing, it means she's having one and the higher they go, the stronger it is."

"Oh, honey," I coo, reaching out for her hand.

THEM

"I'm doing okay, I swear," she replies. "It's only hard to talk during them."

I'll bet.

"Who has Calvin?" I ask Brian.

"Dad's watching him. Our mom and Christine's mom are on their way. If the baby comes before little dude's bedtime, Dad is going to swing by with him."

"Have they given you any idea of how long it might be?"

Christine runs her hand over her belly, "I went fast with Cal and they say babies after the first come even faster, but honestly we don't know."

I nod. "Is there anything I can get either of you?"

Christine lifts a Styrofoam cup from her bedside table. "I can only have ice chips from this point on."

I turn to face Brian. "Do you want anything?"

He drags a hand through his hair and glances softly in Christine's direction. "I'm too nervous to eat anything. Thanks for the offer, though."

My phone chirps from my purse and I pull it out to see a text from Will, wondering what room Christine is in.

I hadn't even looked at the door when I walked in, so I step out in the hall so I can answer him. A return text isn't needed, though, when I see him standing at the end of the hall.

"Will," I whisper-yell, and his eyes meet mine.

I stand rooted, watching his expression warm and him approach me.

"Hey, darling," he murmurs against my temple as he presses his lips to my skin.

"Hi." I squeeze him tightly and lead him into the room.

He's given the same updates as to Christine's condition as I was. Not long after we arrive, we're sent to the waiting room so the anesthesiologist can give Christine her epidural.

"Does Logan know to take the bus home?" I ask, glancing back toward Christine's room.

"I called my mom. She's going to pick him up and take him to her house."

"That makes way more sense than him being all by himself at the house," I murmur, my brows furrowing.

"You're lucky I have more than my good looks to get me by," Will teases.

"Sarah, Will," my mom calls out.

Will leaves me sitting and walks over to hug her.

"How is she? Why are you two out here? Is she already pushing?"

Will glances at me, biting back a grin at my mom's rapid-fire questions.

I pat the seat next to me and reply as she sits. "She's fine. She's getting her epidural. She isn't pushing yet."

THEM

"Oh, whew." Mom leans back into her chair. "I was scared I missed it."

"If you missed it, we'd all be in her room meeting the new baby," I joke.

She frowns. "Well, you make a good point."

The nurses are cool with us hanging out in her room until it's time for her to push. Once that happens, we'll go back in the waiting room while only Brian stays with her for the delivery, depending on how late it is. Will has school tomorrow, and I have no desire to stay up all night. If she hasn't had the baby by eleven, we're going home and to bed.

Since it's her second baby, everyone is convinced it will be here long before that. I'm tired, so honestly, I'm just doing what I'm told. Sit here, Sarah—sure. Drink this, Sarah—okay. Relax, Sarah—I'm all over that. For me, my second trimester can also be called my zombie time. I'm committed to going with the flow, especially now that I can eat without throwing up every time.

I may be a zombie, but I'm an observant one. Christine may not realize it, but I'm mentally taking notes as to how she's handling her labor. For example, before the epidural, she was not a happy camper but after, she took a catnap, with us in the room and everything. I watched the machine thingy next to her bed; she was still having contractions the entire time and slept right through them.

Carey Heywood

Before now, I hadn't put a lot of thought into whether I wanted an epidural or not. The concept of natural childbirth had its appeals, and I figured if my ancestors could do it, why couldn't I? After seeing Christine sleep through a portion of her labor, I was second-guessing not considering it big-time. Seriously, my ancestors went to the bathroom outside. Why would I purposefully do something as painful as labor is, the hard way?

An epidural just moved to the top of my to-do list labor-wise. Making that decision alone relaxed me. *Now there are only a million other things for me to worry over or plan between now and then.* Since we've decided not to find out the sex of the baby, we've somewhat limited ourselves color-wise to gender-neutral hues. Although, pink and purple were historically male colors, and Will is open-minded to the point that I doubt he'd care if our son slept in a pink room or our daughter in a blue one.

The idea of having to correct every stranger we'd pass in the wrong-colored stroller is what's keeping me from making a decision. I could always go with slate and then use any color I wanted as an accent. I pull out my phone. Whether it's the pregnancy or something else, I have lost all ability to remember anything these days.

I can stand up in the living room, walk to the kitchen to get a glass of water and by the time I'm there, I've forgotten what I came into the kitchen for in the first place. Because I forget everything, I send

THEM

Will random texts of things I want to remember. That way, he can remind me or I can check my sent text history and remind myself.

Luckily, the influx of texts hasn't driven him crazy. If I was in his shoes I wouldn't be as patient. Good news for me is he thinks I'm cute.

The nurses come to check on Christine every thirty minutes or so. It's barely past dinner time when our mom's decide we should try and eat now since Christine hasn't started pushing yet, and the cafeteria is still open. Agreeing with them, we head there to grab a quick bite so our growling stomachs won't scare my new niece when we finally get to meet her.

We eat quickly, none of us wanting to hang out in a hospital cafeteria and potentially miss a few minutes meeting the new baby. While the food isn't the most appetizing, since the majority of my all-day, every-day sickness has gone away I wolf down a turkey sandwich.

As fast as I ate, though, my mom and Christine's mom finished way faster. They hurry back to the Labor and Delivery wing and don't bother holding the elevator for Will and me.

"Rude much?" I ask the closed elevator doors when we reach them.

Will chuckles next to me.

"What?" I snap, more annoyed than I need to be. "You don't think it's rude they couldn't wait for us?" I don't wait for his response; I'm hormonal and on a roll. "I mean, geez, it's not like I'm pregnant or anything. Did they expect me to speed-walk along next to them?"

He crosses his arms over his chest, his lips sealed because we both know I'm not done.

"Did they think you were going to abandon me, your pregnant wife?"

He lifts his eyebrows.

"God, and what's up with these elevators? I'm slow-moving these days, but we probably could have walked up the stairs at this point."

Uncrossing his arms, Will drops them to my biceps, gives me a squeeze and leans forward to kiss my forehead. After a beat, he straightens and drops one hand to press the up button on the wall.

I blush. "Oh, probably should have pressed the button before I got all pissed off at it."

He shrugs. "You're cute when you're pissed."

"You're lucky I like you," I grumble as the doors open.

"*Like* me." He clutches his chest as if my words wounded him.

"Don't act funny. I'm still annoyed," I huff, marching into the elevator once the doors open.

He follows me, his hand warm on my back, even through my sweater. If I look at him now, I'll laugh and all of my annoyance will evaporate like a morning mist against the rising sun. I want to hold onto my anger; I still haven't had a chance to let my mom have it.

With gentle pressure on my shoulders, he tries to turn me to face him. I refuse. Part of me expects him to be annoyed in return, but instead, he holds my back to his front and crosses his arms over my chest, hugging me to him. I stand there stiffly, pissed off at everyone and everything for the silliest of reasons, until I notice the slight shake of his body against mine and the muffled chuckle he attempts to suppress.

All at once, my body softens. I melt into him and lift my hands to rest on his arms.

"I'm being ridiculous," I confess, relieved we're alone so I only have to be embarrassed in front of him.

The doors open and he stops me before we can continue on to Christine's room. This time, when he turns me to face him, I don't resist. Cupping my face in his hands, he presses a kiss to my forehead.

"You are never ridiculous," he quietly argues.

"But—" I begin.

He shakes his head and I stop.

"You're exhausted, excited, nervous, and all of those things are affecting you."

"How are you so calm?" I ask.

One side of his mouth tips up. "All a façade. I'm as freaked as you are. This is going to be us in four months."

"You don't seem freaked," I grumble and he laughs.

"As long as I have you near me, I'm fine."

My brows furrow, my lips pinching tightly as tears sting my eyes. Furiously, I blink them away, cursing my hormones and over-emotional state at the moment. Tucking my face to his neck, Will doesn't say anything as I pull myself together. There is nothing worse than crying in public.

After the threat has passed and I sniffle a few times, I lift my head to look up at my husband. "How did I get so lucky?"

He shakes his head, clasping my hand in his and bringing our joined hands up to his lips. "Trust me; I'm the lucky one here."

Part of me wants to smack him for making the tears threaten again. Instead, I face-plant into his chest and hug him tightly. All too soon, we pull apart and quietly make our way to Christine's room.

"What took you two so long?" my mom asks as soon as she sees us.

I open my mouth to let her have it, but Will squeezes my arm and quickly answers for the both of us. "The elevator took forever."

She shrugs and turns back to her conversation with Christine's mom. I glare at her until I hear a giggle from Christine's bed. I blush and walk over to her, guilty she caught me.

"What'd she do?" she whispers once I'm near her.

"It's silly," I return.

"So what," she replies, her slender hands stroking her belly. "I still want to know."

Will pushes a chair up closer to her bed for me to sit comfortably.

"She didn't hold the elevator."

Christine covers her mouth to muffle her laugh and I roll my eyes at myself. "I know. I'm not sure why it bugged me as much as it did."

She moves one of her hands from her stomach to mine. As soon as I started showing, I was amazed by how comfortable people felt touching me. With Christine, it's cool; random strangers at the grocery store, less so.

"Maybe Baby Price will grow up to be a runner, and he or she was upset your mom got a head-start."

I cover her hand with mine, imagining a little brown-haired boy or girl chasing after Will and gulp.

"I like that."

She laughs. "We'll see if you still say that after chasing that baby around all day."

She's probably right. I'll probably be exhausted and annoyed, just like I am now. Will's hand comes to rest on my shoulder. I look up to see Brian standing next to him, his expression adoring as he looks down at Christine. It strikes me then that the look Will's giving me is no less so.

With my other hand, I cover his. No matter what the future has in store for us, as long as I have my family I'll be fine. The lack of chatter from the other side of the room sinks in and I turn to look toward my mom. Both she and Christine's mom sit quietly as they watch the four of us. My mom is two seconds away from crying; it's written all over her face.

It's good to remember where I got my emotional side from. If I end up being half the mom she was to our baby, I'll be happy. I guess being emotional isn't a bad thing. I never had to guess that she loved me with all of her heart when I was growing up. She had so much love within her that she gave the same love to Brian and then to Will.

Being pregnant has made me more reflective of my own childhood. My family didn't have a lot while I was growing up, but we never wanted for anything either. Will and I will probably never be millionaires on a teacher's salary and what I make. That doesn't mean that our family will be lacking on any of the essentials: love, laughter, and the faith that we'll always have each other.

I drop my hand from Will's to brush a tear from my eye, my mother a mirror image of me as she wipes at her face, as well.

Once it's time for Christine to push, Brian is the only one who stays in the room with her while the rest of us go to the waiting room, across the hall from the nursery. Leaning against Will, I zone out as I stare at the little beds holding all of those precious little babies. My mom tries a couple times to get my

THEM

attention but gives up and talks with Christine's mom instead.

My mind is with Christine and, as my hand lightly coasts over my protruding stomach, on hopes for my own delivery.

Brian hurries into the waiting room not long after, grinning from ear to ear. We all stand and circle him.

"The baby?" my mom asks, her hands clasped in front of her.

He lifts his arm to rest on her shoulder. "Both she and Christine are doing great. Come and meet her."

He doesn't need to ask twice.

Christine looks exhausted and yet somehow too serene considering she just gave birth. Nestled in her arms is my new niece, wrapped snuggly in a striped pastel blanket and sporting a pale pink hat. Christine's mom is the first to reach for her while my mom practically shakes next to her as she waits for her turn.

"What's her name?" Will asks Christine as he stands behind me.

"Reilly Jane Miller," she replies.

Brian takes pity on her after snapping a couple of pictures for Christine's mom, so he passes the baby to our mom. *I'm next. I'm next.*

My mother is a notorious baby hog.

After what seems like twice as long as Christine's mom held Reilly, I finally grumble, "Let someone else have a turn, Mom."

She relents, frowning as she eases my new niece into my arms. Will's arms wrap around me as he looks down at her over my shoulder. I lift her little body to press a gentle kiss to her cheek, inhaling her sweet new baby scent.

"She's beautiful," Will whispers, and my throat swells as I nod and look up at Brian and Christine.

I can't wait until it's our turn.

16

Will

"We're home," I call out into the house, shutting the front door behind me.

"I'm in the kitchen," Sarah replies.

Logan grins up at me. "That can only mean trouble."

I smirk back my agreement. The good news was Sarah hadn't had a bout with morning sickness in weeks, but the bad news was she was now eating the weirdest shit you could think of.

"Let's see what she's created today," I murmur, following him toward the kitchen.

Sarah's back is toward us and she grins over her shoulder at me as I approach. From the back, she doesn't even look pregnant, not until she turns to the side and her basketball-shaped belly becomes visible. I mold my front to her back and peer over her shoulder to see what she's making.

I breathe easy when I see it's just a sundae, piled high with syrup, toppings, whipped cream and cherries.

THEM

"Looks good," I murmur, turning my face to kiss her neck.

She whimpers, tilting her head to give me better access to her soft skin. I send telepathic pleas for Logan to suddenly get the idea to go play outside. I don't know what it is with Sarah these days, but we've both become insatiable in the bedroom.

She turns her head back toward my face, until her lips are at my ear. "After my sundae."

I bark out a laugh. I guess she wants her sundae more than my cock at the moment. She's lucky it looks good.

I lift my chin in its direction. "Gimme a bite."

She smirks. "Please?"

I shift my hips against her backside so she can feel how turned on I am and give me a break. "Please."

Her sigh makes me wonder whether it's the loss of a bite of her sundae she's mourning or the fact that given our audience, now isn't the right time to take her upstairs and have my way with her.

She dips the spoon into the ice cream, making sure to get me a good-sized bite, and lifts it to my parted lips. The cool ice cream melts on my tongue, the whipped cream dissolving into a delicious pool in my mouth. It's at that moment an unexpected flavor assaults my senses.

Doing my best to speak around the bite in my mouth, while avoiding it slipping down my throat, I ask, "Sarah, what's in this?"

She doesn't reply immediately; instead, she takes a bite of her own, moaning as she eats it.

It's then she turns her soft brown eyes to mine and innocently replies, "Bacon bits."

Stepping away from her, I spit my bite into the sink and rinse my mouth before straightening to glare at her. Logan is sitting at the island, his head lying on his arms as he laughs outright.

"Not funny," I toss in his direction before turning back to face her.

Her face is the picture of sweetness as she takes another bite and asks, "What?"

Logan is gasping for air at this point but manages to say, "I can't believe you ate something she made without asking first," between his panted breaths.

"It looked normal," I grumble, marching over to the fridge and pulling open the door.

I grab a Gatorade and turn back to them, twisting off the cap.

"How was school, honey?" Sarah grins at me, still eating that disgusting sundae.

"My day was wonderful until about five minutes ago," I grumble.

She pouts, even though she of all people knows my bark is worse than my bite. I cave, setting my drink down before tugging her bowl out of her hand and setting it down, as well. Then I fold her into my arms and kiss the top of her head. She may have just attempted to poison me, but seeing her after a long day of work will always be the highlight of my day.

"It's better now that you're in my arms," I confess, my annoyance all gone.

She tucks her head under my chin and rests her hands on my chest. I'll never want to let her go, but it would be hard to spend each moment of the rest of our lives with her in my arms. Besides, she has that awful creation to eat and Logan has news.

I shift her until we're both facing Logan and hand her back her bowl before draping my arm across her shoulder. "Logan had something interesting happen today."

In an instant, his face is red and he tries to look away.

"Where's Rascal?" he asks innocently.

"In the backyard," Sarah answers. "Now, don't try and distract me. What happened at school?"

"It's about Amber." I grin until she smacks my chest with her free hand.

"How does Will know before me?" she cries and Logan ducks his head.

"He told me on the ride home," I brag, loving that I know more than her and it's driving her nuts. It's the perfect revenge for what she tried to feed me.

"Tell me," she pleads. "Did you ask her out? Are you guys going to go on a date?"

Her theories are pretty spot-on.

"Um, *she* asked *me* out," Logan shyly admits.

"Yay!" Sarah whoops and then pauses. "You said yes, didn't you?"

He nods, his face getting red.

"I like her." Sarah celebrates with another bite. "Tell me everything."

I kiss the side of her head as Logan starts retelling how she was waiting by his locker after final block. Since I've already heard this part, I head toward the backdoor to let Rascal back in. She's gotten so big over the past few months. She'll never be huge, but she's solidly medium-sized. The rottie in her is clear as day in her coloring and build.

I'm guessing it's the lab that has her acting crazy. She excitedly jumps and paws at my legs the moment I open the door.

"Hey, girl. Who's a good girl?" I murmur, bending down to rub her head.

My current level of attention isn't enough apparently. She barks and continues to jump on me until I cave and sink down to the floor. She's in my lap in an instant, her tongue going for my face as she excitedly tries to lick me. I hug her to me, laughing at the way she's humming with happy energy. With the

THEM

exception of a couple of destroyed shoes, she's been the best dog we could ask for.

Now that Sarah is working more, Rascal gives her an excuse to get away from her desk to play. During the time when her morning sickness was at its worst, Rascal was her constant guardian. She wouldn't leave Sarah's side no matter what.

Logan has finished telling Sarah all about the impending date by the time Rascal and I walk back into the kitchen. Thankfully, Sarah has also finished her disgusting sundae.

"Do you know what movie you're going to go see?" Sarah asks Logan.

He frowns. "I was going to let her pick since she asked."

I pick up my Gatorade and lift it in approval in his direction. "Smart man."

"I guess that's okay, as long as it isn't R-rated," Sarah adds.

Logan nods. He's a good kid. He's been one since the day he moved in and before that, when I only knew him as a student in my class.

Sarah and I are considering adopting him. We both want to; the only thing stopping us is our own nerves about asking Logan if he wants it, as well. Will he think we're trying to replace his family? Will the idea of being stuck with us until he's eighteen upset him? We're going to talk to his counselor before we try and do anything.

"I visited with Christine and Reilly today." Sarah grinned.

I slip onto the stool next to Logan. "How're they doing?"

A dreamy look passes over Sarah's eyes before she focuses back on us. "Reilly is so sweet. I held her for an hour and she slept the whole time. Her little lips would purse in the cutest way and oh, my God, she smelled so good. All I want to do is go back over there right now and smell her little head."

Logan raises his brows at me and I shrug. I'm pretty sure I'm going to act the same way once our little one is here. Until then, I'll let Sarah have all the fun gushing over our new niece.

"Was Calvin there?"

She shakes her head. "Brian and Christine thought it would be easier on her if he went back to preschool. That way, she can sleep when the baby sleeps and not have to worry about him getting into anything."

"Is Reilly sleeping better?"

She grimaces. "Not even a little bit. Christine dozed off while I was holding Reilly, she's so exhausted. They have a bassinette in their room, so it's not like she has to go far to get her when she wakes up to eat, but she's waking up every couple of hours."

My eyes widen. All I can picture is how our baby's birth will coincide right with the start of school. Good thing zombies are so popular. There's a good chance

THEM

I'll be a walking, talking version of one next school year if I don't get any sleep.

"Can Brian do anything to help?" I ask, really just to get ideas for myself.

"She's trying to let him sleep since he has to go to work, and being a sleep-deprived lawyer won't impress the partners. She has a breast pump. She's going to start pumping on the weekends, so Friday and Saturday nights they can trade off with feedings and she'll get some sleep."

Logan wrinkles his nose. "Is your baby going to be up all night, too?"

Sarah and I both laugh. It's a fearful, forced-sounding laugh for both of us.

"I hope not," Sarah replies.

I elbow him. "At least we'll have you around to help out. You want to volunteer for all the night feedings?"

His panicked expression has me laughing outright.

Sarah does her best to try and calm him back down. "Don't listen to Will. You know he's teasing. Besides, if anyone is volunteering for all of the night feedings, it will be him."

Logan laughs while I reply, "Hey!"

Sarah ignores and asks, "What do you boys want for dinner?"

Logan and I both jump from our stools to usher her from the kitchen. There's no way we're letting her cook again. She keeps coming up with the craziest combinations and unfortunately, she's the only person in the house who likes them. Even Rascal refused to taste her tuna-macaroni-guacamole disaster when some of it fell on the floor.

"You need to rest," I murmur as we lead her to the living room.

Logan pushes the coffee table closer to her. "Here. Put your feet up."

I hand her the remote. "Why don't you watch one of your HGTV shows?"

She accepts the remote but sets it on the seat next to her before crossing her arms over her chest. "I know what you both are doing."

Logan and I glance at each other before giving her our most innocent looks. "What do you mean?" I hedge.

She rolls her eyes and shoos us away before picking up the remote. Logan and I head back to the kitchen and high-five once we get there.

"That was close," he whispers.

I nod. "Only three more months."

He cringes. "She's going to try and cook again."

I pat his shoulder. "One day at a time, man. That's all we can do. So, what should we make for dinner?"

He glances out the kitchen window into the backyard. "Want to grill?"

17

Sarah

Will and I sat down with Logan as soon as school was out to discuss our wanting to adopt him. We did this after having a meeting with just the two of us, and Logan's counselor. While his counselor couldn't outright tell us what they discussed during their sessions, she was able to encourage us to discuss adoption with him.

In doing so, we only wished we had talked about it sooner. Logan had never brought wanting us to adopt him up because he was still scared that once the baby came, we would abandon him. After, we explained our only reservation in moving forward with adoption was our own fear that he didn't want that. We would have remained his foster parents forever if that was what he wanted.

In Georgia, the process to adopt a foster child takes months. We'll be lucky if we're his parents by the end of the year, and our situation is already what they considered as fast-tracked because we're his foster parents. The classes and home visits required by the state to adopt him we've already been doing so we can foster him.

THEM

Given his age and the connection he had to his own family, and that we continue to nourish those memories, he has no plans of ever calling us Mom or Dad. We'll always be Sarah and Will to him, and that's okay. Neither of us cares about that as long as he can rest certain each day with us of how deeply we've come to love him.

Logan, apart from Will, may be the sweetest boy I've ever met. For someone so young, who has experienced so much loss during his short life, he still manages to face each new day optimistically. Even more so now that the relief of our wanting to adopt him is certain. He is the consummate little gentleman. He carries things for me from room to room, even when I argue with him that I'm pregnant, not invalid.

He and Will have completely taking over all cooking duties, and even when I offer to cook they both jump up demanding that I rest. The only things they'll still let me make food-wise are little snacks for myself here and there.

Having them both home every day for the summer has made me beyond happy. The extra help in getting the house ready for the baby has been huge, as well. Will teases that I'm nesting, and I suppose I am. I have never felt as manic about decorating and organizing anything in my life.

I need the baby's room to be just right. Last week, Will and Logan sent me to spend the day with Christine and Reilly while they painted the nursery. We decided on a pale shade of mint green for the walls. It goes perfectly with the nursery rhyme-inspired bedding and curtains we picked out. Will's mom and my parents bought our furniture for us.

It's a timeless blonde wood with matching crib, dresser, changing table, bookshelf and rocking chair. Sometimes, without even noticing I've gone to the nursery, I find myself rocking in the chair, already imagining holding our baby in my arms, as I will in the future.

I stressed over washing every article of clothing in the right detergent and making sure every gift was put away with care. Each day, I go over a mental checklist of the things we'll still need to get so we'll be ready when the baby comes.

In two weeks, Logan will be gone for a whole week, away at a sleep-away lacrosse camp in Florida. I should be stressing over the pack list his camp sent us, but I can't seem to focus on anything but this room. Even now, I'm once again rocking in this chair.

My eyes drift over the bookshelf, already filling with favorites from Will's and my childhood. The classics we grew up with and will so be reading to our child.

"Darling."

My eyes lift from the shelf to the door and warm as I see Will leaning against the frame.

"Logan and I are going to take Rascal to the park. Want to come with?" he asks.

THEM

I nod, placing my hands on the arms of the chairs and shaking my head when he crosses the room to help me stand. I am moving a bit slower these days, unless it's in the direction of the bathroom. This baby seems intent to constantly bounce on my bladder. I can't go anywhere without a bathroom break anymore.

I meet my boys and Rascal, who is bustling with energy at the prospect of a family walk, at the front door. Logan mans the leash as Will takes my hand. Together, with Logan and Rascal leading the way, we walk toward the park.

There's an ice cream truck parked, its 'Pop Goes the Weasel' tune blaring, when we get there. Logan lifts his brows in a silent plea and grins when Will inclines his head. I wait with Rascal while they both go to get us ice cream.

Logan comes back with an Italian ice while Will has a king cone for each of us, complete with fudge and nuts on top.

"Yum." I trade Will Rascal's leash for my cone.

We find a picnic table and sit, Logan and I on one side, Will with Rascal on the other. I can't help but wonder if the parents pushing their kids on the swings or waiting in line for an ice cream of their own assume that Logan is our son. I would have been a teenage mom long before that show was popular to have a child as old as Logan is.

Logan is looking forward to being a big brother, though. It's something both Will and I have heard him talk to Amber about. She has two little sisters and has been trying to convince him having a younger sibling isn't always as fun as it sounds.

Thankfully, she's mainly teasing when she says this. With the exception of the time her youngest sister dropped her phone and cracked the screen. Although, there could be something in the fact that they're all girls.

Was I just as annoying to Brian? It's not like I stole his clothes or jewelry the way Amber's sisters did.

When I was growing up, I wondered what it would be like to be the big sister. Brian was such a good big brother, so protective and encouraging. I wanted to be that for someone else.

"You still with us?"

I blink away my thoughts and look up to see both Logan and Will are now standing and waiting for me to join them.

"Sorry. I was lost in my thoughts," I apologize, hurrying to stand.

Will passes the leash to Logan and reaches for my hand. "All good thoughts, I hope."

I nod. "Nothing bad. Silly things, really. I was thinking about how I wanted a little sister or brother when I was growing up."

Logan has started and is a few steps ahead of us. Rascal doesn't care where she's going on a walk; she only wants to get there quickly. I'm not moving as fast as I had on the way to the park, and Will hangs back to walk at my pace.

"Did your parents ever want any more kids?"

I shrug. "I don't think so, or at least they never mentioned it."

He gives my hand a squeeze. "I always wanted a brother. Brian was one of the reasons I hung out at your house so much in the beginning. I wanted his brotherness to rub off on me."

"And here I thought I was the sole pull," I joke.

He lets go of my hand to swing his arm around my shoulders, tucking me close to his side. "Once I was smart enough, you were."

I wrap my arm around his waist. "Took you long enough. I had a crush on you from the moment I saw you."

He makes a mock flip of his hair. "How could you not?"

In those days, Will was the guy every girl in our school crushed on. He didn't see me as anything more than a best friend until years after we had known each other. In some ways, he fought against his attraction to me, terrified that if things didn't work out between us romantically he would lose me forever.

It's sad that he was almost right, that our own mutual immaturity had separated us for so long. He hates it when I fuss over what might have been. There's a guilt I carry with me for leaving him all those years ago. I can admit we were both at fault, but in my mind I own the lion's share of it. I was the one who ran. That's a mistake I'll never make again.

Stepping through the front door, I sigh as the air conditioning hits me. July in Georgia can get 'cooking eggs on a sidewalk' hot with an added layer of outdoor sauna-level humidity. The ice cream helped, but I'm soaked with sweat and need a shower.

The heat doesn't seem to bother Logan. He gets a glass of lemonade and decides to mow the front yard since he's already sweaty.

I've only been in the shower long enough to put shampoo in my hair when Will joins me, making me yelp in surprise. When I first started showing, I was terrified Will would think I looked fat. Once my morning sickness passed, his inability to keep his hands off me dispelled that fear.

Showers in particular seem to be his favorite. He's fascinated with my growing belly and doesn't seem to mind the fact that I've gone up two cup sizes in my bras. He would happily spend hours lathering body wash up and over all of me.

He sits on the bench, shifting me till I stand in front of him, the water streaming down my back. With gentle, soapy hands, he strokes me until my knees start to buckle and I have to place my hands on his broad shoulders to hold myself up. It's then that he turns me away from him, easing me down until I'm full of him.

With one hand in my hair, turning my head so he can take my mouth with his, and his other hand gently kneading my swollen breast, he moves in and out of me. I'll never get enough of him, the gentle command he has over my body. I ignore the water streaming down my face and over our mouths as we kiss.

His hand moves from my breast to between my legs, stroking me until I gasp his name against his mouth. It's as if his name from my lips unleashed the power he sought to restrain. He bucks beneath me, both hands now vise grips to my hips as he pulls me downward to meet each upward stroke. My hands cover his as I hold on. Moments later, he groans his release, his arms lifting to wrap around my chest and hold me close as he catches his breath.

He buries his face in my neck and kisses me there. Neither of us moves to stand, both content to let him stay within me for as long as we can. If there wasn't the chance of Logan coming to look for one or both of us, Will probably would have moved us right from the shower to the bed. Being responsible adults sucks sometimes.

"Surprise!"

I look up, my mouth dropping open before spinning to smack Will's chest. "You knew."

He grins, leaning down to kiss me before Sawyer hugs me from behind.

I turn, doing my best to wrap my arms around her. "Are Jared and Pascal here, too?"

She pulls back, nodding, a Cheshire-like smile gracing her face. "They're camped out at Mama Price's but are coming over here for dinner after your shower."

I turn back to Will and glance back and forth between the two of them. "How?" I don't wait for an answer before I point my finger at Sawyer. "I talked to you yesterday."

She is clearly better at keeping secrets than I am.

She just laughs and happy-dances in front of me. "Best surprise ever, am I right?"

I lean forward to kiss her cheek. "Best ever."

She loops her arm through mine and pulls me into our streamer and balloon-covered living room. My mom, Will's mom and Christine all stand to hug and greet me.

"You guys shouldn't have done this." I spin, looking at all the gifts and baby-themed decorations around the room.

"My co-workers threw me a shower and we knew that since you're all by yourself work-wise, it was up to us to make sure you didn't miss out on all the fun." Christine nudges Sawyer with her elbow. "Sawyer planned everything."

She shrugs and her eyes meet mine. "You go all out for your best friend, just like you did for me."

THEM

I sniffle as my eyes well and, not trusting my voice, mouth a thank you.

Her eyes crinkle, then she looks over my shoulder to where Will and Logan stand. "Go hang with Jared and Miss Muffet for the next couple of hours. We'll try to save you some cake, but it looks amazing so I'm not gonna make any promises."

After the party, the boys come back to the house. Will and Jared man the grill while I get to hang with Sawyer.

"You guys need to move to New England," she moans, fanning herself.

"It's not that bad," I argue.

"Right." She lifts her arm and points to her armpit. "I was outside for five minutes and I'm sweating my ass off."

"It's the humidity," I explain. "It makes it feel worse than it actually is."

"Will it still be this gross at that laser thing?"

Before I can answer, Logan dashes into the living room. "We're going to the laser show at Stone Mountain?"

Sawyer cringes since she knows it's supposed to be a surprise.

I shoot her a look before turning to face Logan. "We are."

He pumps his fist into the air. "I've always wanted to go."

"Sawyer and Jared have never been, either."

His brow's furrow. "Is Pascal coming?"

I shake my head, glancing at Sawyer's daughter, who is playing on the rug in front of us. "The music can get loud and it won't end until after her bedtime, so Mama Price is going to babysit her."

He drops to the floor and crosses his legs in front of him. "You are going to have fun with Mama Price," he murmurs to Pascal.

She grins up at him and offers him a block.

"Thank you."

Sawyer motions for me to look at her and once my eyes meet hers she mouths, 'He's so sweet.'

I nod and mouth back, 'I know.'

Before long, Logan gets up to go hang out with Will and Jared.

As soon as he's out of the room, I turn toward Sawyer. "He's amazing."

"Did you see how cute he was with Pascal?" Her question is clearly rhetorical.

"I know. He's a great kid. He offers to walk Rascal every day and is a huge help around the house."

"How's he dealing with everything?"

I shrug. "He was seeing a therapist every week, but at her recommendation he's going to be going twice a month now." I pause to look at her. "That has to be a good thing, right?"

She nods. "Sounds that way. Are you still thinking about adopting him?"

I lean forward to put one hand on her knee while smacking my forehead with my other hand. "I completely forget to tell you. I blame these pregnancy hormones; I swear I can't remember anything these days."

Neither of us says anything for a minute until Sawyer laughs. "So, what'd you forget to tell me?"

I cover my face as I laugh. "God, I'm such a mess. Okay, we talked to Logan about it and we *are* going to adopt him."

She moves forward to wrap her arms around me. "That's fantastic news."

I curl my arms around her back as my eyes start to sting. "We were so nervous he wouldn't want us to."

She gives me an extra squeeze before leaning back into her seat. "Why would you think that?"

I dab at my eyes and look up at the ceiling as I blink tears away. "We were wondering if he'd think we were trying to replace his dad."

"Oh, honey," she whispers, squeezing my knee.

"It turns out he was scared we wouldn't want him after the baby came."

She shakes her head, pressing her hand to her chest. "That poor boy."

"I'm trying not to cry," I grumble before taking a deep breath.

Sawyer waits patiently while I pull myself together.

"He just fits us, you know?" She nods, so I keep going. "He skateboards and plays lacrosse with Will, but he also grocery shops and watches my movies with me and we go for walks just the two of us sometimes with the dog. I've heard people talk about how difficult teenagers can be, and maybe he's trying extra hard to be good because he's scared we'll send him away."

"He has to understand by now that you guys would never do that," Sawyer argues.

"I hope so."

Before I can say anything else, Logan comes back into the room.

"Dinner's ready."

So our northern friends won't melt, we eat in the dining room. Will told Logan we were leaving for Stone Mountain as soon as his mom got to our house. After the third time Logan asked where she was, Will mock-threatened to leave him at home if he asked one more time.

Logan did his best to not laugh. Sawyer and I fail, though, and giggle. Will as a disciplinarian? He shoots me a look and it only makes me laugh harder.

When the doorbell rings, Logan leaps from his chair, exclaiming, "She's here. Let's go!"

THEM

"That's an order if I ever heard one," Jared remarks, pushing his chair back.

Will quickly clears the table while Sawyer picks up Pascal from her travel booster seat and together, we go greet his mom. She only has eyes for Pascal, her smile from ear to ear as she reaches for her.

Sawyer puts her arms around my waist and says, "Yep, you are going to be covered babysitting-wise once Baby Price is here."

I hadn't ever thought of it before, but her comment makes me wonder what they do since Jared's dad lives in Colorado and his mom is in Alaska.

Sawyer is eerily observant to my inner musings and answers my unspoken question. "We have amazing neighbors who love to babysit whenever we need a break."

I don't say it, but I wish we lived closer. I can't fault her for not wanting to move out of her grandmother's house, though. If Atlanta wasn't home for us, I could see Will and me moving to New England. On second thought, Will hates cold weather, so maybe not.

Once Sawyer points to where all of Pascal's things are, we head out. Jared sits up front and since she's the smallest, Sawyer rides in the middle of the back seat. At every red light, Will and Jared play air guitar to whatever song is on the radio while the rest of us laugh at them.

Logan pulls out his phone to record them, threatening to post it to YouTube. By the time we've parked, I don't even care about the laser show. I've already had one of the best days of my life just having all of my favorite people around me.

18

Will

"You know you want to wait."

Sarah's forehead wrinkles as she pouts up at me. "I'm not sure I can anymore."

I smooth my hand down the side of her face, all the way to the column of her neck, and let it rest there. "We're so close, darling."

"I know," she whispers, her eyes holding mine.

"We can do it."

She bobs her head, bringing her hand up to grip my forearm. "I'm sorry I even mentioned it."

"Hush," I murmur, leaning down to silence her with my lips.

We've reached the stage of her pregnancy where we'll be visiting the doctor each week going forward. That seems to have Sarah panicking that we don't know the sex of the baby. There's no way I'm repainting the baby's room, though, so we're sticking to our original waiting plan.

"Did you think it was weird, what he did?" Sarah asks when I pull away.

"The part where he fisted you?" I joke, making her blush.

"I have to ask Christine if her doctor did that, too."

During our appointment today, Sarah's doctor confirmed her cervix is softening and that she's already dilated a bit. Enough so that he massaged the top of the baby's head. He said that would encourage and stimulate the baby to stay head down. Sarah's eyes almost bugged out of her head when the doctor said that.

From where I sat, all I wanted to know was exactly how far he had to reach to do that. Makes me rethink sex. Last thing I want to do is give my kid a concussion before he or she is born.

"You let me know what she says."

I walk her into the house and call out to Logan so he'll know we're back. Logan and I have gone to the high school every day since he's been back from camp to practice lacrosse moves. He's dead-set on trying out for the JV team next year and wants to be ready for it.

There's a private league he's signed up to play on this fall. They also have a spring season, but he wants to play for his school. If he's still all about lacrosse by next summer, we're going to look into him trying out for their travel team. The fact that he wants to share this with me is what has me dragging my ass into the heat to practice with him every day.

There will come a point where he won't think I'm cool. Growing up, all I wanted was my dad to spend time this way with me. I'll never be able to replace Logan's dad, but hopefully I can honor his memory by giving my time to Logan.

"I need five minutes to change. Want to grab the gear and meet me at the car?"

"Yep," he replies, spinning to do what I asked.

Sarah slowly lowers herself onto the sofa, lifting her feet onto the coffee table. Her ankles have been swelling, so she's doing her best to keep them elevated. I make a mental note to give them a rub for her when Logan and I get back.

I jog up the stairs and into our room so I can change out of what I wore to the doctor and into an old t-shirt and some gym shorts. By the time I make it out to the car, Logan is already there waiting for me. I pop the trunk for him to load all of our gear.

"How was the appointment?" he asks as he slides into his seat.

"It was good. Baby's good, Sarah's good, everything is good."

He nods. "Do you think I can come to the hospital when she has the baby?"

I glance over at him, surprised he'd even ask. "Of course you can. If it ends up taking a while, we'll have to touch base about you staying the whole time."

"How long does having a baby take?"

"No clue, man. They say it's different for everyone. Sarah knows someone who said it took her 24 hours."

His mouth drops. "That sucks."

"Yep. So, if it takes that long, we might need to send you home with someone to get some sleep."

"That makes sense."

One thing I like about Logan is how level-headed he is. With the exception of the time right after his dad died, when he was dealing with more grief than any kid his age should, of course. Other than that, as long as you explain stuff to him, he's happy to go with the flow. He doesn't argue but also doesn't have an issue letting Sarah and I know what he wants.

"We'll have to wait and see how it goes."

"Is she going to do the thing where they cut the baby out of her?"

"A caesarean?"

He nods.

"Nope, she wants to do it the old-fashioned way but with painkillers."

"It's supposed to hurt a whole lot, right?"

"That's what they say."

"Last night, I got to feel the baby kicking."

"Where was I?" I get selfish when it comes to hogging all of the baby's kicks.

Sarah never misses a thing, since it's all happening real-time for her. Half of the time, when the baby starts kicking, by the time I get there he or she has stopped. My future son or daughter has already learned how to toy with me.

"You were washing dishes." He laughs.

Once I park, I turn and point at him. "You're on dish duty for the next week."

He cracks up. The fact that the baby always stops kicking once I touch Sarah's stomach has become a running joke between the two of them. I swear it's like everyone is against me.

"I should make you do laps," I mumble as we walk onto the field.

Instead, we work on passing until I'm out of breath. Then I defend the goal and have him try to score on me. His confidence has gone way up since camp, so now the only thing going against him is his height. Unless they're built like a tank, it's the smaller guys who make great forwards. They're fast, and their height makes a smaller target for the defenders to go after.

Logan is taller than I was at his age, and I'm 6'3.

"Have you considered playing defense?" This isn't the first time I've asked him this question.

"Defense is boring," he moans.

"What about midfield? You can run as much as you'd like if you played midi."

THEM

He frowns. "Am I that bad at playing forward?"

Shit. "It's not that. I only want you to understand that your height is working against you. This has nothing to do with your ability." His shoulders slump and it's clear he has his heart set on playing attack. "How about X?" I hazard.

He lifts his eyes to mine. "The forward who plays behind the goal?"

"Yep. You'd still be a forward, but your strategy would be more as assists than scores. X is not an easy position to play. Your passing has to be flawless so the other team won't tag your passes mid-air."

The hint of a smile plays at the corners of his mouth. "You think I can do it?"

I slip off my glove and reach to muss up his hair. "I think you can do anything you set your mind to."

I send him behind the goal to practice passing to me as if I were a forward facing the goal. We pass back and forth until I call uncle. I miss the days of unlimited energy. There's a better chance than not I'll be hobbling out of bed tomorrow.

When we get back to the house, Sarah takes one look at me and offers to run a hot bath with Epsom salt for me to soak in. Before I follow her upstairs, Logan asks if he can go over to Amber's house, because her neighborhood has a community pool. Part of me wants to tell him only if I can go with, but I'm too tired to joke around so I nod.

Amber lives close enough to our house that Logan can ride his bike or skateboard there.

By the time I make it upstairs, the bath is almost full. Sarah is bent over it, one of her hands on the lip. At first, it looks like she's pouring something in it, but then her head turns and her eyes meet mine. I see then that her other hand is clutching her stomach. That and the wild look in her eyes send a shiver straight up my spine. Something is wrong.

Any soreness I had is forgotten and I'm at her side in an instant. "Sarah, what's wrong?"

I try to ease her back to sit on the toilet but she's rigid, locked in that curled-forward position.

She hasn't answered me. Instead, all she does is pant and rasp. The only woman I have ever seen in labor, and I'm assuming that's what's happening here, was Christine and she acted nothing like the way Sarah is acting right now.

I drop to my knees in front of her and look up at her. "Please talk to me, baby. What's wrong?"

All she does is shake her head, so I pull out my phone and call 911. Part of me wonders if I'm overreacting, but Sarah is the strongest woman I know and her fear is palpable. While I'm on the phone with the emergency operator, I turn off the water and run downstairs to unlock the door. I almost carry Sarah down with me so she'll be closer to the EMTs when they arrive but don't want to risk accidentally hurting her or the baby in any way.

THEM

She hasn't moved an inch by the time I'm back by her side. She hasn't spoken other than to cry out or whimper in pain, either. Each one hits me like a physical blow. The love of my life is in pain, and I'm powerless to take it away from her. It's an agony I had not known existed.

It takes five seemingly unending minutes for the ambulance to arrive. Sarah cries out as they ease her onto a cart and then down the stairs, my hands clawing at my shirt to stop from reaching out for her. What would that do? I'd have to push an EMT helping her out of the way while they're busy navigating the cart down our stairs.

It's not until she's in the front yard that I can touch her again. The EMT has the presence of mind to close my front door, since my attention is only on Sarah. We're loaded into the ambulance and I clasp her hand in both of mine. An EMT who, once I'm in such a confined space I finally notice, is checking her. He is an older Hispanic man, his voice smooth and sure as he relays information to the EMT driving. Half of the words out of his mouth mean nothing to me. They could be good or bad.

A heart rate is elevated. Sarah or the baby's? Can pain elevate a heart rate? Why is she in so much pain? Is this labor? This is early; we're not supposed to be going into labor for another month.

"Mr. Price."

I shake my head and look up at the man on the other side of my wife. "Yes."

Rapid-fire questions come: how far along is she? Who is her doctor? Family history? Allergies? I answer them as fast as my brain can process them.

After I answer everything, I ask if it's okay if I make a call. The EMT nods and I call Mrs. Miller to let her know we're on our way to the hospital and that Logan is with Amber at her pool. With that one call, I'm certain she'll call my mom, Christine and Logan. I had to call the one person who could handle all of that so I can focus all my attention on Sarah.

When we reach the hospital, we're taken straight to Labor and Delivery. A nurse, who introduces herself as Dana, and I help Sarah undress and slip on a hospital gown, leaving the back open. I recognize the monitor they hook Sarah up to from when we were here when Reilly was born. After that, they give her an IV. A nurse informs us that Dr. Stacey is on the way, but another doctor is going to examine Sarah in the meantime.

This doctor is a woman, on the short side, with short black hair.

She shakes both of our hands and introduces herself as Dr. Abbott. Sarah groans as the monitor shows a contraction starting. Before that, the pain Sarah was experiencing had seemed to lessen.

"Are they all right?" I ask the doctor, holding Sarah's hand as she grimaces.

"Her water has not broken, but I'm concerned about the fetal heart rate. It is lower than the range we should see. We're going to try having Sarah lie on her side and monitor it from there."

"Is there anything we can do for her pain?"

The doctor makes eye contact with Sarah. "Have you discussed your pain treatment for your delivery with Dr. Stacey?"

Sarah nods. "Yes, I want the epidural."

"We'll need to see the baby's heart rate come up and stay within a normal range first. The anesthesiologist will come and discuss options with you," she replies.

"If her water hasn't broken, how do we know for sure she's in labor?" I ask.

"That's a great question, Mr. Price. There are multiple signs that lead us to believe Mrs. Price is in actual labor. She is 100% effaced, dilated to 4 centimeters, there is evidence that the mucus plug is gone, and her contractions have been consistent and strengthening since she was in the ambulance."

Sarah's eyes widen and all I can say is, "Oh."

Dr. Abbott chuckles and pats my arm. "Breathe, Dad," she encourages and leaves the room.

Once she's out of sight, Sarah covers her face with her hand not attached to the IV. "I'm so embarrassed."

I gently push her hand away. "Why?"

"I don't think I needed the ambulance. They all must think I'm a big wuss."

Pulling a chair over so I can be at eye level with her, I sit. "Don't say that. If it turns out we were overcautious, I'd rather that a million times over than the alternative."

She reaches for my hand and I squeeze it. "You sure?"

With my free hand, I tuck some of her hair behind her ear. "Positive."

Her face softens as someone knocks on the door. It's the anesthesiologist. He goes over how the epidural works with Sarah and has her sign a consent form. He explains that since there was concern already about the baby's heart rate, we'll need to monitor that for another thirty minutes to an hour before he feels comfortable administering the drug. In the meantime, while we wait, he can insert the catheter. That way, once the baby's heart rate is steady in the range they want it to be, he can get the epidural drugs going without any further delay.

Since Sarah is already on her side, she doesn't have to move at all for him to do it. He preps her back and waits for her contraction to be over before inserting the catheter. Sarah squeezes the shit out of my hand as he does it but stays perfectly still.

"You're doing great, darling," I whisper against her forehead, and I press my lips into a kiss there.

Once the anesthesiologist is done, Dana pops in to check on Sarah. Lying on her side has somehow helped the baby's heart rate. The nurse has barely left the room when Mrs. Price and Christine dash in and make a beeline for Sarah.

"I'm so sorry I worried you all," Sarah hurries to say before her next contraction starts.

Her face pinches as she squeezes my hand. I try my best to murmur words of encouragement, but I'm struggling with the fact that I can't take away her pain. Hadn't they said she could have the epidural if the baby's heart rate was steady? How long did it need to be steady before they would do something for her?

"Logan?" Sarah asks once her contraction has passed.

Christine rests her hand on Sarah's calf as she replies, "He's going to spend the night at our house and help Uncle Brian with Calvin and Reilly."

"And Dad?" She looks up at her mom.

I stand so Mrs. Price can have my chair but move up toward the head of the bed so I'm still within eyesight of Sarah.

"He picked up Will's mom and they're both on the way right now."

For the next hour, Sarah faces each of her contractions like a trooper and when Dana comes back to check on her, we're told she's dilated to 5 and can get her epidural. I wish I had my phone out and could have taken a picture of the relieved expression on Sarah's face when she heard the second part. My girl is ready for some drugs.

By the time Mr. Price and my mom make it to our room, the effects have started to kick in. The monitor is still showing the rise and fall of her contractions, but she isn't feeling a thing. If anything, she's sleepy.

Another hour goes by and Dana pops back into our room to check on Sarah. I'm the only one who stays while the rest of the family steps out into the waiting room to give Sarah privacy.

I'm waiting to find out what the latest dilation update is when Dana surprises me by hurrying out of the room without a word. Sarah and I glance at each other and I shrug. Within moments, Dana is back with both Dr. Abbott and Dr. Stacey.

They all take a moment to examine Sarah before Dr. Abbott leaves the room and Dr. Stacey moves to stand next to me.

His eyes are on Sarah. "Hello, Sarah. Will." His eyes briefly meet mine before moving back to her. "Your water has broken. It appears the umbilical cord has come down, as well. This is called cord prolapse, and we need to move forward to deliver the baby via Caesarian section immediately."

Dana hands me a set of scrubs complete with a face mask and cap for my head. I hurry to pull them on as Sarah is shifted from her hospital bed to one with wheels. In what seems like only a blink of an eye, we're in the hall and moving to another room on the same floor. Sarah's panicked eyes hold mine as I tightly grip her hand. Dana is behind me, pushing the bed.

THEM

"What about our family?" I ask, not bothering to look back.

"One of the other nurses is letting them know right now."

I gulp. Any fear or concern I have, I command my body to conceal any outward display of. I need to be strong for Sarah even though I'm not sure if I've ever been more scared in my life.

They ask me to wait outside of what I assume is an operating room. Once they let me in, I quickly cross the room to reach Sarah. There's a fabric half-wall settled over Sarah to prevent her from seeing her stomach. I weigh my desire to see the actual procedure and decide I'd rather not witness Sarah cut open. That means I am staying on this side of the curtain wall. I drop to my knees next to Sarah so she doesn't have to look up at me.

Tears have welled in her eyes. "Do you think our baby is okay?"

My throat is thick as I nod, unable to form words.

"I'm scared, Will," she whispers.

"Shhhh." My hand drifts over her hair, smoothing it away from her face and hopefully comforting her.

My focus is one hundred percent on her. In the background, I can hear our doctor giving directions to one of two nurses who are now in the room with us. It's all white noise, though, almost as though I'm underwater.

I focus on her, holding her face in my hands. Her normally chocolate-brown eyes are wide with concern, but I don't know what to say to reassure her. All I can do is stay by her side, letting all the love I have for her speak through my eyes.

Suddenly, there's a baby crying, our baby. I want to celebrate, but Dr. Sterling is now barking orders and frantically working on his side of the curtain. The door to the room swings open and another doctor rushes in. They don't offer to have me cut the cord, and the fact that they don't causes me to stiffen as I try to get Sarah's attention.

Her eyes are closed. The moment they reopen, after she blinks, I know something is wrong.

"Will? Is th—" Her face pales and her eyes are unfocused as mid-sentence her jaw relaxes.

"Sarah." I reach down to squeeze her hand and am alarmed when it remains limp within mine.

"Sarah!" I shout and realize at that moment the white noise around me is gone.

I drop Sarah's hand and press my hands to either side of her face, my nose inches from hers. "Sarah, darling, please wake up. Please, please, please wake up. Sarah, I need you, darling, please."

Someone grips my shoulders from behind and tries to pull me from her.

"No!" I howl, grabbing onto the side of her bed. "I won't leave her."

EPILOGUE

5 years later

"But Daddy, I need to have the shoes with the sparkles on them."

My daughter, a veritable force of nature, is standing, feet spread western shoot-out style, in the kids' shoe aisle of Target. Our current shoe mission is for a pair of rain boots, not the sparkly Mary Janes Chloe has her eye on. *If only Sarah were here,* I wistfully think.

"Chloe, darling, you already have sparkle shoes. Today we need rain boots. See these ones with the flowers all over them? Aren't they pretty? Or what about the ones with the ladybugs? You love ladybugs."

Her bottom lip pops out. "No, I don't."

I take a deep cleansing breath, not my first since becoming daddy to a mini drama queen, and I'm certain it won't be my last. "Chloe Marie Price, you have five seconds to pick a pair of boots, or I'm going to pick them for you. Five, four, three, two."

She dashes forward, grabs the ones with the ladybugs on them and drops them into our cart with a huff.

THEM

"Was that so hard?" I grumble.

She elects to employ her trademark silent treatment in response and steps onto the bottom shelf of the cart, facing forward and gripping the side in her nonverbal display that she's ready to go.

When we reach the cash registers, she turns her big blue eyes back to me. "Daddy, can I please have a red slush drink?"

Those damn drinks are half sugar. She'll be bouncing off the walls if I get her one.

She latches on to the immediate lack of a no and asks again, this time a couple decibels louder. The woman in line in front of us looks back with a judgy expression on her face. I smirk at her and stare her down until she drops her eyes and looks away. Chloe asks again, even louder this time, as if there was any possibility that I hadn't heard her the first two times.

I ignore the smirk on Logan's face when we pull into our driveway twenty minutes later and he sees Chloe holding a red slush.

"I thought you said you were never getting her one of those again" he says, walking over to help me unload the car.

"It was that or face World War 3 in the check-out aisle," I grumble.

"Amber!" Chloe shrieks, racing across the yard to hug Logan's girlfriend.

"I see you've patched things up," I murmur, tilting my head in her direction.

He nods solemnly. "I'm going to marry her someday."

I set the last of the bags from the trunk to our asphalt driveway and shut the lid before reaching up to muss his hair. "Just remember I'm not ready to be a grandfather yet."

He rolls his eyes and starts toward the house. I stand, watching him go. He's grown into an amazing young man, a freshman at University of Georgia on a partial lacrosse scholarship. Amber has stayed home and is going to a local community college. Over the summer, it seemed like they were going to break up.

Logan said she didn't want to hold him back and was miserable as she tried to push him away. It was then, one night, I pulled him aside to tell him the cliffnotes version of Sarah and me. How, when we were their age, something drove us apart and we lost seven years we could have spent together. I told him to fight for Amber and, if he loved her, to trust in that love.

Seeing her here can only mean he took my advice. I grab the bags at my feet and make my way toward the house. Amber holds the front door for me before walking out to tie a bundle of balloons to the mailbox. I can see they've been busy since I took Chloe to Target so she would be out of their hair while they got the house ready for her birthday party.

THEM

The living room is a riot of pink, purple, and green streamers and balloons. The latest Disney princess's face is plastered everywhere. I continue on to the kitchen. The bags I carry are full of chips which need pouring into the bowls laid out on the kitchen island.

"Daddy, did you see my cupcakes?" Chloe cries, her mouth and lips red from her slush.

For a moment, I'm struck motionless as it hits me what a carbon copy of her mother she is. Except for her blue eyes, every little molecule of her is Sarah.

"Will."

My eyes snap to the brown eyes of the woman who owns the other half of my soul. She's standing next to Sawyer, her hip leaned against the island.

"Look at her dress! She got red slush all over it," Sarah groans, resting her hands on top of her head. "People are going to be here any minute."

I lean down to capture her lips with mine, ignoring Chloe's muttered, "Eww, gross," in the background. Once I'm sure she's thoroughly kissed, I lift my face and gaze into her blinking eyes.

"You are so lucky you're still hot," Sarah teases before pulling away to empty the chips I bought into bowls. "Now, hurry and take her upstairs to change into something else."

"But I want to wear this," Chloe howls from the other side of the kitchen.

"So sad, too bad," I advance, grabbing her and tossing her over my shoulder to carry her up the stairs fireman style.

"But, Daddy," she cries.

"Do you want to wear one of your princess gowns?" I ask.

That shuts her up fast. "Can I?"

"Sure. It's your birthday, baby girl. Live it up."

She squeals when I set her on her feet and runs straight to her toy chest, pulling a pale pink tulle explosion from it. "Will you put pink clips in my hair, Daddy?"

Five years ago, I never would have thought I'd turn into a toddler hairdresser. Sarah still does the pig and ponytails better than I do, but I can hold my own when it comes to clip placement.

"Sure, honey. Let's get you changed first."

Once Chloe is fit to see her subjects, er, party guests, I take her back downstairs. The doorbell rings as we walk back into the kitchen. Chloe takes off like a shot to go answer it and I sneak a cupcake.

"Will." Sarah laughs as I toss its paper cup into the trash.

"What?" I ask innocently, tugging her toward me. "I needed some sustenance before our house is overrun with twenty five-year-olds."

"Ten. There are only ten five-year-olds coming," she corrects, kissing my cheek.

"And Calvin." I widen my eyes in mock fear and she laughs.

"Calvin is a handful, but Brian promised to wrangle him this time."

I'm still annoyed that the last time my demon nephew was over, he broke a new lens for my camera. Brian offered to replace it but Sarah refused, saying it was an accident. Accident, my ass; I saw the gleam in that brat's eye when he did it.

"Hmp," I reply.

She smacks my arm and shakes her head up at me. "Babe, let it go. It was two years ago."

I ignore her and kiss her instead. I've never been shy of showing my affection for her, but I tend to hold her longer and tighter around Chloe's birthday. I'll never forget the day our daughter came into the world. I almost lost them both. Sarah had an emergency C-section because of cord prolapse which cut off Chloe's oxygen supply.

Once Chloe was delivered, Sarah started hemorrhaging. They pulled me from the room as they worked to stop the blood loss and save her. I was a wreck, terrified that I could lose her but desperate to see Chloe. Even though she was delivered, she was by no means out of the woods.

She had trouble breathing initially in addition to already being born four weeks early. Once Chloe was stable, I was able to see her first. I'll never forget her little body, covered with wires in the incubator. She needed to stay under the lights so I couldn't hold her. All I could do was reach my gloved hand through an opening in the glass and hold her little hand.

I don't know how long I sat there like that, just holding her little hand. The movement of time didn't impact me. All I did was pray to every single God I had ever heard of that Sarah would make it. I swore to cherish each and every moment forward with her. I offered up my life for hers. There was nothing I would not do if it came down to it. I found out later that I had sat there, praying as I held my baby girl's hand, for over three hours.

I only left Chloe when Sarah's doctor came to get me and bring me to her. She was asleep. I collapsed into the chair next to her bed and laid my head on her hand before exhaustion took me. Sarah's recovery was slow—she was in the hospital two weeks—but Chloe's was slower. Chloe was in the NICU (neonatal) unit for a little over a month. She developed a heart murmur, but thankfully she did not need surgery.

I took disability from work to care for them both. Our family, community and the school all rallied around us. Logan stayed with my mom while Sarah was still in the hospital. When she came home, she wasn't allowed to walk up or down the stairs for the first week, not that she had the energy to even consider it.

The hardest part of that time was how distraught she was to be away from Chloe. The emotions from having her and then recovering were heartbreaking for her. She was certain she was a failure as a mother, and nothing I could say or do would convince her otherwise. It wasn't until Chloe was able to come home that she was able to shed those fears.

The cloud of gloom that had settled over our home lifted when Chloe was released from the hospital. Between Sarah, Logan, even Rascal and myself, she had no shortage of admirers. Sarah's mom lectured us that we held her too much, but the three of us would just ignore her and continue right on with showering Chloe with as much love and attention as we could.

Even now, our little girl will never turn down a cuddle from her mom, big brother or me. Chloe wasn't even six months old when people around us started to ask when we would have another one. Christine was pregnant again, Sawyer was pregnant again, but Sarah and I weren't ready to even consider going through another pregnancy. After a while, given how difficult her pregnancy and then the delivery was, we decided Logan and Chloe were all we needed.

The pop of a balloon brings me back to now. I glance around and notice Calvin hiding the evidence behind his back. The noise had scared Jacob, Brian and Christine's third child, who Logan was unfortunately holding at the time. Amber rescues him, sweeping a sobbing Jacob into her arms and cooing at him until he settles.

I shake off the vision of the two of them holding their own baby and mouth 'no babies' in Logan's direction. He flushes but that doesn't stop him from tucking Amber close to his side. I only hope those two will graduate college before they start having kids of their own. I collect the remnants of the balloon from Calvin and throw it away.

"Can I do anything to help?" My mom comes to stand next to me, her hand warm on my forearm.

She's blossomed in her role as a grandmother, starting with caring for Logan right after Chloe's birth. Those two have a bond that still surprises me. Logan takes her on what they call 'Nana dates,' going out to lunch or to the movies. She loves showing off her handsome grandson to all her neighbors in the retirement complex she lives in.

There are times I envy their relationship. I can't undo the past, though, so instead, I live vicariously through the gentle way she accepts him. She never missed any of his lacrosse games and has even worked out a schedule with Sarah and me to make his home games now that he's in college.

Already bonded with Logan, once Chloe came home, she was comfortable and confident in her role as Nana. Being there for us during that time helped show her we needed her. Her acceptance and support of our family has healed our personal relationship in ways I never thought possible.

"I think we're all set, Mom. Go hang out with Logan, since he's home this weekend."

THEM

Her face lights up. "He's coming over for lunch tomorrow and he's doing the cooking."

"I hope he isn't trying anything too complicated," I joke. "You may want to have a back-up ready just in case."

"William," she huffs. "My grandson is an excellent chef. I'm positive I'll love whatever he makes."

I take her hand in mine and kiss the back of it, her eyes crinkling as I do. "He adores you."

She presses her lips tightly together and nods, her eyes wet as she looks across the room to where he stands. "You have a beautiful family."

The pride in her tone makes my throat tighten, and I gulp before thanking her. She gives my hand a squeeze before leaving me to go spend time with her grandkids.

Our living room is now filled with family and kids and parents from the neighborhood.

"Daddy."

I look down to the pink princess tugging on my jeans. "Yes, baby girl?"

Her brows furrow. "Daddy, I'm not a baby. I'm a big girl now."

I pull her up and into my arms. "You are the biggest of big girls, but no matter what, you'll always be my baby girl."

She rolls her eyes, and I have to stop myself from laughing at a move she's perfected from her mother.

"Daddy." Her little hands frame my face and direct me to look toward our loveseat. "I'm going to marry Timmy Bonham."

"What?" I choke, glaring down at this five-year-old boy who will obviously never be good enough for my daughter.

Sarah interrupts my plans to question the boy by collecting Chloe and letting all the kids know the bounce castle in the backyard is ready for them to play on. There's a mass cry of excitement and then exodus of all little people toward the backyard.

We could not have custom-ordered a more beautiful day for a backyard birthday party. Heavy rains over the summer have made our grass lush and green, so the kids all lose their shoes and run screaming to bounce around inside the inflatable castle. Bright blue skies with a smattering of cotton ball clouds and a gentle breeze keep the day from being overly hot.

Logan and Amber carry out the bowls of chips while Sarah slides up next to me and wraps her arms around my waist.

"Look at her." She beams as her gaze holds our little girl bouncing like a maniac.

I curve my arm around her shoulders, relishing the fact that even after all these years, Sarah still fits me perfectly. "They'll all sleep well tonight."

She laughs, the prettiest sound I've ever heard.

"Thank you, Sarah."

THEM

Her now-confused gaze moves from our daughter to me. "For what?"

I dip my head to brush my lips cross hers and murmur, "For making me the happiest man alive."

Her warm brown eyes soften, her voice thick as she replies, "You're going to make me cry."

"No crying" I tease.

She takes a couple breaths, tightening her arms around me before looking back toward the bounce castle. I let her go so she can mingle with the other parents when it's time for me to man the grill. Logan watches the burgers and dogs long enough for me to take some pictures of the kids and partygoers.

I've never lost my photography bug; we only need more wall space for Sarah to hang up all the pictures I take. She's settled on a couple of those electronic frames that scroll through images in lieu of buying a bigger house. We'll never move if I can help it. I want our first house to be our forever house.

After I'm done taking pictures, I reclaim the grill from Logan. The next two hours are full of family, friends, food and fun. By the end of the party, both children and adults alike are worn out. Our little family are all that remain: Logan, Chloe, Sarah, Rascal and I.

Chloe and Logan are passed out on the couch, a Pixar movie on, while Sarah and I try to put the house back together. Sarah pauses in the doorway of the living room and motions me over. Side by side, we watch our children sleep.

"I still can't believe Logan is in college," Sarah whispers.

"I know. He looks so young," I reply.

"Especially when he's sleeping," she adds.

"Don't even get me started on how big Chloe's getting." I drape my arm around her shoulders.

"Is it still weird that we're parents? I mean, we made her, Will."

I chuckle. "You don't have to remind me. I was there," I tease.

"Maybe we should make her drink coffee to stunt her growth."

She's only half-joking.

"She told me she was going to marry Timmy Bonham today."

Sarah's head tilts so her eyes can meet mine. "Is he the blond one?"

I nod, smirking.

She laughs at me. "I'm surprised you didn't leave the party to go buy a shotgun."

"Trust me, I thought about it."

She bumps me with her elbow. "So, what'd you do?"

THEM

I drag my hand over my face. "I officiated the ceremony."

She folds over laughing, and I take the opportunity to enjoy the view. All these years and she still turns me on like no one else. I'm about to drag her upstairs to have my way with her when Logan turns to look at us, a grin on his face.

"I was the flower boy."

Sarah straightens but doesn't stop laughing. "Where was I? I feel so left out."

"You were playing nurse to Ashley Morton," I reply.

"That scrape took two big princess Band-Aids."

"She's a daredevil, that Morton girl."

"I have a feeling they'll renew their vows at some point," Sarah muses and Logan stands up, stretching before coming to stand with us.

"What makes you say that?" I ask.

"I married the boy who lived down the street at least twenty times between kindergarten and second grade."

My mouth drops open. "Excuse me? Was there ever a divorce?"

She covers her mouth as she laughs but doesn't reply.

"And here I thought I was your first love," I grumble.

She pulls my face down to hers and while laughter still dances in her eyes, she replies, "William Price, I've never loved anyone other than you."

I coil my arms around her, dipping her as Logan laughs at both of us. "Same here, Sarah Miller Price. You're stuck with me for the rest of our lives. There isn't another woman I could love more than you."

I drop my lips to hers. Rascal thinks we're playing and comes over to bark and jump on us, and her barking wakes up Chloe. She does her best zombie impression as, still half-asleep, she walks over to hug our legs, pushing Rascal away as she tries to lick her face.

"Come on, girl," Logan calls, walking toward the back deck.

I swoop Chloe up in my arms and hold Sarah's hand as we follow Logan outside.

Rascal seems to be the only one in our group with any energy left. She races from one side of the backyard to the other, chasing squirrels. With Chloe in my lap, her head on my shoulder, Sarah sits next to me, tucking herself under my arm. Logan sits on the other side of me, opening his arms when Chloe reaches for him and tugging her into his lap.

The earlier warmth from the day lingers now with only a touch of the cool night air creeping in. The sky is still clear, enough for a half moon and stars to shine brightly overhead. Life, work, kids and distractions have a way of making us lose sight of what's truly

THEM

important. Here, surrounded by the people I love most in the world, it's in the forefront of my mind. Five years ago today, I almost lost my world.

To each of those Gods I prayed to that day, I offer my thanks for every moment I've been given since with Sarah, Chloe and Logan. There will be no shortage of ups and downs in our future, and I look forward to it all.

THE END

ACKNOWLEDGEMENTS

First and foremost, I would like to thank you for reading this book. Will and Sarah feel like family to me at this point so I truly hoped you enjoyed their story as much as I loved writing it.

Next, I have to thank my beta readers, without them this book would never have turned out as well as it did. Thank you Kristy, Nasha, Christine, Nicola, Dana, and Amy.

To my Keep Calm and Carey On Facebook group, thank you for cheering me on, and being so friggin awesome all the time. You guys rock!

I have to give a big shout out to my big sister Joy. She is a nurse midwife and was such a big help to me in making sure the medical scenes I wrote were accurate.

A huge thank you to my cover designer, Sarah Hansen with Okay Creations; my formatter, Integrity Formatting; my editing team, Hot Tree Editing; and my proofreader, Vanessa Brown.

I feel so blessed to be part of the indie author community. It is amazing to call so many of these brilliant authors friends. I would like to thank one author in particular, Heidi Mclaughlin, for being the first person to read and love Them.

THEM

To each and every blog who has read one of my books or shared a link or quote pic, thank you so much for helping new readers find me. I'm my own marketing team (and I fail at marketing!) so I appreciate your help so much.

Lastly, I need to thank my family. My husband Seth, who I have to admit, was part of my inspiration for Will Price, thank you for loving me. To Zachary, Aydan, and Emma, even though you three were a distraction from writing this book, I wouldn't have had it any other way.

ABOUT THE AUTHOR

New York Times and USA Today bestselling author with six books out and many more to come. She was born and raised in Alexandria, Virginia. Ever the mild-mannered citizen, Carey spends her days working in the world of finance, and at night, she retreats into the lives of her fictional characters. Supporting her all the way are her husband, three sometimes-adorable children, and their nine-pound attack Yorkie.

I'd love to hear from you!

info@careyheywood.com

www.careyheywood.com

ALSO BY CAREY HEYWOOD

The Carolina Days Series
The Other Side of Someday
Yesterday's Half Truths

The Him & Her Series
Him
Her
Them
Sawyer Says (Spin off)
Being Neighborly (Spin off)

Standalones
A Bridge of Her Own
Uninvolved
Stages of Grace
Better

being
neighborly
a novella

New York Times Bestselling Author
Carey Heywood

BEING NEIGHBORLY

Copyright © 2014 by Carey Heywood

All rights reserved. Except as permitted under the U.S. Copyright Act of 1976,no part of this publication may be reproduced, distributed, or transmitted in any form or by any means, or stored in a database or retrieval system, without prior written permission of the author. The scanning, uploading, and distribution of this book via the Internet or via other means without the permission of the publisher is illegal and the punishable by law. Please purchase only authorized electronic editions and do not participate in or encourage electronic piracy of copyrighted materials. Your support of the author's rights is appreciated. Sawyer Says is a work of fiction. Names, characters, places, and incidents are either the product of the author's imagination or are used fictitiously. Any resemblance to actual persons, living or dead, events, or locales is entirely coincidental.

being
neighborly

Beau Hamilton spends his days working the family farm, leaving him no time to worry about finding a girlfriend. He wants to settle down and start a family, but his prospects aren't looking up. He knows what he wants; a nice country girl, who doesn't mind living on a farm, a girl nothing like his new neighbor Bethany. Bethany screams "city" and it's only a matter of time before she hightails it out of farmland and back to the land of coffee shops on every street corner. She's not the type of girl who would be happy, living on a farm for the rest of her life. Despite all the reasons he shouldn't be, Beau finds himself drawn to her in ways even he can't dismiss as only being neighborly

dedication

This book is dedicated to all the readers, who each night stay up past their bedtimes to take in the words we write. Thank you.

note to the reader

Beau, the main character of this book, was introduced in my novel ***Sawyer Says***.

chapter
one

"Did you hear someone bought the Wilson place?"

I glance up from my breakfast and into Bess's pointed stare. What'd I do? "What does that mean for me, Bess?"

A Cheshire-Cat-like grin spreads across her face. "I wondered if you could run this apple pie I baked over to her."

Her?

I shrug. "Sure. When?"

She turns her back to me and nonchalantly replies, "How about before suppertime, after you've showered and changed?"

This smells like a setup. I've known Bess my entire life. She's like an unrelated aunt and a second mama. She's been more prone to meddle now that my dad's retired.

I've been slowly taking over my parents' farm since his health deteriorated. My mom and dad even moved out of the main house, moving down to a cabin at the back of the property. My dad's always been a go getter. Our hope is that tucked away back there, he'll

being neighborly

be forced to take it easy and relax. So far it's been working.

Our farm, while owned by my family, is also home to three other families in search of a simpler life. We eat what we grow and barter for the things we need and donate any surplus to the local food bank.

Bess would like me to settle down and start a family of my own. I have nothing against women. I've just been so busy that none of the single women I know have held my attention.

I had a serious girlfriend a few years back, but farm life wasn't what she was looking for. From what I hear, she's married and has a kid living in the city. It'll take a certain kind of girl to want this type of life. I love the families who call this farm home, even when it feels like I can't get a moment of peace to myself.

With the weather turning warmer, I'm moving from the main house to another cabin on the property. It's within walking distance of the main house but gives me peace and quiet during the spring and summer months.

I live in the main house during the winter just because it costs less for us to heat one place. The cabin my parents have moved to has no electricity, but is small enough that the wood stove is all they need for the winter.

"Want to tell me more about this new neighbor, Bess?"

Her cheeks redden and it's clear she knows I'm on to her. "Her name is Bethany, and Mrs. Brendal said she was a cute little thing, so I didn't think there'd be anything wrong with you going over and being neighborly."

"You know I don't like setups, Bess," I warn.

"It's not a setup. I've never even spoken two words to the girl. I just figured, since it sounded like she was around your age, it made more sense for you to go over rather than me."

I cock a brow at her. "And why's that?"

"You need more friends your age, Beau."

I groan, but it in no way stops her.

"You work your tail off on this farm. When was the last time you went out or did something just for yourself?" I start to speak but she lifts her hand cutting me off. "You are just like your father, and if I have to banish you from the farm so you'll relax, I will."

My shoulders sag. I push back from the table and cross the room to pull her into a hug, dropping a kiss on the top of her head. "Message received, loud and clear."

"We all love you, Beau. We just want what's best for you."

Nodding, I swipe a muffin and head for the door before talk can get any deeper than it already has. I pass Ben, one of the kids living on the farm. He's maybe ten and likes to think he's grown.

being neighborly

"Women," he mutters as I walk past.

Snorting, I nod. "Tell me about it."

My morning passes quickly, the grumble in my gut letting me know it's time to head inside for lunch. After spending most of my morning caring for the few animals we have on the farm, a quick whiff confirms I now smell like them. I head straight for the shower. Bess will want me to deliver that pie after lunch, and if I'm already clean by the time I see her again, she'll have no reason to fuss at me.

In no mood to impress our new neighbor, I pull on an old t-shirt and a pair of faded jeans. The insoles of my work boots are wearing thin, so I pull on an old pair of sneakers before I head back downstairs. Once this pie is delivered, I'll spend the rest of my day moving back into my cabin.

Bess frowns when she sees what I'm wearing but silently passes the pie. No words are needed to tell me she had hoped I'd be wearing a dress shirt and slacks. She's lucky I'm going willingly seeing as how I'm the lamb being led to slaughter.

My precious cargo, the pie, rides on the passenger side foot well. I can't risk the hell that will befall me should it slide off the seat.

Mrs. Wilson was our closest neighbor until she passed away. It's still a five-minute drive from our farm to hers. Mrs. Wilson didn't have as much acreage as us, but did have a pretty little pasture and stable setup to board horses. Pulling up to her house,

I glance around, looking to see if our new neighbor is planning the same thing.

The stables don't appear to be recently used. It's rained the last three days, and unless she's using the back entrance, there would be more signs of traffic. I walk around my truck to retrieve the pie from the passenger side. There's only one other car parked by the house, a small coupe with no trailer hitch. At this point, I'm guessing no on the horse boarding.

I amble up the front steps and rap my knuckles on the edge of the screen door. A crash, followed quickly by a yelp, has me pulling open the screen door and opening the front door.

"Hello? My name is Beau. I live on the next farm over. Are you all right?"

A muffled groan coming from the back of the house has me dashing toward the kitchen, pie still in my hand. The sight I come upon catches me so off guard I almost drop it.

There're two bare legs sporting some hot pink flip-flops peeking out from underneath a toppled over two-legged table. How in the world? I skip asking questions and jump into action. Quickly setting the pie on the counter next to me, I reach forward to lift the table off my new neighbor.

Judging from the tools scattered on the floor around her, she was putting the legs on. I'm just not sure how. I twist the table top onto its side and rest it against the wall before reaching my hand out to help her up.

"Are you all right?" I ask.

Curly auburn locks are pushed back to reveal hazel eyes as she reaches her other hand to meet mine. "Uh huh."

I lift her slowly. "Were you hurt?"

She shakes her head, her curls bouncing. "Just startled."

It takes a moment before I realize her hand is still in mine. She's tall for a girl, coming almost up to my nose in her flip-flops. In some sexy heels, I wouldn't even have to dip my head to kiss those plump lips. It's hard not to stare at her. Most of the tall girls I grew up around were built like men. Bethany was all woman. Hell, I'd even sign up for a geometry class dedicated to studying her curves.

She slowly pulls her hand from mine and starts to take a step back, but her foot lands on a screwdriver and she loses her balance. I catch her, pulling her tightly to my chest before she pitches backwards. Her hands grip my shoulders as she looks up at me, wide-eyed.

Gulping, she glances behind her before moving to step away from me again. This time, I don't let her go right away.

"I didn't get your name."

She wets her lips, and stills in my arms. "I'm Bethany."

Her chest rises and falls rapidly; movement I cant ignore given her warm body is pressed to mine.

"I'm such a klutz," she groans,

"Maybe you should sit. If you want, I can finish putting your table together."

She nods, and then gasps as I lift her and set her gently on the counter next to the pie.

"Thought it'd be safer for you up there. I wink.

Turning quickly so my back is to her, I'm not sure what compelled me to wink at her. I don't wink at people. Focusing on things I understand, like furniture assembly, seems safer.

I crouch in front of the table, still leaned against the wall, and start to attach the third leg.

After a few moments of silence, I break it by asking, How did the table fall on you?

She chuckles behind me. I know I should have flipped the table on to its back and put all the legs on that way, but I thought I was being clever by setting it up on a couple chairs so I wouldn't have to flip it back over when I was done. It didn't work out as well as I thought it would.

Turning back to her, I ask, What would you have done if I hadn't shown up?

She shrugs, one flip-flop precariously dangling from her foot. Wiggled out from under it somehow."

being neighborly

Her eyes widen. "I haven't even thanked you. You must think I am the rudest person ever."

Holding up my hand in an attempt to stop her, I shake my head. "It's fine really."

She continues, "And now you're putting together my table and I'm just sitting here."

After leaning the table back up against the wall, I cross the small kitchen and stand in front of her, taking her wringing hands into mine. "Bethany, it's no big deal. I'm happy to help. It's what neighbors do."

Her shoulders sag. "Not where I'm from."

I tilt my head and smile. "Aren't you glad you moved here then? So, where're you from?"

Her eyes drop to our still joined hands, a blush racing over her pale cheeks. "Baltimore, Maryland."

"A city girl. What brought you out here?"

"One day, it hit me that after my parents moved, I had nothing keeping me in Baltimore. I needed a change. I'm my own boss so I can work anywhere. I stumbled across this listing and could picture myself better here than where I was living. My parents think I'm crazy for moving out to what they would call the 'middle of nowhere', but I'm looking forward to unplugging. I wanted to live somewhere peaceful."

I reach up to tuck a curl behind her ear. "Can't argue wanting an uncomplicated life. I've had to do a little bit a traveling for the farm. I think I'm allergic to city life."

She laughs, the skin around her eyes crinkling as she looks up at me, and it's like someone knocked the wind out of me. Needing some distance, I release her hands and abruptly take a step back.

"I'll just finish up," I mumble, focusing on the table and not my new neighbor.

The slap of her flip-flops hitting the floor behind me has me turning to look back at her.

"Would you like a drink? I feel awful just sitting here watching you work."

Can't argue that logic. Not knowing what she has on hand since she just moved in, I ask for a glass of water.

When she hands me a bottle, I frown. "Tap water is fine for me."

Her brows come together. "Is it safe to drink?"

"Course it is."

She doesn't look convinced, but reaches to take the bottle back from me. I'm almost done putting the final leg on when she brings me a mug of cold tap water.

I lift the mug, turning it to read it. "Smarty Pants?"

She blushes. "It was a gift. I haven't unpacked all my other kitchen stuff yet and it was already out."

"I like it." I hold her eyes as I lift its rim to my lips.

What I don't say is I like smart girls too, even the clumsy ones.

being neighborly

After draining the mug, I hand it back to her. Out of habit, and seeing how she was assembling it in the first place, I give the two legs she already attached a quick once over. With a couple of extra turns of the screwdriver, I am confident they aren't going anywhere.

"Ready to flip her?" I ask.

"Um, sure." She is still holding the mug, almost cradling it. She turns and sets it on the countertop, and then comes to stand opposite me. Mirroring my movements, we both bend, and then lift the table before setting it upright on its legs.

"Nice looking table," I remark, rubbing my hand across the worn blonde wood.

"Thanks. I've had it forever. It was my first adult purchase."

"No cigarettes or nudey magazines for you?" I tease.

She laughs again. This time, any self-preservation instinct that moved me to flee last time vanishes. Just like a bloom turns toward the sun, I need to be closer to her. I've forgotten the table between us, until I bump into it, breaking the spell her laughter cast on me.

"I should go." I start to back away.

She arches a brow. "And make me eat this pie all by myself? That doesn't seem very neighborly."

My eyes find Bess's apple pie and I hesitate.

Then she goes in for the kill. "I have vanilla ice cream."

Dammit. That's just downright irresistible.

"You've found my weakness," I smile.

As she digs through a box for a couple plates, I pull the chairs over and place them around her table.

"Is there anything I can do to help?" I offer.

Shaking her head, Bethany motions for me to sit. She joins me not long after with a plate for each of us.

Waiting for her reaction to Bess's pie, I hold off eating any of mine and just watch her. She loads her fork up with a good amount of pie and pulls it through her ice cream for good measure. She hasn't noticed my attention is solely on her. Her full lips circle then close around her fork. Riveted, I watch her eyes widen as she pulls the fork from her mouth.

She chews, covers her mouth as she appears to start to say something; she then shakes her head and moans. Her incredulous eyestrain themselves onto mine and she slowly chews. After one final gulp her mouth opens.

"Oh, my God. Seriously. Oh, my God."

I nod, finally able to take my own bite. "I know."

Unfazed, she continues, "Seriously, this is the best apple pie I have ever had."

My mouth is full so I nod again and raise my brows. This is not the kind of pie that allows for conversation while it's being eaten. All thought, focus and attention being *neighborly*

must be solely on the heaven on earth that is this pie. The addition of slow churned vanilla ice cream makes heaven taste downright sinful. Wait, ice cream?

I gulp down my current bite. "So you've already been to the grocery store?"

She shakes her head. "No, Bess and I have been talking on the phone for a couple weeks now. She knew I was getting in late last night and offered to stock the fridge for me."

Smirking to myself, I can't help but notice how easy it would have been for Bess to leave this pie for Bethany herself, last night.

"She even stopped by this morning to check on me."

Must have been while I was working.

"She didn't tell you?" Bethany continues.

Shaking my head, I look forward to finding out exactly what Bess is up to.

After we've both finished, I clear the plates and set them in the sink.

"I should really be taking off now." I take a step toward the door and she follows me.

"I've totally kept you. I'm so sorry. Of course you have things to do."

I shrug. "It's no problem, really. I'm happy I was able to help and thank you kindly for the piece of pie."

After opening the front door, I half step out, letting the screen door lean against my back and reach out to shake her hand. "It was nice meeting you, Bethany. If there is anything you need, you just give us a shout."

Her small hand is warm in mine. "Thank you, Beau. It's nice to know I have great neighbors."

When I release her hand, Bethany follows me out on to her front porch, leaning against the railing as I walk down to my truck. I give her a quick wave, which she returns before I back out her drive.

chapter *two*

"Can I have a word?" I interrupt the kitchen chatter, my eyes on Bess.

"Oh, you're back. What did you think of Bethany?" Bess's eyes light up as she crosses the room to me.

She's a sweet soul, with a habit of meddling.

"I didn't realize you had already met her when you sent me to deliver the pie."

"I didn't tell you?" she asks innocently.

I smirk, draping my arm around her shoulders and kissing the side of her head. "I'm on to you."

She grins. "She's a real pretty girl, isn't she?"

I almost argue her use of the word girl, in my opinion Bethany is all woman; instead, I only nod my agreement.

"Well," she pushes, "didn't you think she was pretty?"

Smoldering hazel eyes, plump kissable lips, and auburn curls flash through my mind. "She's pretty."

Gorgeous, really.

"It's so nice to have someone your age living so close to us now. Maybe you could ask her on a date."

"Bess," I interrupt, "she just moved here. Let the poor woman settle in before you try and get her a man."

She glares up at me, a sight that would have had my eight-year-old self quaking in my boots, but now just makes me want to hug her. "This is the reason you're still single. You are too relaxed about women. You need to be more forceful and get what you want."

I grin down at her. "I haven't had any complaints."

It takes everything I have not to laugh when she starts muttering, "No complaints." She pushes away from me and opens the front door. "I don't see a line waiting to go out with you."

Ouch.

Frowning, I walk out onto the front porch and slump into an old wooden rocker. She follows me cautiously, possibly regretting the bite in her words. I don't say it, but I'd love to be settled down, married with children of my own. I've dated, but shit always came up, differences. I'll be thirty in less than a year and I'm happy where I am, on this farm. I have no desire to live anywhere else.

I grew up here. My dad's health started declining when it would have been time for me to go away to college. I decided to stay home, take courses at the local community college so I could help my dad. I wouldn't go back and do things differently; it just made meeting girls hard. I was too busy with work and school to socialize.

being neighborly

Besides, it seems like every girl who's ever sparked my interest has moved away. A girl I grew up with, Sawyer, came back into my life last year. Never thought I'd be interested in a woman with pink hair, but it didn't matter anyway. She was in love with someone else. They're already married and expecting a baby now. Story of my life.

As cute as Bethany is, there's no guarantee she'll even like country life. There's a fifty-fifty chance she'll be gone within a year. I'm a watcher, a planner and a patient man. If she's still here this time next year, maybe I'll ask her out.

Bess breaks the silence. "I'm sorry I was rough."

Shaking my head, I smile up at her. "You didn't say anything I don't already know."

I skip dinner with the rest of the house in favor of my quiet cabin, still full from pie and ice cream. There's a loft above the main room with a thick mattress and soft cushions. A porthole window offers a gentle breeze from the orchard. I've spent many a day sprawled out up here with a book. It was my hideaway even when I was younger.

Unless someone takes the time to climb the wooden ladder leading up here, there's no way to know I'm here. I'm a solitary man. I need time to myself, and after the long winter in the main house, I need it more than ever. Today, instead of reading, I contemplate the surprise that is Bethany.

It'll take a while to not picture her on her back, long bare legs sticking out from underneath the table. Pairing that image with the noises she made as she ate that pie, I groan as the two moments combine in my mind and send blood rapidly to my painfully hardening cock. I may be solitary, but that does not mean I don't enjoy the feel of a woman underneath me.

At this moment, I'm wishing it was a certain woman with eyes that can't make up their mind between green or brown. Last thing I should be thinking of is dragging those cut-off jean shorts down her legs and tasting her. What I should be doing is taking a long cold shower, but climbing down that ladder with a stiff dick will be a pain in the ass.

I unbuckle my belt, then pop open the button on my worn jeans. My cock pushes almost painfully against the zipper as I ease it down. Once I'm free, I grip, picturing Bethany on her knees and those luscious lips wrapped around it. Her eyes blink up at me as she sucks me down deeply. With each blink, they change colors only slightly, one time looking more brown, the next more green.

In my mind, I fist her hair, pumping my hips as I come down her throat. Sadly, in real life I'm alone, coming all over my hand and shirt and not a towel in sight. I wipe my hand on my shirt and carefully pull it off without making more of a mess. Once I'm zipped, buttoned, and buckled up, I toss my shirt down from the loft and climb down the ladder.

being neighborly

I'm on the last rung when someone knocks on the door. I'm shirtless but otherwise dressed, so I cross the room quickly to answer it.

Words fail me as I find Bethany on my doorstep. Her mouth hangs open as she openly ogles not my face but my chest. All I can think, looking at her, is how I just pictured my cock in her mouth. Her standing here with it hanging open sends blood rushing that direction again.

I clear my throat, crossing my arms over my chest in the hopes she'll look up at me and close her mouth. "I wasn't expecting to see you again so soon."

Her eyes snap up to mine, looking more brown than green. "Bess called and invited me over for dinner. I just got here and she sent me over to collect you since it's almost ready."

I'll bet she did, I think to myself. "I was just changing my shirt."

Hoping that explains my appearance, I turn and grab my soiled shirt from the floor. "Give me just a minute. Umm, make yourself comfortable."

She tiptoes into my cabin and her eyes dance around the room, from the wood carvings on the walls to the old worn throw blankets hanging off the back of the sofa. I flee to my bathroom and fill the sink up with water before tossing my shirt in it. I usually don't do my own laundry and do not want to explain that spot to anyone. On my way back to the front room, I grab a Henley from my closet and drag it over my head.

"It's a nice surprise, you joining us for dinner," I say once I'm back in the room with her.

"It was sweet of Bess to ask me," she replies.

Is that saying she wished I had asked her? I frown but wipe it from my face when I see her watching me.

"You're always welcome."

She's lost her pink flip-flops and changed into a dress and a pair of worn-in cowboy boots. She was showing more leg in her cutoffs, but knowing I could easily push that dress up and over her hips is one hell of a turn-on. Shit, she could even leave the boots on.

"I might be a crazy person. You shouldn't just make a blanket invitation like that."

I push open the door, holding it for her. "Just being neighborly."

"Oh, so that invitation isn't specific to me? It's open to all of your neighbors?"

"Never said that." I sweep my arm in front of me. "After you."

She eases past me, her arm brushing mine as she does. "Thank you."

Once outside, I frown when I notice how cool it's become. "Will you be warm enough?"

She nods, but the slide of her hands up and down her arms tells a different story.

being
neighborly

"Wait right here."

Hurrying back into the cabin and back into my room, I pull an old hoodie from my closet. It's small on me but good for layering under bigger coats during the winter. I'm back outside and by her side in no time.

"Put this on," I say, passing it to her.

"You didn't have to," she argues even though she's already putting it on.

I have to admit, my clothes look good on her.

"Didn't want you to catch a cold."

The main house is a short walk from my cabin. Her long legs match my stride easily and I use the opportunity to point out different sections of the farm along the way.

"So you donate whatever you don't use to the food bank?"

This has been a bone of contention with other girls I've dated. "Yep, we make enough to sustain our needs, barter for things we need in the community, and donate the rest. We're technically a nonprofit."

She spins around, almost trying to see the whole place at once. "That's so cool."

"Really?" I push, she needs to understand I'll never been a wealthy man.

She nods, her eyes meeting mine. "I moved here to take a step back, live more simply. I love what you're doing here."

I look away, suddenly embarrassed by her praise.

"I see you found, Beau," Bess calls out from the front porch.

"I wouldn't have made her come and get me if I knew you had invited her," I retort.

Glancing around, I look for her car. "Where'd you park?"

Bess tsks. "I went and picked her up. Didn't want her to have to drive at night on our dirt roads."

"I told her she didn't have to," Bethany adds.

Shaking my head, I stop her from saying anything else. "She's right though; these country roads can be tricky at night."

Bess leans slightly over the railing toward us. "I hoped you would drive her back. You know how my eyesight gets in the dark."

Puppet master all the way.

She smiles sweetly as she opens the door for us. I take over for her and kiss her cheek as she passes by me. Meals on the farm are a well-oiled machine at this point. Everyone helps out in one way or another. Bess and two other families currently live in the main house.

The kids set the table and clear it before dessert. The older kids and adults all take turns preparing meals. I'm not much of a cook, but put in my time on a regular basis doing food prep. I do dishes most nights being *neighborly*

as well. Washing dishes is safe. I've never burned one or undercooked one.

Everyone is sitting when we walk into the dining room. After introductions are made, we all sit and dig in. I had planned to skip dinner earlier, thinking I was full. One look at the roasted chicken and mashed potatoes proves I was wrong. Over dinner, it's nice to learn more about Bethany through other people's questions.

She is an only child. Glancing around the table, she explains she always wished for a big family. Her parents are still living; they retired and moved to Florida a couple years back. She had no desire of moving that far south but figured Tennessee was closer than Maryland when she decided to move.

Money was the main reason she researched moving here in the first place. Tennessee has no state income tax. There is still a tax for investment related income but not income she earned through her business. Florida is another state without income tax, but the idea of living there never appealed to her. Once she spent some time online researching communities, she could see herself living here.

The Wilson place had been on the market for a while and fit her budget.

The reason it was in her price range though were the updates needed to it. That didn't deter her; she had a plan and it involved doing some of the work herself. All I could picture was her underneath that table, and her all by herself if something else like that happened. That's the only excuse I have for opening my mouth. "I could help you."

She shakes her hand and her head at the same time. "No, I'm perfectly capable of—"

Bess cuts her off before she can get any farther. "Beau, that's a wonderful idea. Bethany, he is so good with his hands. He'll get you taken care of in no time."

I'd like to show her just how good with my hands I can be.

Bethany looks back and forth between us, clearly debating my offer to help. Her gaze finally rests on me. "Are you sure?"

I'm not, but I won't let her know that. "Wouldn't have offered otherwise."

Her lips pull tightly, a wise smile settling in. "That would be amazing. I've watched 'how to' videos but never tackled anything like this on my own before."

"I'm happy to be of assistance"

The look of sheer delight on Bess's face was not lost on me. As much as I give her grief for trying to set me up with any available woman near my age, I get how lucky I am that she cares. Bess might not be blood, but she's family. Someone loves you, and tries to do a kindness for you, that is something you acknowledge. I do this by giving her shoulder a gentle squeeze on my way to the kitchen. I'm on dish detail and figure Bess and Bethany can gab. I am elbows deep in hot suds when Bethany comes up beside me.

being neighborly

"Can I help"

"You're a guest. I can take care of this" I reply, waiting for her to argue.

She grabs a towel and reaches for a plate. "I don't mind."

We make short work of the dinner dishes. Since dessert is another apple pie, I ask Bethany if she'd like to go for a walk instead. I try to invite Bess, but am turned down in favor of pie and a firm suspicion she wants Bethany and me to be alone.

Dusk is in full effect, shadows growing into night with each minute passing. The path to the orchard is so well worn and imprinted on me, the lack of light is no concern. It has a happy side effect, however, of Bethany grabbing my arm when she stumbles, and she doesn't let me go after I right her.

If she's still here in a year, I am definitely asking her out.

"In the summertime, these trees will be full of fireflies."

She stops walking and sighs. "I can't remember the last time I saw a firefly.

Shaking my head, I give her arm a little tug to get her moving again. "You'll be seeing them almost every night in a month or so, as long as you look outside just after the sun's set."

"Another thing to look forward to."

We fall into an easy pace, her arm still around mine. "Another thing? Do you have a list going?"

It's still light enough that I can see her nod. "I do, not written down or anything." She taps her head. "All up here."

We're almost out of the orchard and I point out the small grouping of gravestones.

"Do cemeteries scare you? We can avoid it if you'd like."

Her pull on my arm toward the gravestones answers my question. "Has this always been here? How old are these? Is it like your family plot?"

"Not just immediate family, but we still consider it the family plot if that makes sense."

She peers at the stones, the light probably making the markings hard to read. "I'd love to come back here during the day."

"You're welcome anytime."

The absence of sunlight in no way diminishes the brightness from her responding smile. It lights up her face and eyes in a way that makes my chest tight. Were I not exhaling and inhaling without struggle, I would think she takes my breath away. Dizzy, and not from lack of oxygen, I dumbly blink at her.

As if realizing the effect a full blast of her smile is having on me, she looks away. "That's so nice. Thank you."

being neighborly

Once we return to the main path, we are back to the main house in no time.

"I should be probably be getting home" she murmurs.

Nervously, I wonder if something from our walk bothered her. "Oh, right. Hang tight. I'm going to give Bess a heads up that I'm running you home."

Hurriedly, I find Bess and let her know where I am going. Only reason I do is so she won't worry. The gleam in her eyes makes me second-guess it though. Making the excuse that Bethany is waiting for me, I leave before she can encourage me to ask her out.

Ignoring the attraction I feel for Bethany is impossible. I'm just trying to be smart about it. She's our closest neighbor. With any luck, she'll stay a while.

If it turns out country life doesn't suit her and she leaves, at least there won't be any feelings on either side complicating things. If she's still here in ten months, maybe I'll ask her out.

She turns when I open the front door, the light resting on her face. "Ready"

Her lips curve. "Yep"

Offering my arm, more for the feel of hers than anything else, we walk toward my cabin. Walking around to the passenger side, I open the door for her. In theory, the act screams gentleman and my mama would be proud, as long as she didn't know how much leg I get to enjoy as Bethany settles in her seat. The thoughts running through my mind are anything but gentlemanly.

Attraction is there. An internal debate sparks between my common sense and go-with-the-flow self. Repercussions of things ending badly with my closest neighbor keep me from acting on that attraction. Besides, if she still lived here in ten, er, make that nine months, I'm asking her out.

chapter
three

"What do you think about this color?"

I squint at the twelfth paint chip I've been asked to give my opinion on in the last five minutes. "Did you show me that one already?"

Her face lights up. "Just making sure you were paying attention."

I lean forward against the cart, resting my chin in my hand. "And I'll tell you what I said the first time. That's an excellent choice."

Her brows come together and her lips pucker into a pout. "But you said that for all of them."

Grinning, I reply, "I meant that for all of them. It's paint. If you don't like what you get, we can just repaint it."

"But which one do you like the most?"

I stand and step toward her, draping my arm across her shoulders. "It's your kitchen."

"Fine," she huffs, going with the pale mango shade.

"Did you still want to paint the cabinets too?"

She shakes her head. "I want to see how the walls look done first."

Passing over the paint color to the store employee to mix it, she waits while I go and fill our cart with the supplies we'll need. It's been two weeks since she came over for dinner and we've fallen into an easy friendship. She likes to cook and has talked me into coming over a couple nights every week so she can try stuff on me. Apparently, my palate is too countrified. I grew up eating simple meals we made based on what the farm produced. I have nothing against other types of food, just haven't had them.

She's been paying me in meals for the help I've been giving her around the place. The first thing she asked for my help with was installing a new rain showerhead in the master bathroom. Standing in her tub, guessing by her still damp hair, that she was naked in there earlier was hard. Not hard to do, as in made me hard.

That reaction was repeated the next day thanks to the mental picture I got when she went on and on, telling me how wonderful her shower felt. Luckily, since then I've been mainly assembling bookshelves and rescreening her porch.

I'm still trying to figure out whether it's expanding my culinary horizons or my company she likes more. I'm hoping it's the latter. If she still lives here in eight months, I am asking her out.

The paint is ready by the time I have everything we'll need. Once everything is paid for, I push the cart out to the parking lot. A gentle breeze carries the scent of Bethany's honeysuckle conditioner past me.

being neighborly

It hits me then, that so far, there isn't one thing that I don't like about her. Windows down, we drive back to her house, I add another thing I like about her to my mental list; she looks seriously hot in my truck.

She runs upstairs to change while I tape off the room. I work on a farm, I'm not worried about paint getting on my clothes. When Bethany comes back down, I have to fight to not stare at her. She's changed into a tight tank top and a pair of rolled-at-the-waist plaid boxer shorts. I can only hope she bought them; that's easier to swallow than them belonging to an old boyfriend.

"You mentioned starting your own business before, but you never said what," I ask as she climbs a stepladder to start edging.

"I'm a freelance editor."

Dipping the roller into the tray, I glance up at her. "What kind of stuff do you edit?"

She sets down her brush and straightens her shoulders. "Novels, mainly fiction, though I did edit one autobiography."

"I've never met an editor before. Would I know any of the books you've edited? I don't read as much as I'd like to, but I still follow new releases."

She giggles, her eyes mischievously holding mine. "That depends, do you read any romance?"

I shake my head and start painting the wall in front of me. "I mainly read mysteries, but Bess inhales those romance novels. She loves that Sparks guy. He's the only one I know of for romance. Oh, and those grey books, something shades of grey."

"Everyone knows those. I'm afraid I don't edit for Nicholas Sparks or E.L. James. If I did, I might've bought an island, not a farmhouse."

"Fair enough."

"Would you like to read something I've edited?" she asks with a hopeful lilt in her tone.

There is only one right answer to this question. "I would love to."

"Really?" she beams.

Yep, that was the right answer.

She climbs down the stepladder and motions for me to follow her. Leading me into her den, she immediately starts rummaging through a box on the floor.

"I have an old eReader you can borrow. I just have to find it."

I glance around at all the books on her shelves. "Do you have a paperback?"

She gasps and looks up at me. "My paperbacks are signed."

My brows furrow so she explains, "If you read one of those, you might crack the spine."

"That sounds like a bad thing," I hedge, even though I'm not certain I understand why that's a bad thing.

being neighborly

Her attention turns back to the box, and after another moment of shuffling through it, she brandishes a small tablet victoriously. "Found it."

Her face is a picture of elation as she crosses the room toward me and pats my arm. "I'll hook it up to my charger while we paint and it should be good to go for you to read tonight."

Following her back out to the kitchen, I ask. "Tonight?"

She stills and I almost walk into her. Her face turns so I only see her profile and she nods solemnly.

Guess I have homework tonight. After she plugs the eReader in, we get back to painting. Her kitchen isn't overly large, and since we're not painting the cabinets, of which there are many, it does not take us long to get the first coat up. We share lunch on her screen porch while it dries.

"So what kind of book would you prefer, heavy steam or low steam?"

I drop my elbow on to the table and rest my chin on my hand. "This your way of telling me you edit dirty books?"

She blushes which is a definite yes.

"I want to read whichever one is your favorite."

We finish lunch and head back inside to do the second coat. When we're finished, it looks great. Sure, it needs to dry, but a coat of paint is always an easy way to change the look of a place. She pulls the tape as I pack the other supplies up.

"I'm going to go wash the brushes outside."

"I'll come along with you," she says, following me.

I use the hose, the overspray getting her legs, making her dance away with a squeal. Painting has never been fun, but somehow with Bethany, it didn't feel like a chore. We leave the brushes and roller heads outside to dry and head back into the kitchen. There are still things I need to take care of on the farm, so I start to take my leave.

She stops me, unplugging the tablet and pushing a few buttons. "This eReader has an awesome battery life, so you should be good. The book I want you to read is opened to page one."

She goes on to point out how to change the font size if the text is too small.

"Thank you, Bethany. I look forward to reading this."

"Guys who read are sexy."

Excuse me?

Either the room just got warm or I'm blushing. "Good thing I like to read."

"I can't wait to hear what you think of it. Are we still on for dinner Tuesday night?"

Tucking her eReader under my arm, I grin. "Wouldn't miss it."

being
neighborly

If she still lives here in six months, I'm so asking her out.

※·※

This book is hot as hell. I realize I am alone in my cabin, but I still glance around to make sure no one can see that words on a page just gave me a hard-on.

Words on a page.

My eyes settle on my alarm clock and nearly pop out of my head. I hadn't meant to read this late. I'm just having a hard time putting this book down. There's this guy and a girl who grew up together and fell in love, but some bullshit happened and she left town without a word. He's still in love with her and sees her again after a few years.

I need to go to sleep but I'm still reading to try and find out why she left in the first place. Every time they're together, you can tell they just want to tear each other's clothes off. Sexier than what I was expecting. The digital glow of my clock catches my eyes again and I turn off the eReader. There's a ton of work I need to do tomorrow so I have to get some sleep.

Even though I'm not running at one hundred percent, the next day I carry Bethany's eReader around with me. Every chance I have a couple free minutes, I pull it out and read. I'd like to be able to finish it before our dinner tomorrow night.

"What do you have there?" Bess asks, peeking over my shoulder.

I pass the eReader to her. "It's a book Bethany wanted me to read."

"And you can read on this thing." She moves the eReader back and forth from her face, squinting at it.

I shrug as she hands it back to me. "It's nice for reading without a light. It's got one built right in."

She shakes her head. "I like the feel and smell of a book. There's nothing like turning an actual page."

There's no point in arguing with her, so I give her a small smile and nod.

"When are you seeing Bethany again?"

Without even meaning to, I glance in the direction of her farmhouse. It's too far to actually see from where I'm currently sitting, but no matter where I am on my land, I know where her house is in relation. She's west, just like the setting sun.

"Tomorrow night."

"Are you gonna quit sniffing around her and ask her out already?"

My jaw drops and it takes me a moment to respond. "I'm not a dog, Bess, and I'm just being neighborly."

She snorts, and then chuckles at my raised brow. "Neighborly my rear. You like her and you're being silly for not telling her how you feel."

I take a deep breath. "You know not everyone is cut out for farm life. She grew up in a big city. I'm partly waiting to see if she'll stay."

being neighborly

Her hand comes to rest gently on my shoulder, squeezing it. "I was born and raised in a big city too, Beau. I don't think she's going anywhere."

"There's nothing wrong with giving it some time to know for sure."

Her hand squeezes my shoulder again before she lifts it, and starts walking away.

She pauses, turning back to look at me. "Sometimes you wait too long and lose an opportunity that you can't ever get back."

I've known Bess my whole life. That's the most melancholy I've ever seen her. As far as I know, she's never married, never had a long-term relationship. I don't even know what brought her to the farm in the first place. Maybe someday she'll share her story with me.

Watching her figure retreat, I can't help but wonder if my caution toward making a move on Bethany is a mistake. What would be worse, never having a chance to ask her out or doing it too soon and pushing her away instead?

It's a question I mull over quite a bit that day and into the next. I'm no closer to knowing what to do than when I started. The few female relationships I've had have been initiated on their side. My very first girlfriend was the cousin of the Jackson's, a family who still lived and worked on the farm.

She came out for a visit the summer I turned seventeen. Angel was nineteen, and looking back, was probably bored staying on the farm. She decided to fill up her free time with being my first everything. By the end of the summer, I was convinced I was in love with her. Unfortunately, that feeling was not mutual and she headed back to college without even looking back.

In my defense, I was still on the scrawny side back then. After her came my first local girlfriend, Sylvia. This time around, I was twenty and happy to practice all the things Angel had taught me. Again, I was sure I was in love. That was until Sylvia started talking about moving away together. I told her in no uncertain terms that I had no interest is living anywhere else.

She didn't even tell me to my face she was moving; she just up and left one day. I had to find out from her mother when I was picking up fertilizer from the farm supply warehouse. The next girlfriend I had, like Bethany, moved out to the country for a change of pace. Her name was Josie and that change of pace only suited her eight months before she got bored and moved back to Atlanta.

Whatever woman I end up with, if I end up with someone, will have to understand that being a farmer is part of who I am. I enjoy waking up early, except for this morning after staying up too late reading. Most mornings, I'm the first one up and out the door. Being outdoors is where I am most comfortable. Walls, no matter how tall, always seem to close in after a while.

being neighborly

There's a hope though, after spending time with Bethany and learning more about her, that maybe she'll stick around long enough for me to take that chance. Once I've finished my work for the day, I head back to my cabin to shower before dinner at Bethany's. I need a haircut, but otherwise, I clean up nice enough. I wasn't able to finish the book; work of the farm and needing a good night of sleep took precedence over it.

Hopefully, that's okay with Bethany. I'd hate for her to think I wasn't interested in what she did. I did manage to make it to 68%, or at least that's what the bar on the bottom of the eReader said. I still have plenty, book-wise, to talk about with her even though I'm not done. I change into a newer pair of jeans and a grey collared t-shirt. It had been a hot week seeing as how summer was fixin' on moving in.

It won't be too long before I'll be taking evening dips in the pond out by my parents' cabin to escape the heat. Hell, it might be fun to see if I can talk Bethany into swimming some night. More nervous than I thought I'd be, I leave to head over to her place. When I get there, I see she's setting up supper outside.

She looks up as I park and waves. I suddenly feel underdressed in my jeans and t-shirt when I see her in a dress.

I pass the front door and head straight for the porch, smiling as she opens the door for me. "That's some dress, Bethany. I feel like I should be taking you somewhere fancy."

She looks away quickly, blushing. "That's sweet of you to say."

The table is already set, so I offer to help in the kitchen, but she refuses, telling me it's all done. It feels foreign not helping her. I sit stiffly, wanting to help her as she starts bringing stuff out.

Finally, I give up and stand. "Sorry, I gotta help."

She shakes her head at me, but doesn't argue when I take the platter from her. She's prepared lobster and crab legs. Seafood dishes appear to be her specialty. We don't eat much seafood on the farm so it's a nice change.

Bess usually sends me over with a dessert, and tonight is no different. We've finished our main course and are about to have some pecan pie when Bethany jumps out of her chair and runs into the yard.

"Where are you going?" I laugh, following her.

Her hair bounces around her face as she glances back at me. "I saw a firefly."

Our dessert is forgotten as we race around catching and releasing fireflies.

chapter four

"Bethany?"

"I'm in the kitchen. Hurry," she shouts.

If there wasn't water spraying out from under the sink, the sight that greeted me as I rushed into her kitchen would have been funnily similar to our first meeting. Legs, long, pale, freckle-kissed legs, one fine ass encased in a pair of cutoff jean shorts and the rest of Bethany's body disappearing from sight into the cabinet under her kitchen sink.

"I can't turn it off," she groans.

I crouch down beside her and tap her thigh. "Let me try."

She wiggles out, her green t-shirt soaked and molding to her breasts. She squints at me, probably wondering why I'm staring at her and not trying to shut off the water.

I quickly duck my head under the sink and go to turn the shut off valve. It's stuck, maybe rusted, but with sheer force and a layer of skin off my palm, I get it to turn. I'm breathing heavily by the time I move out from under it. Bethany is standing over me, panting and dripping. I can't deny under different circumstances, I'd love to be making her pant and drip all over again.

Just thinking of her that way sends blood flowing to my cock. I shift, using my now sore hand as leverage and wince.

Lifting it to inspect the damage, I'm grateful the pain is killing whatever budding erection I was about to sport until Bethany gasps, "Your hand."

Standing, I wave her off. "It's not that bad. It's my own damn fault for not putting on a pair of gloves or using a wrench."

She ignores my brush off and comes closer, pulling my hand into both of hers, cradling it at she takes a look. She's so close and is touching me, in a wet shirt. Any pain I'm feeling vanishes as desire returns. Over the past few weeks of getting to know Bethany better, I can't deny there is something more than a simple attraction going on here.

I like her. Even when she's trying to do something harebrained to this old farmhouse, it's fun to just be around her. More often than not, I've found myself gravitating toward her farmhouse, a pull I cannot ignore. Even if she's working, she'll save her place and offer me a glass of lemonade and her company. In all my unexpected visits, not once has she seemed anything less than happy to see me.

Her call to my cell for help is the reason for my visit today. Even when I'm busy on the farm, a call from her makes me stop whatever I'm doing. Bess notices but hasn't said anything. She doesn't have to. She already looks like the cat who ate the canary. When I first met Bethany, I planned to keep any feelings I was developing for her on hold. I'm a farmer. I know a seed takes time and nurturing to take root.

At first, I planned to wait a year to ask her out and I've been reevaluating and lowering that time frame mentally every time I see her. Just two days ago, it was down to two months. Standing here, in this kitchen I helped her repaint a couple of weeks ago, my patience has reached its end. She's cradling my hand in both of hers. Quietly, flustered since I got hurt, not noticing my other arm snake around her waist until I've crushed her body tightly to mine.

Her hands are still between us, one now pressing against my chest, the other protecting my hand. Her wise eyes are more green than brown, her pretty lips forming an O. Gently, I tug my injured hand from hers and slide it up her back and into her damp hair. Any pain I feel is outweighed by how right her skin feels against mine.

I keep my eyes locked on hers as I slowly dip my mouth to hers. This way, I know she knows it's coming. She has plenty of time to stop me. So close I can almost taste her, my eyes drift to her lips and have just enough time to see the corners tilt up before I claim them. Her hands drift up to wrap around my neck. The dampness of her shirt seeping through mine is nothing compared to her firm breasts rubbing against my chest.

I have no plan in place for this kiss, other than the absolute certainty that I need to put my mouth on hers. Once I have, it becomes another absolute certainty that I need to taste her tongue. When I have, I am absolutely certain I'm not going to stop anytime soon.

She seems as greedy to consume me as I am for her. Her tongue sweeps into my mouth, changing my outlook on patience as she does. Her teeth nip at my lips lighting the spark to my fuse. I only hope, as her hips rock against my very apparent appreciation toward every single thing she is doing, I won't embarrass myself by blowing a load in my pants. Turning, I lift her and set her onto the counter, my lips never leaving hers.

Stepping between her legs, my hands flex on her waist as her fingers dive into my hair. Bess has been after me for a couple weeks now to trim my hair. I can safely say I may never cut it short again. I'd hate to risk losing the almost painful jolt of pleasure it brings as Bethany tugs it. Her shirt is wet, and clinging to parts of her I'd like to explore. *It'd only be polite to remove it, right?*

My hands drift under the damp material. Similar to the start of our kiss, I move slowly. I wait for her hands to release my hair and stop my hands and their upward progression. This does not happen; instead, her lips drift from mine to my ear.

She kisses my neck first before her nose ghosts over the shell of my lobe as she whispers, "Do it."

being *neighborly*

Verbal confirmation heard and acknowledged, I tug her shirt from her and fling it behind me. It lands somewhere with a slap. My hands reach to cup her breasts. Her swift intake of air as her back arches, pushing them further into my hands, a giant turn on. She inches forward on the counter, hooking her legs around my waist as she grinds against me.

My thumbs massage her nipples through the lace of her mint bra. I drop my mouth to one, sucking her nipple into my mouth through the lace as my hand works the cup down of her other breast. She gasps, her hands once again in my hair as she holds me to her. One of her hands moves downward and slips into my jeans to grip my ass.

All I want to do is love her long and hard until she's panting my name. With a mouthful of her tit, I'm curious if that's something she'd like as well. My fingers trace the seam of her bra, all the way to the back closure. I lift my head. Her eyes are closed; her lips parted. When her eyes flutter open and her gaze rests on mine, I unhook her bra.

Our eyes stay locked as my fingers move up to her shoulders and slowly drag the straps down.

"What do you want, Bethany?" I ask, dropping her bra next to us.

She gulps. "You."

Good answer.

My lips drop to her neck. "And what do you want me to do?"

"Whatever you want."

Even better answer.

I take her mouth, lifting her as she clings to my shoulders. Her bedroom is on the second floor. I sample her lips, throat and collarbone with each step. I grin against her lips when I see how messy her room is. There are boxes from her move still piled in one corner. Another corner boasts an overflowing laundry basket. Her bed clearly unmade. Instead of annoying me, somehow I find her haphazard mess endearing, or I could simply not care since I plan on burying myself in her.

Depositing her gently onto her sheets, I take a step back to imprint the sight before me permanently. Naked from the waist up, eyes wild with lust, she beckons me. Reaching over my head, I tug my shirt forward and off. She's seen me shirtless before, but watching her lips part in appreciation, ratchets my desire impossibly higher.

I fumble to take my boots and socks off as quickly as possible as her body writhes with want. My fingertips crawl up her legs until I get to the button of her little jean shorts. Her hands fist the sheets on either side of her as I undress her. Once I've rid her of every stitch she wore, I kiss my way up her legs. I focus on and worship each freckle that has tormented my dreams along the way.

Patience is a virtue and I plan to take my time loving Bethany. Her attempts to rush me along are noted and appreciated. There is a time and a place for a fast and hard screw, but seeing as how she's been an itch I've been wanting to scratch these long weeks, I plan to fully see to it. Besides, I've never been a halfway kinda guy.

"Just watch, darling. I'm gonna take real good care of you."

I hold her gaze, her eyes widening and hands fluttering to my head as I taste her. She's perfect. Every single thing about her in this moment has me more turned on than I think I have ever been before now. With my fingers and my mouth, I take my time drawing pleasure from her. When I'm certain she is completely satisfied, I start my ascent up her body.

Her hands go straight for my jeans, but I almost stop her, wanting today to be only about her, but I'm too weak with want. She pushes me onto my back and then rids me of my jeans and boxers. I'm ready for her, long and hard. My hips buck when her fingertips wrap around my cock. Christ, her touch is heaven, sending a sensory overload through me. I'm a bundle of exposed nerves.

Her eyes land on mine and I watch as her tongue darts out to wet her lips. She doesn't break our eye contact as she lowers herself to take my cock in her mouth. There's nothing hotter than her hazel eyes locked on mine as she goes down on me. This feels really good, like winning the lottery or scoring the game winning touchdown.

That's a guess since I've neither won the lottery nor played high school football. Problem is what she's doing is so freaking amazing; I'm about to come straight down her throat. I'd rather be balls deep in her pretty little pussy though.

"Darling." I sit up, reaching to lift her and pull her into my arms.

My mouth needs hers. "Shit, Bethany, you are so gorgeous. I want you so bad."

Her mouth moves against mine as she tries to kiss and speak at the same time. "I want you in me, Beau. Please."

"I want in you so badly, darling. Do you have any condoms?" I can't break our kiss either, replying against her mouth, holding her body tightly to mine.

She pulls me with her as she leans right, her hand going for her bedside drawer. Her hand disappears into the drawer once she has it open and she groans, shuffling stuff around. I try not to laugh, but she's so frustrated it's cute.

"Let me." Shifting her off my lap, I move closer to the edge of the bed so I can see inside her drawer. I find her vibrator first and lift it and an eyebrow up at her. She blushes and covers her face so I set it on the top of her table.

"We're playing with this later."

Once I find the condoms, I take no time opening one and putting it on. Bethany has turned so her back is to me, hands still covering her face. I crawl over to her and kiss my way up the side of her body, turning her onto her back.

being neighborly

"Don't be embarrassed, sweetheart. I think it's sexy as hell you can make yourself come. Now, it's my turn to." Her mouth drops as her hands fall away from her face. "You know that right, Bethany?"

She shakes her head so I continue, shifting her legs until I'm between them. "Just how sexy I think you are. Hell, you've been the reason for every cold shower I've had to take since I met you. Does that turn you on?"

She nods, her lips still parted. I dip my mouth down to hers as she tilts her hips up to meet my cock. I was wrong earlier when I thought heaven was my cock in her mouth; nope, that wasn't even close to burying myself between her thighs. She wraps her legs around me and her fingers bite into my scalp. Her lips are the path to my salvation as I pump in and out of her.

"You feel so perfect," I groan against her lips.

Not moving her lips from mine, she replies, "Oh, God, right there."

"You tell me what you want."

"You, don't stop."

I can't stop kissing her and she seems to feel the same way. Neither of us fully stops speaking as we continue to kiss. I tell her how her body is the most beautiful thing I have ever seen. She tells how me what feels right, don't stop, there, there, there, harder, yes, yes, oh God yes.

Amazing is only way to describe what being with Bethany feels like. Her hands come to rest on my shoulders as I lift her up and down and then back down onto my shaft. Moving one hand back behind her to brace herself, she twists her hips, grinding against me each time I'm deep inside her.

I lower my head and pull her nipple into my mouth, running my tongue over it before nipping it. She groans, her movements becoming jerky, her body tensing. I repeat my attention on her other nipple and she cries out loudly, her tight core convulsing around my dick. I come hard after that, gripping her slick body tightly in my arms.

I push her backwards, following her and tucking her to my chest. "That was . . ."

"Incredible," she finishes, dusting my collarbone with gentle kisses.

"Give me just a moment." I stand, the heat of her eyes on my bare ass as I cross the hall to her bathroom to dispose of the condom.

She's waiting for me, all sated and luscious on her bed. I tackle her, grinning as she squeals. "I want to kiss every inch of you."

She wraps her arms tightly around my neck. "Best house call ever."

I pull back. "Shit. Forgot about your sink."

She shrugs, pushing a curl out of her eyes. "It'll still be there when you're done kissing me."

being
neighborly

I pull her back into my arms. "Fair enough."

chapter five

The weeks that followed our first time together were full of laughter, good food, getting to know each other even better, and the hottest sex I've ever had. Every spare moment I'm not working on the farm, I'm over at Bethany's. I can talk about anything with her and she with me. I finished that book she edited and am reading another one; only I'm not doing it alone this time. Now, as I read, I do it with her feet in my lap as she works.

Together, we've also worked on and gotten frisky in just about every room of her house. She's still just as messy as ever. There's at least one unpacked box shoved in a corner of each room, but otherwise, her place looks great

I've questioned a couple of her paint selections, but after seeing those off the wall colors actually on the wall and surrounded by her things, I can't help but like them. Each room has Bethany written all over them. There's even some of me as well. The other day I mentioned how much I liked Ansel Adams pictures, just in passing. Next time I came over, there was one hanging up in her living room;

being
neighborly

it's like she's unconsciously fitting me into her future.

At the farm, it's assumed that I'm eating over at Bethany's place unless I let them know she's coming over to eat with us. She's heading to Florida for a week in a couple days and it's already messing with my head. Stupid what ifs that have zero basis is in reality plague me. What if she decides she wants to move to Florida? What if she tells her parents about me and they don't think I'm good enough for her?

I've been short and snapping at everyone around me all week. I'm on my way to my parents' cabin, hoping the walk will clear my head and relax me. I try and stop by at least once a week to check on my folks. I haven't told them anything is going on with me and Bethany yet. At this point, they just think we're friends. I plan on telling them just how much I've grown to care for her today, and see if it'll be all right for me to bring her by to meet them.

I've told her all about them. She's too married to technology to ever go off the grid like they have, but she still thinks the idea of it is romantic. It's hard to think of my parents that way, as romantics. It's almost as weird as knowing they had to have sex at least once for me to be here. I'm maybe fifty yards from their front door when it happens.

Trying not to think about my parents sexual relations and not paying attention to where I'm walking is not wise in a wooded area. I step right on to a cottonmouth snake and thoroughly piss him off enough for him to bite me.

"Damn it."

They aren't extremely venomous, but I'll still need to go to the hospital. This isn't the first snake bite we've had on the farm, so I know not to panic. Thankfully, my mom keeps a four-wheeler at the cabin in case of emergencies. This qualifies. I limp the rest of the way to their place.

Man, my leg hurts. The bite is on my left calf. Halfway to the cabin, I stop and call the house line.

Luckily, Bess answers.

"Bess, I got bit by a cottonmouth. I'm maybe twenty yards from Mom and Dad's cabin, but it's killing me to walk. Can you come get me?"

"Be right there," is all I hear before she hangs up.

A half-assed glance behind me is all I can manage before sinking to the ground. I drag the back of my hand across my forehead to find I'm soaked with sweat. Something isn't right. I've seen reactions to a cottonmouth bite before and they weren't this bad. This is my last clear thought before I pass out.

My eyes swim as I try and figure out where I am. It hurts, correction everything hurts, but my attempt to turn my head to look around hurts enough to make my head spin.

being neighborly

"Hey, Beau."

It takes a moment for my eyes to focus on Bess. I'm still not sure where I am, but my nerves settle a bit at seeing a familiar face. That doesn't stop my head from spinning. I've never been so dizzy lying down before.

"What?" My throat burns so badly I stop at that one word.

"Well, big guy. You gave us quite a scare. You had an allergic reaction to the snake bite and have been unconscious for the last two days."

I start to shake my head, but it makes the room spin.

"Is somebody awake?" An unfamiliar voice precedes a woman in light blue scrubs entering the room.

"Beau, this is Lilly, one of your nurses," Bess explains.

She turns my hand over, her fingers taking my pulse. "How are you feeling, Beau?"

"I'm dizzy," I rasp, keeping my eyes closed. "And thirsty," I add.

"I'll grab you some water in just a minute. That sound good?"

A slight nod of my head is all I can manage.

She takes my temperature and checks my blood pressure. I zone out, trying to remember what happened.

"Can you feel this, Beau?"

Huh?

"Can I feel what?" I ask, my eyes opening.

She's standing next to my left leg, a grim expression on her face.

I lift my head to try and see what she's doing. Even though my vision blurs and the exertion of lifting my head is exhausting, I need to see. She has my foot in her hand and is turning it from side to side.

I'm watching her move my foot. I see it. My brain recognizes that I see it, but I can't feel it. Time stands still as I tell myself to feel it, as if mind over matter could come into play.

"Well?" she asks again.

I let my head fall back to the bed allowing the exhaustion to win. "I can't feel it."

There's a gasp from the doorway and I turn my head, opening my eyes to see who it is. Bethany. Her eyes are wide, her hands covering her mouth. She clearly just heard I can't feel my foot.

"Darling," I breathe and she rushes to my side.

Her hands are on my face, her lips on mine. "Oh, my God, Beau. I was so scared."

being
neighborly

"Shh." I want to put my arms around her to comfort her, but I'm either too weak or medicated to.

My nurse interrupts us, letting me know she is getting me some water. Bethany is so busy fussing over me; I barely notice when the nurse returns with my water. I open my eyes slightly, risking the dizziness to see Bethany. She's holding my water, her hands shaking as she brings the bendy straw to my lips. Even here, no makeup, clearly sleep deprived Bethany is beautiful.

When I notice the redness around her eyes, my chest tightens and my throat swells, making it hard to sip the water she's offering me.

"What happened?" I manage.

Bess walks around to other side of my bed, opposite to where Bethany is standing and pulls a chair forward before taking my hand in hers. "You were unconscious when I got to you with the truck. Thank God, Bethany was with me when you called. If I'd have come by myself, I never would have been able to get you into the truck."

A sniffle pulls may attention to Bethany and I watch her wipe fresh tears from her eyes. I try to lift my hand again, but am only able to raise it a couple inches before it falls back onto the bed, useless.

"Don't cry," I plead.

She shakes her head and attempts a brave smile. "I was so scared," she croaks, her voice thick.

"I'm okay," I try to reassure her.

She leans over me, pressing her forehead to mine, her eyes squeezed tightly shut. Frustration bleeds from my inability to take her pain away, pain I caused. She drops a kiss on my lips before pulling away to collect herself.

Bess clears her throat and I turn my head back toward her. "You had an allergic reaction to the venom and were in shock when we found you."

"Allergic reaction?" I repeat.

"Yes," a new voice confirms, entering the room.

"Hello Beau. My name is Dr. Vanson." An older gray-haired gentleman in a lab coat says.

I lift my chin in reply.

"Ladies. I need a couple moments with Mr. Hamilton." "They can stay," I breathe.

He goes right to examine my foot, turning it from side to side before lifting it asking me what that nurse had asked. I confirm that I still can't feel what he's doing. Instead of stopping like the nurse has, I watch as his hands move up my leg. He stops every inch to ask if I can feel anything. He's almost to my knee before I do.

As scary as the loss of sensation is below my knee, it's a relief to know it doesn't go farther than that.

being
neighborly

Bess asks the question on the forefront of my mind. "Is it permanent?"

"Allergic reactions can present themselves differently from one patient to the next. Partial paralysis is not unheard of, and unfortunately, only time will tell if it is temporary or not."

He starts to explain a condition called foot drop or drop foot. This is important; this is stuff I need to know about. Unfortunately, my body has other ideas, and exhaustion claims me.

The next time I wake, the room is much darker, only dim lights above a sink in the corner are on. I'm less disoriented and dizzy this time around. Light breathing to my right draws my attention. Even in the dim room, I know it's Bethany. She's curled up on a recliner, a long sweater as a blanket, her shoulder a pillow. Not wanting to wake her, I watch her sleep.

Her being here, not leaving me is an unexpected relief in this otherwise scary moment. I'm not sure how long I've been watching her when a nurse, a different one from before, comes in to check on me. Her movement wakes Bethany. She rubs her eyes, groggy in a way I've grown used to from our occasional overnights. It takes a moment for her to realize I'm awake.

When she does, she takes my hand in both of hers and presses it to her cheek.

"Beau."

"Hey," I rasp.

"Are you thirsty?"

I nod and she releases my hand to get me water. I only take a few sips before shaking my head to let her know I'm done. Then her hands grasp mine again.

"I'm sorry I fell asleep before."

She squeezes my hand and kisses it. "You need your rest."

"I feel weak," I grumble.

For a moment, she looks as though she might cry. "Shh."

"I do," I argue.

One of her hands comes up to push hair back from my forehead. "Just give it time. The doctor said you're going to be just fine."

"What about my foot?"

"You might be unsteady but you should be able to walk, and since it's your left foot, drive an automatic. He said something about needing to lift your leg higher when you walk since you won't be able to lift your toes."

I rub my thumb back and forth across the back of her hand. "How are you?"

being
neighborly

She gulps, dropping her forehead onto our joined hands, her body shaking.

"Get up here," I plead.

She shakes her head.

"Dammit, Bethany. Get up here." I just about beg.

She slowly climbs up onto my bed and tucks herself against me. Sleep finds us both not long after. When the nurse comes back around to check on me again, Bethany doesn't wake. The nurse takes pity on me and doesn't make a fuss about her sleeping on the bed with me. After she leaves, sleep eludes me. Each time I wake, I'm not as weak. Relieved to be feeling like myself again, I just want to go home.

Bethany wakes first the next morning, her sleepy stretching against me waking me as well. I'm sitting up comfortably the next time a nurse comes to check on me. The doctor visits me not long after. He's pleased my strength seems to be returning and has me stand next to the bed. After he seems happy I won't keel over, he okays the removal of my catheter. Thankfully, Bethany steps out of the room for that.

The mind is a curious thing. No matter how many times my foot and leg have been poked and probed, I'm still surprised the first time I go to put weight on it that I can't feel it. If Dr. Vanson hadn't caught me,

I would have fallen on my face. There's just nothing there, no pins and needles, no soreness, nothing.

I've delivered a couple of foals in my days, and I'm pretty sure my first steps weren't that far off from theirs. I am motivated though, not wanting to piss myself in front of Bethany is inducement enough for me to figure it out.

Hobbling over to the bathroom takes some getting used to. Getting to shower and brush my teeth makes it worth it. Bethany brought some sweats I was able to change into. It's hard to feel manly taking small uncertain steps with your ass peeking out from a hospital gown.

The next day, I still haven't regained feeling in my foot, but it hasn't stopped me from walking though. Reminding myself to lift my left leg higher is taking time. I've tripped more than once, dragging my toes since I can't lift them. I should be able to go home today.

I've got doctor's orders not to walk in the woods in shorts and sneakers again and a prescription for an EpiPen to carry on me. No matter what, if I ever get bit again, I'll still need to go to the hospital, but with the EpiPen, the hope is my reaction won't be as extreme.

It all makes sense to me, including the follow up appointment with a physical therapist to get fitted with a brace for my ankle. The brace should help keep me from rolling my ankle if I step weirdly. I'm

being neighborly

working with the assumption that what's happened to my foot is for good. Either way, there's a farm I need to get back to whether my foot works or not.

I hate to see Bethany so anxious. Being in the hospital, and her being here with me made our feelings for each other pretty clear. I'd like her to be in my future and am moving forward with that goal in mind. She wants the same thing, but I know she's also worrying herself sick over me; I see it with every touch and every glance. I haven't said anything yet, but I need to before she drives me crazy.

She checks on me when I'm sleeping; worries about me working the farm, and tenses up at the mention of me driving. I respect that she doesn't want anything bad to happen to me. Problem is, I need her to be my woman, not my mother.

chapter six

"I'll be fine," I grumble.

Bethany glances at her suitcase and back at me. She canceled a trip to go to Florida and visit her parents when I got bit by that snake. I've been out of the hospital for a week now and convinced her I was well enough for her to reschedule her trip. Now that she's supposed to leave tomorrow, she's having second thoughts about leaving me.

What happened was scary. Life goes on. I limp now; it sucks, but it could have been so much worse. I'd rather move on at this point. The hovering, the babying, and her nonstop nervous energy around me needs to stop, for both of our sakes. She moved out here to get away from the city and relax. She's unfortunately doing the exact opposite of that.

"What if you come with me?"

Arching a brow at her, I groan. "It's just a week."

She tries not to pout. Thank God I think she's gorgeous and it comes off more cute than annoying. I should be thrilled she cares about me enough to want to take care of me. I'm just not that guy. Call

being
neighborly

me old fashioned but I want to take care of her or bare minimum meet her halfway.

"I know," she grumbles.

I snake my arm around her waist and pull her into my lap. With that pout, those plump lips of hers are too much of a temptation to not sample.

"Just think of how much I'll miss you while you're gone," I tease, my hands full of one very fine ass.

"I don't want to leave you," she breathlessly confesses against my lips.

Figuring any argument to that is futile, I opt to give her a sendoff kiss she won't forget anytime soon.

I start to stand about to pull her up with me, but she slides off my lap before I can. A month ago, she wouldn't have done that and it burns. I avoid her eyes, tense from her unspoken declaration of my inadequacies. Did she think I was going to stumble with her in my arms, or worse, that I was going to drop her all together?

She goes to grab her suitcase but I stop her, my hand on hers. Our eyes, hers more brown than green, wage a silent struggle in which she relents and lets me win. I'm extra careful as I carry her bag so I don't drag my toes and trip by mistake. We're both tightlipped as we make our way out to my truck.

The tension in the truck lessens when she reaches for my hand. Lifting her hand to my mouth, I hold her gaze as my lips caress her knuckles. When her mouth falls open, I have to shift in my seat as my body reacts. She's been handling me with kid gloves since I got out of the hospital. My guess is she's scared it'll hurt me. Not something you want your woman thinking about you when it comes to sex.

It's a bit of a haul to the airport, but these days I'm more relaxed in my truck than anywhere else. You can't trip if you aren't walking and I don't look like a gimp when I'm driving. We're almost at the airport when I sense her tensing up.

Trying to keep her mind from worrying about me, I give her hand a squeeze. "Promise not to get into any trouble."

She huffs, "I'm more worried about you."

"I'm a big boy, darling." I pull up to the curb. "Don't you worry about me."

She gives me a shaky smile before we both get out. I hold up my hand to stop her from grabbing her suitcase from the back. It's already bad enough I'm dropping her off at the curb and not walking her in. Carefully, I set it down in front of her and pull the handle up for her.

Her eyes soften, and I pull her to me for one long goodbye kiss. When my mouth leaves hers, she stumbles slightly as she steps back, my hands lock onto her waist to steady her. She presses her fingers to her lips, her cheeks flushing prettily.

"I'll call you when I land." The husky lilt to her voice makes me want to kiss her stupid all over again.

Watching her walk away from me is harder than I thought it would be. It's just a week, I remind myself. We've fallen into this undefined relationship so easily. Dinners turned into overnights that became days that evolved into weeks of being together. Am I what she wants because there's nothing else better around? She's only had a taste of country living. Will it still be as idyllic after she's had a chance to be back in a city again?

"It's time for you to move along, son." A police officer gestures to my truck.

"Yes, sir." I nod before glancing at the doors Bethany disappeared through one last time.

It's a tossup between overthinking things and blasting some tunes on the way back to the farm. I opt for Metallica. I've been in my head enough already. The drive back is strangely invigorating. When I get back to the farm, I've almost forgotten about my foot, until I stumble and it all comes back to me.

I'm still jacked up; what in the hell can a girl like Bethany see in me now? I'm never going to be a rich man; that's not the point of the farm. I'm no slouch, but now with my foot, I can't even guarantee I can walk across a flat service without tripping. I'm an embarrassment. Maybe she'll figure out that she'd be better off without me.

"Take Bethany to the airport?" Bess asks as I slowly make my way to the main house.

"I did."

"You gonna sulk the whole time she's gone?"

Frowning at her, I reply, "I might."

She makes a face at me. "Don't make me take you over my knee."

I laugh at her idle threat. "You never spanked me when I was a kid. Why would you start now?"

"To get your head out of your butt."

Gripping the railing tightly as I work my way up the stairs, I say, "My head is not up my ass."

Her head twists, as she looks around her. "Language, Beau, what if one of the kids was around."

"I don't curse around kids, Bess."

She pats my cheek as I near her. "Cause you're a sweet boy. Please try and remember that and not get so annoyed at that nice girl for worrying over you."

Leaning against the frame of the front door, I glance back at her. "I already have a mother, two counting you. I don't need another one."

being neighborly

"Did Bethany ever tell you she was engaged once?"

My mind races as I turn fully to face her. "Excuse me?"

She sinks onto one of the rocking chairs and folds her hands across her lap. "It probably isn't my place to even tell you that, but just know I think you're being too hard on that sweet girl when all she is doing is worrying over you."

"What happened to her fiancé?"

"I think you should ask Bethany to tell you."

Groaning, I turn back toward the house, pulling open the door. Problem is if Bethany wanted to tell me what she clearly told Bess, she would've already done it. Does she trust Bess more than me? I had thought we were moving toward something long term. If she has another guy waiting in the wings, maybe she's toying with me.

I don't like that one bit.

There's some paperwork I need to take care of for a couple upcoming deliveries. It is the one aspect of the farm no one hassles me about doing since I've come home from the hospital.

That night, instead of having dinner at the main house, I see my parents. The whole point of them living in the far cabin is for them to not have to deal with the day-to-day worries of running the farm. Since I got bit, my mom has been spending more time at my cabin and the main house to keep an eye on me. I tried to tell her, just as I told Bethany and Bess, that I am fine. Doesn't stop her from needing to take care of me.

I've finally convinced her that I'll live so she's back fulltime at their cabin. Now when I go see them, I take my truck the whole way. Any walking I do in the woods, which isn't much, is in long pants and boots. My days of walking in shorts and sneakers are over. That's more in my head than anything else. I have the EpiPen on me at all times, so in theory, if I were to get bit by another snake, or hell, have a similar allergic reaction to anything, I should be all right if I use it.

My nose tells me before I get to the cabin that we're grilling tonight. The cabin my parents live in does not have electricity. My mom cooks on the wood stove in the winter months and my dad mans the charcoal grill. The pond behind my parents' cabin is loaded with fish for grilling.

I skip the front door and walk straight to the back porch where I assume my folks will be. My mom is setting the table while my father is tending the grill.

"Hey, Mama," I greet, giving her a kiss on the cheek.

She pulls me in for a hug. "How are you feeling?"

Shrugging, I lift my foot. "Still no feeling, but I'm getting better walking around on it."

being neighborly

My father comes over to pat me on the back. "That's good to hear."

"How are you doing, Pops?"

"Better than most so I can't complain."

It's not in his nature to complain. He's a simple man. He'd rather cut off a limb than complain. Unfortunately, because of that, it had taken almost losing him to a heart attack for the rest of us to realize he was overdoing it.

"Pity Bethany couldn't join us," my mother adds, looking at the three place settings on the table.

"I dropped her off at the airport earlier today," I explain, then pull my phone out of my pocket to see if she's called. Her flight should be landing soon.

"How are the fruit trees looking this year?" my dad asks, glancing at my mom.

He knows we purposefully keep him out of the loop so he has no excuse to worry. "I'm not happy with a couple of the pear trees. I'm not sure what it is, but some of the branches are looking diseased. I've been treating them, but if I don't see improvement in the next week or so, I'm cutting them down."

"That would be a shame." My mother frowns.

"I could take a look at them if you'd like," my dad offers.

I glance at my mother before looking back at him. "Nah, I've got this covered, Dad."

The orchard is probably the prettiest part of the farm, especially when all the fruit trees are in bloom. I spent my childhood climbing those trees and agree with my mom; it would be a shame to lose a couple. It'll be even worse to lose all of them. I love those trees. Do some of my best thinking under their boughs. There's a better chance than not I'll end up in the orchard tonight to process what Bess told me.

I haven't even decided if I'll ask Bethany about it when she calls. Part of me is not even sure I want to talk to her. I slip my phone out again to see if she's called. An emotion I can't define, that's somewhere between relief and frustration when I see she hasn't, fills me. Shoving my phone back into my pocket, I focus on spending time with my parents instead. We've finished the main course and my mom is about to serve the cake I brought with me when my phone rings.

"It's okay, son. You can take it," my dad says after witnessing my hesitation to answer it.

After pressing accept, I hold the phone to my ear. "Hello."

I push back from the table and slowly make my way down to the pond.

"I just landed. I'm still on the plane. There's another plane at the gate we're supposed to pull up to so we're just sitting on the runway until it moves."

"How was your flight?"

"Good until now," she grumbles.

"Are your parents picking you up from the airport?"

"My mom is. Oh, we're moving."

"That's good." I hesitate, knowing now is not the time but my curiosity gets the better of me. "Why didn't you tell me you were engaged?"

Her gasp is clear through the phone. "How did you—"

"Bess told me," I cut her off.

"It's a long story."

"One you trusted Bess with but not me."

"It's not something I like to talk about."

A firefly lights up not far from where I stand, painfully reminding me of the night we laughed and chased them behind her house. "I'm sorry to hear that."

"Beau—" she starts.

"I hope you have a nice visit with your parents, Bethany. I should go now."

"I see."

"Goodbye."

I end the call after I hear her subdued voice in return.

"Bye," she whispers.

chapter *seven*

"You want me to what?"

"You heard me," I groan.

"Why can't you pick her up? She's expecting you."

Bethany and I haven't spoken since the call where I asked her about her engagement. She'd called a couple times but I ignored them. I wasn't prepared to deal with what she had to say.

"I just can't."

Bess stands, wiping her hands on her apron. "This behavior is not the Beau I know."

"What's that supposed to mean?" I stand firm.

"When I told you about her fiancé, it wasn't for you to push her away. It was to explain why she was acting the way she was."

"Your plan backfired, Bess. All it did was make me question why she never told me about this guy. What? Does he want her back?" I snap.

"I can see now it was a mistake to say anything at all, but just so you know, her fiancé passed away two months before they were supposed to get married."

"He what?"

"You heard me," she throws my own words back in my face.

Here I was acting all jealous and insecure over a ghost. "I'm an asshole."

She doesn't even fuss at me for swearing. "Sometimes."

"I won't be needing you to pick her up from the airport."

"I figured as much."

Hell, I've made a big mess out of everything. First, I pushed Bethany away for caring about me. Now, I've distanced myself even more because I don't feel good enough for her. It's about time I got over my shit and started acting like a man worthy of the attention Bethany was giving me.

I have a lot to think about on the drive to the airport. Whether the outcome be good or bad, I need to tell Bethany how much she means to me and the reason I pushed her away in the first place. I'm scared, scared I'm not man enough for her after the bite, and scared she will leave me after I found out she had been engaged before. Those were embarrassing things to admit to myself, let alone her.

I made good time on my drive, and since I beat her plane, I decided to park and meet her at the baggage claim instead of on the curb. Walking

being
neighborly

around on paved surfaces is much easier than almost anywhere on the farm. I focus on taking my time. That, plus the smooth walkways makes my limp less noticeable.

Once I find the carousel her luggage is being sent to, I wait. There's a rush of people; I'm assuming from her plane, but I don't see her. It's when I head in the direction of the gates. That's when I find her, walking slowly, pulling an extra bag for an older gentleman. He's walking with a walker peacefully chatting with her as they make their way to baggage claim.

She looks amazing, her long pale green sundress showing a hint of her ankle with every step she takes. Her auburn curls shine as they frame her beautiful face. I'm a fool for pushing this stunning creature away.

That's when it hits me; this is just who she is, a caring person. How lucky am I that she cares for me! How blessed I should feel that she wants to be with me and how stupid would I be to not treasure the gift of it. I meet them halfway.

"Bethany."

She seems surprised to see me, smiling, widely. "Beau."

"Here, let me help you with that extra bag."

She passes it to me quietly, a small smile hinting around the corners of her mouth. "This is Mr. Williamson. We met on the plane."

I dip my head. "Nice to meet you, sir."

He glances between us. "This your boyfriend?"

I answer for her, bending down to kiss her cheek before I offer him my hand. "Yes, sir. Beau Hamilton."

He lifts one hand from his walker to shake mine. "You have a very sweet girlfriend, Beau."

I nod, my eyes on Bethany as I reach for her hand. There's still plenty for us to discuss, but this is the first time I have acknowledged myself publicly as her boyfriend. She doesn't correct me. I don't know if that's for my benefit or for Mr. Williamson's, but we'll have about an hour alone together in my truck for me to find out.

When we reach the carousel, a relative of Mr. Williamson meets him and I pass over his rolling bag. He shakes my hand a second time telling me to take care of Bethany. She smiles widely and gives him a hug before he leaves. I reclaim her hand as we stand together waiting for her suitcase.

We walk in a comfortable silence back to my truck once we've retrieved it. It's once I've loaded it into the back and we're both seated that I break the silence.

"I'm sorry I've been acting like an ass."

being neighborly

"I'm sorry I didn't tell you about my engagement," she replies, lifting my hand into hers.

"You don't have to tell me if you don't want to. I don't want you to feel pressured."

She sighs, turning her head to look out the front windshield. "It's hard to talk about, and that's why I haven't brought it up before. I told Bess while we were waiting for you to wake up at the hospital. What happened with you reminded me of what happened with Kurt. He wasn't bitten by a snake though. He had been in a car accident. Waiting for you to wake up brought me right back to when I waited for him to wake up; only in his case, he didn't."

"I'm so sorry."

"Life goes on. His death inspired me to make so many changes in my life. A part of me will always mourn the life we never had, but I'm also grateful that I still have the opportunity to live mine. I don't know if I ever would have been brave enough to leave my job and move out here. If I hadn't have done that, I never would have met you, Beau."

"You are so brave."

"I'm just trying to live my live without regrets. I don't want to look back and wish I would have done something but was too scared to."

"That's sorta how I feel right now. I've been scared since the bite that now you don't think I'm man enough for you. Then, after finding out you were engaged, I let that push me even further away. I was scared there was something wrong with me and that's why you hadn't told me. I'm realizing now what an idiot I was."

She squeezes my hand. "We're human, Beau. We're all going to make mistakes. I only ask that you talk to me first next time and I'll do the same."

I lift her knuckles to my lips. "Deal."

"I noticed you didn't correct Mr. Williamson about being my boyfriend."

I nod, my eyes flicking from the road to hers. "I'd like to be. My stupid streak seems to be over for the time being and I'd like to take advantage of it and make you my girlfriend. Also, I want you to know I love you."

I've known I was in love with Bethany for a while; I was not planning to just spit it out like that though. Terrified, I wait for her reaction, hoping she feels the same way.

She leans across the seat and kisses my cheek. "I love you, too."

Without the tension that's been holding me down, I feel lighter than I have in days. We laugh and joke the whole ride back to her house. The moment I kill the engine though, the mood shifts from lighthearted to something more intense.

being neighborly

"I've missed you." The husky tone of her voice lets me know just how much.

"We've got some catching up to do."

She makes it to her front door before me, but squeals when I swoop her up into my arms. "Your foot?"

I shake my head. "Don't you worry about a thing."

Concentrating on lifting my leg high enough takes most of my attention as I carry her up the stairs to her bedroom. The way she nips at and kisses my neck on the way has me wondering if she'd be cool with me taking her right on her stairs. I'd do it too if spreading her out across her bed was a temptation I could pass.

It has been too long since I was inside her and a quickie on the stairs is not what I have in mind. Patience is a virtue, right? Sure the Good Lord probably meant waiting till marriage, not waiting till you reached her bedroom though.

I'm no philosopher and am more interested in the willing woman I am quickly falling in love with than anything else. Gently setting her on her bed, I kneel before her, slipping her dainty silver sandals from her feet. Using my hands and my mouth, I drown myself in the pleasure that is the silken softness of her skin. Sliding her dress up as I go, from ankle to thigh, I leave no inch unloved.

Save a pair of lace panties, she's bare to me from the waist down. She's restlessly waiting for my next move. Her body arches for my touch while I sit back and admire her. Over waiting, she stands, one foot on either side of me and pulls her dress off over her head. Her panties taunt me, shielding me from her. I drag them off as she lifts one leg, then the other for me to rid her of them fully.

She sinks into my lap, kissing me as she unbuttons my shirt. Once it's off, she pushes me back onto the floor before moving to remove my shoes and jeans. Before long I'm naked beneath her. All I want is to taste her and start to move her until she hovers over me. I start to kiss her thighs when she turns around and takes my cock into her hand and then her mouth.

Groaning at the sensation, I attack her with my tongue. She wiggles against my face and I wrap my arms around her thighs so she can't move. My hips lift as I rock into and out of her mouth, her fingers pumping me. I release one of her legs to ease my finger inside of her. The sensation is too much for her; she lifts her head from my cock and groans loudly as she comes. I lap at her clit until her body stops shuddering. Once it has, I lift her, shifting her in my arms so I can capture her lips with mine.

"You are so beautiful."

She blushes at my words and I stand, Bethany in my arms, to lay her across her bed. She's almost limp, sated as she lazily grins up at me. I quickly

being
neighborly

sheath myself before spreading her legs and driving myself into her. My eyes roll back at the feel of her. Her body seems made for mine, fitting me like a glove. She alone seems able to lift me to the highest levels of pleasure.

I've missed not only her, but also the physical connection we've shared. She isthe first woman I've craved body and soul. I want it all, her laughter, her tears, her smiles, and her ecstasy. I will be the man deserving of the gift that is her company. Taking her lips once more, I groan as I find my release. I shift onto my side, pulling her with me, tightly in my arms.

"That was one hell of a homecoming," she teases.

"I'd greet you this way every time I saw you if I wouldn't get thrown in jail for public indecency."

"We'll just have to limit ourselves to private property."

That gave me an idea. "Have you ever camped out?"

She grimaces. "I wouldn't really call it camping, but when I was younger, I went to a Girl Scout summer camp."

"You were a Girl Scout?" I grin.

She nods. "Sold cookies and everything."

"You taste better than any cookie I've ever had," I joke, nibbling her neck.

"I doubt that, but whatever you're doing feels good so don't stop."

"I have no intention of ever stopping when it comes to you, Bethany."

Her fingers thread my hair as she pulls my mouth up to hers. Traveling and our unique way of making up, exhaust her. Even though it's barely past nine, she curls up on her bed and falls asleep. I take the time to go back out to my truck and collect her suitcase. In our haste to get inside, we forgot it earlier. Since she's asleep, I move slowly up the stairs with it, careful not to bump it against anything and wake her up. I want to take care of her, just like her impulse is to take care of me.

Once I have it up in her room, and in a corner ready for her to unpack, I undress. Sliding under the covers I pull her flush against, my lip curling into a satisfied grin as her body molds itself to mine, even in sleep. I was an idiot to consider throwing this away. Pushing her away is a mistake I'll only make once. I know now it was wrong to think because of my injury that maybe I wasn't man enough for her. What I've learned is it takes a true man to admit their weaknesses.

I'm lucky enough to have the love and support of Bethany despite them.

epilogue
eight months later

"We're going to be late," Bethany groans, arguing but not really arguing as I lift her dress up.

"No such thing as being late to a picnic." I ease her down onto me and we both moan as I fill her.

Number one perk of moving in with Bethany, other than just being around her all the time, has been the on-the-fly sex. We can be on the sofa just hanging out and she'll slide into my lap, or at breakfast, if I catch a glimpse of her gorgeous breasts, I can just bend her over the kitchen counter, and lastly like right now, some hard and fast up-against–the-wall sex before we walk out the door.

Is it strange owning and working a farm I'm not currently living on? Some days, but being able to fall asleep next to Bethany every night makes it worth it.

Slipping my hand between us, my fingers furiously circle her clit until she comes all over my cock. Ladies always first, I wait till she's done before I follow. She teases me about it, but ever since I regained feeling in my foot, sex standing up has been my downfall. I can't lie; it makes me feel powerful, and knowing I'm not going to trip or drop her takes all the anxiety out of it.

"Ready, hornball."

I lower her legs and kiss her. "I love your pet names, darling."

She gives my ass a squeeze before going to the bathroom to clean up. Ever since she went on the pill, we've been condom free. I've never experienced that before her, the feeling of absolutely nothing between us. If I thought sex was addictive before, it's even more so now.

"All better?" I joke once she's all done.

"I should have just left it and had you explain to your parents why I had cum running down my leg."

I cringe and shake my head as she laughs at me. Once she's close enough, I pull her in for another kiss.

She pulls away, grabbing my hand and tugging me to the door. "No way, mister, we're already late enough."

"Like being outside will stop me," I argue, vividly recalling the time I bent her over the back of my truck, that time on the front porch or the time chasing fireflies turned into chasing each other.

She slips into the driver's seat. I let her drive my truck one time and now it's her favorite thing to do. She's lucky she looks so sexy behind that wheel; only thing I love more than my truck is her.

"Are we bringing anything?" I ask, suddenly realizing my hands are empty.

being
neighborly

She tilts her head to the back of the truck. "I carried the cooler out when you were in the shower. There's extra ice and a fruit salad in it."

"I would have carried it," I argue.

"I know but I didn't want to forget it so I just loaded it while I was thinking about it."

That's my girl. She doesn't wait for someone else to take care of her. She just does it. It doesn't always work out well. I smile to myself remembering the first time I met her. If she hadn't been stuck under the table she was trying to put together all by herself, she might not have made as great of an impression on me. I won't ever know for sure, but either way, she's had me hook, line and sinker since day one.

Bethany parks not far from where the tents are set up. We're lucky it's a good day for a picnic. We've had nothing but rain the past week but it was sunny yesterday and there isn't a cloud in the sky today as well. The ground has dried up nicely so it's grassy and not muddy where the grills are set up.

The kids are running around blowing bubbles while the grownups are socializing in circles not far from the keg. There's a table with drinks and cups for folks to serve themselves.

I grab Bethany's hand, lifting her knuckles to my lips. "Uh oh, somebody brought a box of wine. I'm guessing I'm driving home tonight."

She giggles, covering her mouth. My girl loves some wine in a box.

I carry the cooler over to the drink table and take out the fruit salad, passing it to Bethany. I watch her walk it over to the dessert table, my eyes glued to the gentle sway of her hips. She turns, right before she reaches the table and gives me the 'stop looking at my butt' glare. I ignore her and just keep on staring. She goes around to the backside of the table and starts talking to Bess so I grab a beer and head off to find my dad.

As I suspected, he's manning one of the grills. "Hey, Pops."

He lifts his bottle to mine and I clink it. "Hi Beau. Farm is looking real good, son."

"Thanks. We've had a good year. The food bank is thrilled and we've been able to barter for a new tractor."

I should have known better than to mention a new tractor to my dad and expect him not to want to see it. I just didn't expect him to leave mid-conversation and stick me with grill duty.

"How'd you get stuck grilling?" Bethany asks a bit later as she walks up.

"Mentioned the new tractor to my dad and he took off. I didn't want the fish to burn so I figured I'd hang out here until he got back."

"What glass is that?" I tease, pointing to her wine.

She smacks my stomach lightly. "My first."

being neighborly

My dad makes it back not long after to reclaim his grill duties. Bethany and I make the rounds together to chat and mingle with everyone in attendance. Once the food is ready, we head over to some picnic tables and chow down. As the sun sets, we light tiki torches while the kids start roasting marshmallows. I ease down into an Adirondack style chair and pull Bethany into my lap.

"Mmm," she mumbles, snuggling against me.

"When do you want to head home?" I ask, gently kissing the back of her neck.

"Soon if you keep that up."

"Let's go."

I collect our cooler from the drink table while Bethany says our goodbyes. She's had a few glasses of wine so I drive with her cuddled up to my side.

When we get to the house, she pops into her office to check her email while I head out to the back porch. After a couple minutes, I ask her to join me.

"It's dark out here. Want me to turn on the porch light?" she asks from the doorway.

"It's not that dark. Come here, baby."

Silhouetted from the light inside the house, she almost glows before she closes the door and joins me out on the porch.

"I poured you a glass of wine," I say, passing it to her.

"Oh, baby, I'm already a sure thing," she teases, taking it.

"And I'm sure about you." I lean over and kiss her cheek.

"It's so beautiful out here," she murmurs.

"I have something for you," I say, handing her a glass jar with a firefly inside.

"Aww. Little guy. When'd you catch him?" She sets down her wine and lifts the jar to get a better look.

As she moves it the ring slides across the bottom, clinking on the glass. Her eyes widen as they focus on the ring. "Beau?"

She looks up at me but I'm not there. Her mouth drops when she looks down to see me on one knee in front of her.

I take her free hand and wrap both of my hands around it. "Bethany. In a moment you are going to free that little firefly from that jar and I hope let me put that ring on your finger. You freed me, darling, from the fear that I wasn't good enough. Even when we didn't know if my foot would get better, your feelings for me did not waver in the slightest. You are the most caring, generous, crazy, beautiful woman I know and I'd be honored if you would consider becoming my Missus."

Even in the dim light the hint of tears glisten in her eyes as she nods her head. I stand, pulling her into my arms and kiss her. She stays wrapped up in me as she opens the lid of the jar to release the firefly. I lift one

being
neighborly

arm from around her and reach into the jar to collect her ring.

"This was my grandmother's ring on my mom's side of the family. She's been saving it for me and swore I couldn't have it without her blessing. She was thrilled when I asked for it for you."

It slips right on. "It's a perfect fit," she sighs.

"You're my perfect fit."

the end

acknowledgements

You.

If you are uncertain if this applies to you, please allow me to elaborate. If you are reading this, it applies to you. If you have written a book I've read or read a book I've written, for all the mint chocolate chip ice cream in the world this applies to you. If we're related, by choice or not, this most definitely applies to you. If you tell friends about the books you've read and loved, and if any of my books fall into that category, it abso-freaking-lutley applies to you. If you've reviewed a book and or emailed me or any writer after being moved by something they've written, it will forever apply to you. If you help craft an author's words into its beautifully finished product by editing, proofing, or creating a gorgeous cover to show it off to the world, it without a doubt applies to you. If you've been there for me during my moments of self doubt and offered me words of encouragement on this incredible journey, until I have no stories left to tell, it will apply to you.

Thank you.

Made in the USA
Charleston, SC
28 April 2015